**TO GRISSOM'S DISAPPOINTMENT, THE
EXPOSED SAND APPEARED NONDESCRIPT
IN NATURE, OF THE SORT WIDELY
AVAILABLE IN THE DESERTS
OUTSIDE THE CITY.**

Still, perhaps Trace would be able to discover something more distinctive in the soil sample. If they could determine where exactly the sediment came from, that might bring them a step closer to identifying the headhunter—and the victim.

They still didn't know for sure that it was a murder investigation, but he was getting a bad feeling about this case. "There was a note enclosed with the *tsanta*," he stated. "Just two words: *tumashi akerkama.*"

"That mean something to you?" Robbins asked.

"Not at first, but I looked it up once we got back to the lab. It's the Jivaro term for 'blood-guilt.' A crime against a person or a clan that can only be avenged through bloodshed."

"Not exactly a friendly sentiment," Robbins noted. "More like a threat."

"That's what I'm afraid of," Grissom said.

Original novels in the CSI series:

CSI:

CRIME SCENE INVESTIGATION™

HEADHUNTER

a novel

Greg Cox

Based on the hit CBS series "CSI: Crime Scene Investigation" produced by CBS PRODUCTIONS, a business unit of CBS Broadcasting Inc.

Executive Producers: Jerry Bruckheimer, Carol Mendelsohn, Anthony E. Zuiker, Ann Donahue, Naren Shankar, Cynthia Chvatal, William Petersen, Jonathan Littman

Series created by: Anthony E. Zuiker

POCKET STAR BOOKS
New York   London   Toronto   Sydney

Pocket Star Books
A Division of Simon & Schuster, Inc.
1230 Avenue of the Americas
New York, NY 10020

This book is a work of fiction. Names characters, places and incidents either are products of the author's imagination or are used fictitiously. Any resemblance to actual events or locales or persons, living or dead, is entirely coincidental.

First Pocket Star paperback edition November 2008

POCKET STAR BOOKS and colophon are trademarks of Simon & Schuster, Inc.

For information about special discounts for bulk purchases, please contact Simon & Schuster Special Sales at 1-800-456-6798 or business@simonandschuster.com.

Cover design by Richard Yoo
Scanning Electron Micrograph photo by SMC Images (Getty Images)

Manufactured in the United States of America

10 9 8 7 6 5 4 3 2

ISBN-13: 978-1-4165-4500-2
ISBN-10:   1-4165-4500-X

Dedicated to the next generation of Cox's:
Stephanie, Sarah, Cadence, Terra,
Nicholas, and Rory.

1

THE DISTINCTIVE SKYLINE of the Strip could be seen from the third floor of Wright Hall at the University of Nevada, Las Vegas. The Eiffel Tower, or at least a reasonable facsimile thereof, shared the view with a giant neon Coke bottle, a forty-five-foot-tall golden lion, and other eye-catching landmarks. Vivian McQueen gazed longingly at the glamorous hotels and casinos, barely more than a mile away. Maybe she could talk her husband into a night on the town after work? It had been too long since they'd gone out to dinner somewhere nice. *Bellagio*, she mused, *or perhaps the MGM Grand?*

Sipping on a late-afternoon cup of coffee, she strolled back to her desk at the center of the college's Department of Anthropology and Ethnic Studies. Professors, aides, and students filled the bustling corridors surrounding her cubicle. Her in-box was overflowing with schedule changes, budget reports, grant applications, scholarship requests, and other paperwork. As office manager, Vivian liked to think that she kept the entire department running smoothly, but she wouldn't have objected to a few more administrative assistants. A UNLV calendar, extensively annotated, was pinned to her bulletin board, next to various memos and news clippings. A plush college mascot perched atop her computer monitor. Framed photos of her kids added a personal touch to her desk. A bowl of Hershey's Kisses betrayed her sweet tooth.

"Excuse me?" A nervous-looking freshman approached her desk. Judging from his gray complexion and hungover body language, he had been doing more partying than studying lately. "Is it too late to transfer out of Dr. LeGault's Cultural Studies class?"

She reached automatically for the appropriate form. "Fill this out, and get it signed by Friday."

Clutching the document as if it were a stay of execution, the student awkwardly retreated from Vivian's domain, nearly bumping into the mail cart as it parked right outside the cubicle.

"Hey there, Viv!" Henry greeted her. The jovial mailroom guy glanced at the clock on the wall, which was steadily creeping toward five P.M. "Ready to call it a day?"

"And then some." She could practically taste the Grand's exquisite Kobe beef. "What have you got for me?"

Nothing too urgent, she hoped. *I'm getting out of here on time for once.*

"Don't ask me." He dropped a stack of correspondence on her desk, along with a package wrapped in plain brown paper. About the size of a shoebox, the parcel was addressed to the head of the department, Professor Malcolm Kim. Colored labels, reading "Fragile" and "Handle with Care," were affixed to the wrapping. "I just deliver this stuff."

He continued on his rounds, leaving her alone with the daunting stack of mail. Unwilling to face all of the various envelopes just yet, she contemplated the parcel. *That's funny,* she noted, *there doesn't seem to be a return address.* She hefted the bundle experimentally and found it lighter than, say, a textbook. *Wonder what's inside.* It was the wrong size and shape for a manuscript. *Maybe some sort of lightweight fossil?*

As far as she knew, Professor Kim wasn't expecting any new artifacts, but perhaps one of his colleagues or former students had dropped one in the mail anyway? Dr. Kim was a popular instructor with many successful former protégés, after all.

Succumbing to curiosity, Vivian reached for her letter opener. She routinely screened Dr. Kim's mail for him, so she knew he wouldn't mind. The brown paper was quickly consigned to the wastebasket beneath her desk, exposing a plain cardboard box with no obvious markings. Lifting the lid, she found the interior packed with crumpled tissue paper. A folded piece of paper, about the size of a memo pad, rested on top of the tissues. Intrigued, she unfolded the paper to read the inscription printed inside in bold red type:

"TUMASHI AKERKAMA."

The foreign-sounding phrase meant nothing to her. Was it a message or the name of the sender? Putting the note aside, she looked to see what else was in the box. *Careful,* she reminded herself. *The wrapper said "FRAGILE."* Her fingers gently peeled away the protective tissues.

A shriveled little face looked up at her.

A startled yelp escaped her lips. Vivian yanked her hands back as though she had accidentally touched a red-hot coal. Her dinner plans—and appetite—completely disappeared.

Inside the box was a shrunken head.

2

GIL GRISSOM WAS FASCINATED by the specimen.

The fiftyish crime-scene investigator waited patiently in the entrance to the cubicle while his younger associate, Nick Stokes, took several photos of the shrunken head in its box. It was unclear at this point if the grisly trophy was a historical relic or evidence of a murder, but Grissom was not taking any chances. Even though he couldn't wait to examine the head himself and get it back to the crime lab, he wasn't going to risk compromising the evidence by rushing the initial stages of the investigation.

Let's do this by the book, he thought. *No matter how tantalizing the puzzle.*

Night had fallen, and the offices of the Anthropology Department had been largely cleared of prying eyes. Outside the cubicle in question, Captain Jim Brass was busy taking statements from a handful of university personnel, including the office manager who had discovered the shrunken head. According to Brass, the trophy's startled recipient, one Vivian McQueen, had insisted on contacting the police regarding the unsolicited, anonymous delivery. She had personally handed over the cryptic note accompanying the head, which now resided in a plastic bag in Grissom's hand.

Tumashi akerkama. The exotic phrase sounded familiar, and vaguely disturbing, to Grissom, but he couldn't quite recall its meaning. *I need to look that up at the first opportunity.*

Brass jotted something down in his notebook, then strolled over toward Grissom. His rumpled, hangdog face bore a typically dour expression. A tan sportcoat and striped pants testified that his uniformed days were well behind him. His badge was affixed to his lapel pocket. "Having fun?"

"I admit to being intrigued," Grissom said. Technically, it was a bit early in the evening for Gil Grissom and his team; they ordinarily handled the graveyard shift. But with the regular swing-shift crew tied up with the aftermath of a bloody gangland shoot-out in Henderson, Grissom had readily volunteered to take on this case, especially once he learned that a shrunken head was involved. "One doesn't often get called in to investigate a suspicious *tsanta.*"

"*Tsanta?*"

"The native Jivaro term for a shrunken head trophy," Grissom explained. He had a small *tsanta* collection of his own back in his office at CSI headquarters.

Brass smirked. "I thought this call had your name

written all over it." A trace of an accent betrayed his New Jersey roots. He sighed wearily. "Me, I like my DBs a little less exotic. Give me an ordinary stabbing victim any day."

Grissom was puzzled by the cop's attitude. "You never found shrunken heads captivating, not even as a child? Didn't you ever try making your own out of apple cores?" Grissom had fond memories of carving faces into apples, pickling them in a salt and lemon juice solution, then hanging them out to dry until they resembled small shriveled heads. He wondered what had happened to them. *Probably boxed up in my storage locker somewhere.*

"Nah," Brass said. "I collected baseball cards instead."

I see, Grissom thought, filing that fact away in his gray matter. The varieties of human preferences and behaviors interested him almost as much as the life cycles of his favorite insects. Which was to say, considerably.

Nick finished checking the exposed features of the *tsanta* for prints. Like Grissom, the young CSI wore a department-issue blue windbreaker. "FORENSICS" was stenciled in large white letters across the back of the jacket. A matching baseball cap partially concealed his short brown hair. His metallic silver field kit sat open outside the cubicle.

"All yours."

"Any prints?" Grissom asked.

Nick shook his head. "Nothing patent," he said. In other words, nothing visible to the naked eye. He waved a cyanoacrylate fuming wand over the mummified face; in theory, the superglue vapor would react with any fingerprint oils lurking unseen on the head's leathery flesh, exposing them to view. The process required a delicate touch and careful timing to avoid overdeveloping any hidden prints; if fumed too long, the individual ridges broadened and overlapped, causing vital detail to be lost. Grissom trusted Nick to carry out the procedure expertly. The younger CSI's frown, however, suggested that his efforts had been in vain. "Nothing latent, either," he confirmed.

"Too bad." Grissom made a mental note to have the rest of the *tsanta* checked for latent prints after his preliminary examination. Slipping on a pair of latex gloves, he carefully lifted the shrunken head from its box. His keen blue eyes inspected the specimen.

Unlike the shaggy mane found on most genuine *tsanta*, this head had short red hair that matched what appeared to be a neatly trimmed mustache and goatee. The red hair suggested Caucasian roots, although the face's dry, leathery skin was brownish-black in color. *Possibly from having charcoal ash rubbed into it?* Grissom speculated. *As per tradition?* About the size of a fist, the macabre curio displayed most of the usual characteristics of a shrunken head. A marked degree of mandibular prognathism caused the jaws to protrude. Lateral shrinkage along the temples gave the head a pear-shaped contour. The eyes and mouth had been sewn shut. Miniature beads adorned the hair and beard.

Brass muttered in disgust as Grissom raised the *tsanta* to his nose. The head smelled faintly of tea, possibly from the tannins used in its preparation. Somebody knew what they were doing, he theorized. The smell was fresher and more pungent than the decades-old shrunken heads in his collection. An indication that this *tsanta* was of more recent origins? The head also seemed less deteriorated than most of the genuine shrunken heads he was familiar with. As though it were created not too long ago?

"Well," Nick asked, "is that the real thing?"

"I believe so," Grissom stated. He always reserved final judgment until all the facts were in. Exiting the cubicle with the specimen, he approached the college staff members still standing by. He held out the *tsanta* before him. "Dr. Kim, do you concur?"

The head of the Anthropology Department was a tall Asian man in his early fifties, wearing a tweed jacket, a turtleneck sweater, and crisply pressed slacks. Streaks of gray at his temples gave him a suitably distinguished look. Clean-shaven, with dark black hair that had yet to recede, he looked fit and well put together, especially for an academic. Grissom wondered if Malcolm Kim's well-groomed appearance had assisted his ascent to the head of the department. *No doubt Catherine would approve.*

Kim stepped forward and squinted at the specimen in Grissom's hand. He kept his own hands clasped behind his back, as though reluctant to touch the *tsanta*, not that Grissom would have allowed him to in any event.

"Amazonian relics are not my specialty," he hedged in a rich baritone that probably lent itself well to lecturing from the podium, "but this appears authentic enough." He stepped back from the grotesque relic. "Although I'm not sure I'd recognize a counterfeit if I saw one."

"I would," Grissom replied. The ears, in particular, looked remarkably realistic. The complicated folds of the human ear, he knew, were difficult to duplicate by counterfeiters. If this was a fake, made from goatskin or a flayed monkey, it was a good one. *It's no dried apple, that's for sure.*

Brass viewed the shrunken head with obvious distaste. "Amazonian? As in the river?"

"The practice originated among the Jivaro tribesmen of what is now Ecuador and Peru," Grissom expounded to the others. "The heads were trophies of raids on rival tribes. Claiming an enemy's head was a way of acquiring his soul and power. The ritual was also intended to prevent a fallen enemy's spirit from taking revenge on his killer." A thought occurred to him. "Excuse me, Professor. Does the department have any *tsantas* in its collections?"

Kim shook his head. "Not that I'm aware of."

Brass smirked at Grissom. "Guess that puts your office one up on the university."

"Come again?" Kim asked, giving the cop a befuddled look.

"Never mind," Grissom said. "What about the Barrick Museum?" The university's celebrated natural history museum, which was only a short walk from Wright Hall, contained an impressive collection of pre-Columbian relics from Latin America, as well as southwestern Native American artifacts, but Grissom couldn't recall ever seeing any *tsantas* on display. "Could they be missing a shrunken head?"

Kim scratched his chin. "I'll have to look into that, but I don't believe so."

"I'll have somebody talk to the curator," Brass

volunteered. He scribbled a reminder into his note-book. "Who knows? Maybe this is just some sort of college prank." He nodded at the *tsanta*. "What I really want to know is, how old is that thing? Does it belong in a museum—or a morgue?"

Good question, Grissom thought. It was funny how the passage of time inevitably transformed a crime into history. In a sense, all genuine shrunken heads were evidence of killings, but he saw the detective's point. A homicide committed along the Amazon several generations ago was well beyond the LVPD's jurisdiction. "Hard to say. I'll know more after we get it back to the lab."

First, though, there was a somewhat awkward line of inquiry to be pursued. "Excuse me, Dr. Kim." Grissom gave the professor another look at the *tsanta*. "Do you recognize this face? Perhaps it re-sembles a student or colleague?"

Kim was visibly taken aback by the question. "I . . . I don't think so." He backed away from Grissom, looking appalled by the very notion. "You aren't truly suggesting foul play, are you? That seems almost impossible to believe."

Not really, Grissom thought. He had once found a human head mounted on a wall like a hunting tro-phy. If there was one thing his career had taught him, besides the fact that evidence never lied, it was that human beings were capable of almost every-thing. "We have to consider every possibility," he said. "Are you certain that this face doesn't remind you of anyone?"

"I'm positive," Kim insisted.

Grissom took the professor at his word—for now,

at least. "All right. Thank you." He approached Vivian McQueen, the office manager, who flinched as he held the shrunken head up in front of her. She was a slight, matronly woman whose permed brown hair was a few decades out of style. Her conservative light blue pantsuit had toner stainers on the sleeves, the battle scars of routine office work. "What about you, Ms. McQueen? Does he look familiar to you?"

She shook her head emphatically. "No. At least, I don't think so." A shiver ran through her body, and she hugged herself to keep warm. "It's hard to think of that . . . thing . . . as a person."

"I can see that," Nick said sympathetically. He fished the package's original brown paper wrapping from Vivian's wastebasket and carefully bagged it for processing. Grissom winced at the thought of all the contaminants lurking in the trash. Was that a fresh ketchup stain on the torn wrapping?

"Better bag up the entire contents of the wastebasket," he advised Nick. "Just in case some trace evidence fell off the packaging."

At least the box didn't end up in the garbage, too.

"Right," Nick said somewhat sheepishly. "I should've thought of that."

McQueen blinked in surprise. "You want all my *garbage*?"

"Simply a precaution to ensure that we don't overlook any evidence," Grissom assured her. "We appreciate your cooperation."

Apparently, there was nothing particularly embarrassing or incriminating in the trash, since the stricken woman raised no further objections to Nick pillaging her wastebasket. Instead she turned her attention back to the disturbing curio in Grissom's hand. "I don't understand," she said, shaking her head in shocked disbelief. "Who would do such a thing, in this day and age?"

"That's what I intend to find out," Grissom said.

Modern science met primitive craftsmanship as a brilliant red laser beam scanned the shrunken head as it rotated slowly on a turntable. Mirrors on either side of the rotating stand reflected images of the *tsanta*'s illuminated features to sensors that then transmitted the data to a nearby computer workstation in the Las Vegas Criminalistics Bureau's well-equipped computer-imaging lab. A luminous green image began to form on the computer's monitor as a sophisticated program calculated the distance from each point on the surface of the shrunken head from the axis of rotation, in order to create a 3-D virtual model of the *tsanta*. Nick carried out the procedure while Grissom stood by, waiting on the results. Assistant coroner David Phillips was on hand to take custody of the head prior to its inevitable postmortem. A bespectacled young man in his mid-thirties, David wore a white lab jacket over his street clothes.

Ordinarily, an autopsy would be the first order of business for any suspicious cadaver, or portion thereof, but Grissom had decided to break protocol in this instance. The intact *tsanta* was possibly the key item of evidence in this case, and there were a number of crucial tests he wished to run on the head before subjecting it to dissection. He also had his doubts as to just how valuable a routine post-

mortem would prove to be this time around. Doc
Robbins was going to have to wait for this particular
John Doe.

Glancing away from the computer monitor, Grissom noted that a small crowd of spectators had
gathered in the corridor outside the imaging lab.
Catherine Willows, Warrick Brown, David Hodges,
Greg Sanders, and miscellaneous "lab rats" peered
through the lab's clear glass walls at the shrunken
head, which was obviously a topic of considerable
interest and gossip. The inquisitive audience did not
escape Nick's notice as well.

"Looks like we should've sold tickets," he
quipped.

"I'm not sure Ecklie would approve of that," Grissom replied, referring to their occasionally thin-
skinned boss. He was pleased to see that all the
extra scrutiny did not appear to rattle Nick or interfere with his attention to his task. The broad-
shouldered young Texan had come a long way since
joining Grissom's team over a decade ago. "This is
supposed to be a crime lab, not a sideshow."

Still, he couldn't really blame the snoopers in the
hall for their curiosity regarding the *tsanta*, especially after he'd rhapsodized to Brass earlier about
the inherently fascinating nature of shrunken
heads. The detective himself was not among the
spectators outside; as far as Grissom knew, Brass
was still trying to track down the curator of the Barrick Museum to see if a redheaded *tsanta* had gone
astray recently.

Grissom glanced at his watch. It was almost
eleven. Scanning an adult human skull generally

took about an hour; creating a digital model of the smaller *tsanta* might go more quickly, he estimated, but still, he probably had better things to do with his time than look over Nick's shoulder for another forty-five minutes or so. Such as refreshing his memory on the history and lore of headhunting. Fortunately, he had several interesting books and pamphlets on the subject in his office.

"Carry on," he instructed Nick before turning toward David Phillips. "Let me know when Dr. Robbins is ready to examine the specimen."

"Yes, sir," David agreed. Like everyone else, his gaze was glued to the wizened, disembodied head on the turntable. His eyes were wide behind the lenses of his horn-rimmed black glasses.

The crowd in the hallway dispersed rapidly as Grissom exited the lab. Brisk footsteps echoed through the aquamarine glass-and-steel corridors of the complex as criminalists, clerks, and technicians suddenly remembered things they needed to be doing. The sprawling facility, which had once served as a warehouse for confiscated firearms and ammunition, was a maze of labs, conference rooms, and offices into which the staff could disappear as needed. Grissom allowed himself a bemused smile. It was good to know that the *tsanta*'s arrival hadn't completely disrupted the crime lab's nocturnal routines, such as they were. Ultimately, it was just another dead body.

Or, at least, a portion thereof.

The temperature in the morgue was a crisp forty-five degrees Fahrenheit, the better to preserve the human remains temporarily taking up residence there. The stainless-steel furnishings and the tile floor were kept meticulously clean. Glass-faced steel cabinets, holding chemicals, containers, and the other paraphernalia of the coroner's trade, were mounted over the sinks and counters. A refrigeration unit held tissue and organ samples until they could be sent for analysis. A hanging scale was on hand to measure brains, hearts, and other organs. The pristine, sterile environment was designed to prevent contamination, not infection, since its visitors were, by definition, beyond medical assistance. The *tsanta* looked strangely out of place on the polished steel operating table at the center of the morgue. A lip around the table was intended to direct bodily fluids to the drain at one end. That wasn't an issue in this instance.

"Well, this is a first," Dr. Albert Robbins observed. The chief medical examiner was not referring to the partial nature of the cadaver; in the past, he had often been called upon to examine severed heads, decapitated corpses, and random body parts. Once he'd had nothing to work with but a single severed finger. He peered at the shrunken head through his glasses. Blue surgical scrubs shrouded his stout middle-aged frame. His metal crutch, a legacy of a long-ago auto accident, was propped up against a nearby counter. "Been raiding horror-movie sets, have we?"

It wouldn't be the first time, Grissom thought. Less than a year ago, his CSIs had investigated a series of gruesome deaths on the set of a low-budget slasher film. Unfortunately, some of the blood had been all too real, as had been the danger. They had nearly lost a promising young intern on that case.

"We didn't want you getting bored," he quipped. He was also dressed out in surgical scrubs.

"I appreciate that," Robbins replied. He enjoyed an easy camaraderie with Grissom. The two men had worked together as peers for many years. "Although you didn't have to import a headhunter to Vegas on my account."

"*If* this head was indeed harvested in Clark County and environs," Grissom hedged, not wanting them to get ahead of themselves, "and not in the jungles of Peru."

Robbins nodded. "Let's see if we can get that sorted out." He glanced over at his assistant. "How are we doing on that fluoroscope, David?"

"Almost ready," David said as he finished positioning the hanging X-ray scanner over the *tsanta*. "I had to replace one of the HV transformers." He activated the device via a laptop computer, and a see-through image of the miniature head appeared on an LCD screen mounted nearby. The three men stared at the *tsanta*'s profile. As with the laser scan, Grissom had wanted to examine the specimen non-invasively before proceeding to the autopsy.

"No skull or brain matter," Robbins observed. "Not much inside at all, in fact." He squinted at the X-ray. "Is that sand in there?"

"Probably." This discovery did not surprise Grissom. "Traditionally, the skull was quickly discarded and tossed into the river as a 'gift to the anaconda.' The skin, which had been carefully peeled away from the skull, was then simmered in hot water to begin the shrinking process. Later, the skin was turned inside out and scraped free of excess fat and muscle before being turned right-side out again. Heated rocks were placed inside the skin to shrink it from within. This process was repeated several times, with successively smaller rocks and, eventually, hot sand. The whole ritual took about a week."

Which puts the time of death at least seven days ago or more, he thought. *Talk about premeditated.*

David repositioned the fluoroscope to X-ray the *tsanta* from several angles. The device often detected foreign objects embedded inside a corpse, and this time was no exception. "What's that beneath the eyelids?" Robbins asked aloud. "Seeds?"

"Exactly," Grissom said. "The Jivaro would place red seeds where the eyes should be before sewing the lids shut. Great care was taken to try to preserve some semblance of the victim's original features. The warrior would mold the skin around the hot sand in order to retain the resemblance. It was quite an art."

"I think I'll stick to music," Robbins said wryly. He stroked his neat white beard thoughtfully. "What about the mouth?"

"The mouth was dried by having a hot knife pressed against it," Grissom explained. "Then the lips were held together by palm pins and sewn shut." He contemplated the knotted hemp cords holding the specimen's lips together. With luck, an examination of the cords themselves would help determine the head's origins and identity. *That sounds right up Nick's alley.*

"All right, David," Robbins instructed the younger man after he had scanned the head from every conceivable angle. "I think we have enough coverage."

He glanced at Grissom, who nodded in agreement, and stepped up to the operating table. "Shall we dig in?"

Grissom conducted a quick mental checklist to make certain that there weren't any more tests he wanted to have performed on the specimen before allowing Robbins to violate the *tsanta*'s virginity as it were. "Let me check one more thing first."

He put on his own glasses and gently lifted the *tsanta* from the table. Using a magnifying glass, he peered into the head's tiny nasal cavities. Tiny filaments were plastered to the interior of the specimen's shrunken nose. *Eureka.*

"Something interesting?" Robbins asked.

Grissom nodded. "Nasal hairs." According to the research he had just conducted in his office, the presence of the minuscule hairs suggested that they indeed had a genuine human head on their hands, not just a cleverly made facsimile. "It's a good way to tell the fakes from the real thing. Imitation *tsantas* usually lack nasal hairs."

Along with the specimen's intricately detailed ears, the hairs left Grissom convinced that the artifact in his hands had once been a living, breathing human being. Now they just had to determine when and how he had died.

He put the *tsanta* back down on the table and stepped back to give Robbins more room. Having produced permanent records of both the shrunken head's exterior and interior, he felt confident to let the autopsy proceed. "He's all yours."

Robbins began by taking samples of the hair and skin. A surgical mask covered the lower portion of the doctor's face, while latex gloves sheathed his fingers. Lifting the *tsanta* from the table, he scrutinized its scalp beneath the spotlight. He used a pair of tweezers to pluck a single strand of hair from the specimen. "Take a look at this, Gil. Our redheaded John Doe appears to have gray roots."

"A dye job?" Grissom's pulse quickened as he confirmed that the reddish strand was definitely gray at the bottom. Identifying the nature of the dye might go a long way toward determining the age of the shrunken head. He quickly bagged the telltale hair and handed it off to David. "Get this to Trace right away. Tell Hodges I want results as soon as possible."

"Got it." David rushed the sample out through a pair of swinging double doors.

Robbins did not object to the temporary loss of his assistant. Working methodically, he extracted samples of the beads in the *tsanta*'s beard and hair and put them aside for processing. A cursory examination revealed that the beads were made from all natural materials: clay, wood, shell, and polished stone. A certain uniformity of size and shape hinted at mass production. He spoke aloud into a digital tape recorder as he examined the stitching holding the head together:

"A vertical antemortem suture, approximately seven inches in length, running up the back of the head, presumably where the flesh was peeled away from the skull. The neck is drawn closed with a string to prevent the contents from spilling out. Additional stitching to hold the eyes and lips shut."

Something caught Robbins's attention, and he held the *tsanta* up to the light to get a better look. He delicately brushed the hair away from the ears, then took a closer look at the chin. "Well, this is interesting," he commented. "Seems our pygmy-sized friend here has had a face-lift."

Grissom arched an eyebrow. "Cosmetic surgery?"

"Yep, and not too long ago." He held out the head for Grissom's inspection. "Note the distinctive scarring behind the earlobe and beneath the chin." Faint white lines betrayed the surgeon's work. "Judging from the look of the scars, I'd guess that this poor fellow had a bit of work done less than a year before his death." Robbins peered over the top of his glasses at Grissom. "I'm no expert, but I'm guessing that they weren't performing rhytidectomies along the Amazon back in the day."

"No, they weren't," Grissom said. The Jivaro had a fascinating culture, but modern face-lift surgery had never been a part of it, and certainly not during the glory days of headhunting, a practice that had been banned for generations. "So it would appear that our redheaded victim here was *not* some unlucky explorer or missionary who came to a bad end decades ago."

"That would be my assessment," Robbins agreed. "But identifying the victim is going to be a challenge. No fingerprints. No dental work. A preliminary examination suggests that the head belonged to a redheaded Caucasian male, but beyond that, I'm stumped." An alcohol-dampened pad had wiped away the ashy residue from a portion of the *tsanta*'s forehead, exposing pale white skin beneath the dark, sooty polish. "I'm afraid you and your people have got your work cut out for you."

Grissom shrugged. "We always do."

The doors swung open and David hurried back into the lab. "Hodges is checking into the hair dye," he reported breathlessly. He pulled his own surgical mask up over his face. "I miss anything?"

"Just the fact that our victim had a face-lift before he got his head shrunk." Robbins succinctly brought the younger man up to speed, then lifted a gleaming scalpel from the tray by the operating table. "I'm making the first incision now." Ordinarily, he would open the cranium to remove the brain at this point, but that was hardly an option today. Instead he slit open the stitching at the back of the head and poured the contents of the head into a small steel basin. Sure enough, the head appeared to hold nothing except a handful or two of gritty brown sand. "You know, this thing is nothing but a glorified bean bag, albeit with slightly nastier upholstery."

To Grissom's disappointment, the exposed sand appeared nondescript in nature, of the sort widely available in the deserts outside the city. Still, perhaps Trace would be able to discover something more distinctive in the soil sample. If they could determine where exactly the sediment came from, that might bring them a step closer to identifying the headhunter—and the victim.

They still didn't know for sure that it was a murder investigation, but he was getting a bad feeling about this case. "There was a note enclosed with the *tsanta*," he stated. "Just two words: *tumashi akerkama*."

"That mean something to you?" Robbins asked.

"Not at first, but I looked it up once we got back to the lab. It's the Jivaro term for 'blood-guilt.' A crime against a person or a clan that can only be avenged through bloodshed."

"Not exactly a friendly sentiment," Robbins noted. "More like a threat."

"That's what I'm afraid of," Grissom said. As a rule, he distrusted hunches, preferring to rely ultimately on the evidence instead, and yet . . . the prospect of a genuine headhunter prowling the neon jungle of Las Vegas gave him pause. If nothing else, the media was going to eat this up with a spoon—which never made the CSIs' job any easier.

The more publicity, the more pressure there'll be to wrap this case up quickly.

Robbins weighed the sand in a hanging scale. "Three-point-five ounces." He handed the basin over to David for processing before returning to what was left of the *tsanta*. Emptied of its stuffing, the shrunken head lay flat against the steel tabletop like a deflated balloon. A few deft incisions opened the eyelids, allowing the doctor to extract the seeds underneath. The black tear-shaped seeds looked as if they had come from a watermelon. These, too, were bagged as evidence, as well as the thread removed from the stitches. Bar-coded labels ensured that each sample could be individually tracked and identified. Finally, Robbins removed the thread from the head's pursed lips.

"Well, that's it." He stepped back from the table and lowered his mask. "I'm afraid there's not much to examine here. No bones. No organs. No bodily fluids. Not much in the way of tissue. Just a dried flap of skin and some hair."

"That may be enough," Grissom said. Each piece

of evidence, no matter how seemingly insignificant, represented a potential lead or breakthrough. Hairs, seeds, sand, fibers . . . if nothing else, the autopsy had given his people a lot to work with. He resolved to have the flattened face scanned as well before Robbins or David put the *tsanta* back together. "Any thoughts regarding cause of death?"

Robbins gave Grissom a bemused look. "Are you serious? I'll have hair and skin samples sent to toxicology, but I'm not optimistic. These remains have been smoked, stewed, and mummified, which is going to make it difficult, if not impossible, to determine the cause and the time of death by biological means."

He spread the empty skin out on the table so that it was stretched taut against the polished steel underneath. It looked like a Halloween mask for a small monkey. "Judging from the lack of bruising, the lacerations along the bottom of the neck appear to have been inflicted postmortem, but I can't swear to it. Still, my best guess is that the head was severed after death."

"That would fit the pattern," Grissom stated. "The Jivaro typically killed their foes in battle before taking their heads." He bent over the table to check out the flattened face's mouth. "Observe the perforations in the victim's lips. The Jivaro would hold the lips shut with wooden pins before sewing the mouth closed. Such perforations are usually missing on imitation heads."

"Sounds like your killer is a sucker for tradition," Robbins said. "Assuming there actually is a killer on the loose." He strove for a hopeful tone. "Maybe someone simply mutilated a corpse?"

Grissom conceded the possibility. "There's certainly precedent for that. Back around the turn of the century, shrunken heads became such hot commodities in the United States and Europe that unscrupulous doctors and taxidermists started manufacturing their own for the tourist trade, using unclaimed bodies from South American hospitals and morgues."

"Disgraceful," Robbins muttered, clearly offended by the very idea. As coroner, he took his responsibility to the dead very seriously. Despite the extremely invasive nature of an autopsy, the doctor always treated the cadavers with respect and did his best to reassemble them after the postmortem was completed. Even the shrunken head would eventually be put back together again—although Grissom was not looking forward to informing the victim's loved ones what had become of his remains. *That's going to come as a quite a shock to them.*

"All of which raises the most pressing question." Grissom nodded at the unidentified face on the table. "Where's the rest of him?"

3

" . . . SO THEN THIS CRAZY voodoo priest brings these shrunken heads to life to fight crime," Greg Sanders said, enthusiastically recounting the plot of some bizarre horror movie Catherine Willows had never heard of. "And they fly around like superheroes!"

The CSIs were seated around the large rectangular light table in the layout room at CSI HQ. Photos from ongoing investigations, many of them brutally explicit, were pinned to the eastern wall. A glass door offered a view of the corridor outside, as well as the entrance to the garage across the hall. The roomy chamber provided a convenient venue when the team needed to meet to review a case. Besides Greg and Catherine, Warrick Brown and Nick Stokes had also gathered to await Grissom's assignments for the evening. A day had passed since the shrunken head's discovery, but the mystery of the university's unwanted package—and shrunken heads in general—was still the primary topic of conversation.

"Wait a second." Catherine tried to follow her colleague's story. "The heads can fly?" An attractive blonde in her mid-forties, she wore a stylish leather jacket over a tank top and slacks. "How can shrunken heads fly?"

Greg shrugged. The former lab rat, who was at least twelve years younger than Catherine, considered himself a real pop-culture maven. Perhaps in emulation of Grissom, he was wearing a gray T-shirt and dark slacks. "Um . . . the power of voodoo?"

"Voodoo has nothing to do with shrunken heads," Grissom corrected him as the supervisor entered the room. An armload of folders was cradled against his black polo shirt. "*Vodou* evolved from West African origins, by way of the Caribbean. Shrunken heads, or *tsantas,* are of South American origin."

Greg looked sheepish, and Catherine felt a twinge of sympathy. Grissom had always intimidated the younger man, who had struggled to work his way up (or down, depending on your perspective) from highly paid DNA technician to overworked field agent. "Don't tell me," Greg said, attempting to brazen it out. "Tell Hollywood."

"I think I have somewhat more important things to do," Grissom said archly, while Greg squirmed uncomfortably in his seat. Catherine couldn't tell if Greg's still-occasional bursts of immaturity actually got on their boss's nerves or if Grissom just liked torturing the kid sometimes. *Probably a little bit of both,* she guessed. *Or maybe this is his way of keeping Greg on his toes.*

Taking mercy on Greg, she changed the subject. "Grissom. Warrick and I wrapped up that hit-and-run from Friday." They had been working the case full-time for three days now. "Sofia just got a confession from the perp. Apparently, he spilled like a piñata once she confronted him with the tire impressions."

"So I heard," Grissom said. "Good work, both of you." He posted a color photo of the shrunken head on the bulletin board, then sat down at the head of the table. "That frees you up to go headhunter-hunting with the rest of us."

Warrick Brown nodded at the freaky-looking photo. "So what's the story with Little John there?"

Grissom arched an eyebrow. "'Little John?'"

"That's what people are calling him around the lab," Warrick explained casually. Unlike Greg, the handsome African-American CSI was much more comfortable around Grissom. A black T-shirt and faded jeans flattered his rangy, athletic physique. Exotic green eyes peered from his rugged features. "Because he's a John Doe, but, um, you know, little . . ."

His voice trailed off as he realized how lame that sounded. *Ouch*, Catherine thought, wincing in sympathy. *If you have to explain a joke . . .*

"I see." Grissom sounded distinctly unamused. "Perhaps I need to remind you all that, despite the more . . . colorful aspects of this case, we *are* dealing with a serious matter here. Whoever Little John was, he was a human being, whose life apparently ended too soon." Peering over the tops of his wire-framed glasses, he swept a stern gaze over the assembled crime-scene investigators. "We need to treat this investigation just as we would for any other dead body found under suspicious circumstances."

He paused to let his admonition sink in. Catherine felt the mood in the room grow more somber. Although he rarely raised his voice, Grissom could put the fear of God into his subordinates when he had to. None of them ever wanted to disappoint him.

"Point taken," Warrick conceded. The other CSIs murmured in agreement.

Catherine leaned forward. "So, are we talking homicide here?"

"Perhaps," Grissom said. Having made his point, he relaxed his body language somewhat. He relayed the findings of the autopsy, even though office gossip had already transmitted most of the pertinent details throughout the building. "We are not dealing with a historical relic or a high-quality replica," he summarized. "This is an actual human head that appears to have been recently harvested. What we need to determine now is the victim's identity, and whether he was murdered or died of natural causes."

We're dealing with a pretty twisted mind either way, Catherine thought. She wasn't exactly squeamish, but the idea of someone turning a human head into a grotesque souvenir made her skin crawl. That sounded like serial-killer behavior to her. *Except . . . don't serial killers usually keep their trophies?*

"I don't get it," she said. "Why go to all the trouble of shrinking a head, then just pop it into the mail to the local college? Wouldn't a true headhunter want to hang on to his prize?"

"Not necessarily," Grissom said. "In fact, the Jivaro usually discarded their *tsantas* once the traditional rituals and celebrations were completed.

Often, they were given away as gifts or even turned into toys by the native children. It was the act of creating the *tsanta,* and displaying it in elaborate ceremonies, that granted a victorious warrior the spiritual power of his enemy, not the actual possession of the head. It may be that our local hunter had no further use for this particular specimen."

"And decided to make an anonymous donation to UNLV?" Catherine still found the whole notion hard to wrap her head around. "How civic-minded of him. Are we talking about an oddly generous alum here?"

"Perhaps." Grissom consulted his notes. "Any results from Trace on the hair samples?"

To Catherine's slight relief, trace evidence technician David Hodges was not sitting in on this meeting. Hodges knew his stuff, but his inflated ego, and eagerness to suck up to Grissom, were more than a little off-putting. Frankly, he got on her nerves.

Nick answered Grissom's query instead. "According to Hodges, the dye used on his hair was 'Just For Men Color Gel.'" The trace analyst had run the hair sample through the gas chromatograph mass spectrometer to get a precise chemical breakdown of the dye, then checked it against a computerized database. "Unfortunately, it's a common brand, widely available in most drugstores."

"Plastic surgery *and* hair dye," Catherine said. "Let's hear it for male vanity."

"Guess we're looking at someone who cared about looking good," Warrick said.

Nick cracked a smile. "Good thing we're not based out of L.A."

"Trust me, La-La Land's got no monopoly on narcissistic males," Catherine said. "Vegas has plenty of its own, both homegrown and imported."

She automatically looked to Sara Sidle for confirmation, then remembered that the other woman no longer worked there. After eight years of working alongside the driven, sometimes acerbic young criminalist, it felt strange not having Sara around, not to mention being the only woman on the team. *We definitely need to get another girl in here.*

"At least the modern hair dye proves for sure that this is a *new* shrunken head and not a museum piece," Greg pointed out. "This is a twenty-first-century *tsanta*."

"Yes," Grissom agreed, "but we already knew that." He fixed his cool, penetrating gaze on Greg. "What's the story regarding DNA?"

The young CSI, who probably knew more about processing DNA samples than anyone else in the room, shook his head. "I don't know what they did to that head to shrink it," he said, "but the DNA we've retrieved so far has been badly denatured."

Catherine wasn't surprised. She'd looked up the basics on Wikipedia; from the sound of it, shrinking the skin involved a lot of heat and herbs. In fact, you had to be careful not to boil the *tsanta* by mistake, or all of its hair would fall out. *Wouldn't want that*, she thought wryly. *Whoever heard of a bald shrunken head?*

"Great," Warrick groused. "Another dead end."

"Maybe not," Greg said. "The ordinary nuclear DNA is toast, but maybe we can still salvage some of the mitochondrial DNA."

There's an idea, Catherine thought. Unlike regular, or autosomal, DNA, which was located in the nucleus of living cells, mitochondrial DNA was hidden away in the mitochondria, tiny organelles that floated in the cytoplasm outside the nucleus. MtDNA was hardier than regular DNA and could be found in places where ordinary DNA did not exist. Nuclear DNA, for instance, could be retrieved from a strand of hair only if the follicular bulb was still attached. But mtDNA could be found in any hair fragment, provided you had the time and resources to extract it. Too bad it wasn't easier to pull off.

"Good idea, Greg," Grissom said. "Mitochondrial DNA has been successfully extracted from ancient mummies. Just a few years ago, a team of German scientists obtained usable mtDNA from mummified Neanderthal remains that were nearly fifty thousand years old."

"Right." Warrick nodded. "That was in *Scientific American* a while back. They've also used mtDNA to trace the ancestry of ancient Egyptian pharaohs and their relatives."

"Okay then," Nick said enthusiastically. "If you can get DNA out of some old freeze-dried caveman, how hard can a shrunken head be?"

"Don't ask," Greg said. "There's a reason we don't do it every day."

Was Greg just stressing the technical challenges involved, Catherine wondered, or was he now worried that he might have raised everyone's expectations too high? *Tough,* she thought. *That's how the game is played sometimes. You want to impress Grissom, you have to go out on a limb.*

"Still, it's our best option at this point," Grissom decided. "Have Wendy get to work on that." Wendy Simms had been the lab's chief DNA specialist for two years now. Catherine had been impressed by the woman's skill and professionalism. "Let me know if she needs any extra equipment or manpower."

Or money, Catherine thought. In the past, they'd had to ship samples to the FBI for mtDNA testing. After an epic budget battle, the DNA lab had recently upgraded its ABI genetic analyzer, but Catherine wasn't enough of an expert to know whether the new machine was up to tackling mtDNA and what sort of special reagents might be required. She wondered how Grissom was planning to get Ecklie, not to mention Sheriff Burdick, to spring for the extra bucks for the mtDNA extraction. *That's not exactly cheap.*

"In the meantime," Warrick commented, "at least we've got a photo of the victim. Sort of." He gestured toward the mummified face on the wall. "I have to ask, Gris, how much of a likeness is *that* compared to the guy when he was still alive?"

Grissom shrugged. "That depends on the craftsmanship of the headhunter. Obviously, the bone structure is missing, as are the eyes and fatty tissue, but a *tsanta* is supposed to retain the features of the fallen warrior."

"I suppose," Catherine said dubiously. In her experience, even an ordinary cadaver looked very different from a living human being. Would Little John's friends or associates be able to recognize the shriveled memento mori as someone they once knew? Frankly, she wasn't so sure. *It doesn't look much like a person to me.*

Nick sighed. "Guess a facial reconstruction is out of the question. No skull, nothing to work with."

He had a point there. Facial reconstructions, whether done in clay by a talented sculptor or via computer, used the skull as the starting point upon which to re-create the features of an unidentified victim. Without even a fragment of the skull, they were screwed.

Or were they?

"What about doing some sort of *reverse* facial reconstruction?" she suggested. "To work up a portrait of what Little John looked like before his skull was removed and his skin was mummified?"

Nick gave her a skeptical look. "Is that even possible?"

Beats me, she thought. It sounded as if it ought to be feasible, but what did she know? *I'm a criminalist, not a forensic anthropologist.*

"I like that idea," Grissom said, visibly intrigued by the challenge. Despite his austere, professional demeanor, Catherine knew him well enough to spot a gleam of scientific excitement in his eyes. She guessed that he was already brainstorming ideas for how to go about it. "Let me look into that."

Grissom glanced at his wristwatch. "Time to get going." He stood up and walked around the table, handing out folders and assignments to the other CSIs. "Greg, I want you to scour the missing-persons case files for our John Doe. Shrunken heads take about six or seven days to prepare, so start with the people reported missing roughly a week ago, then work backward from there."

Greg grimaced at the tedious-sounding chore but,

wisely, did not complain. Catherine didn't envy him
his task. Vegas had a high population turnover;
there were bound to be plenty of missing persons.
"I'll get right on it."

"Nick," Grissom continued. "Keep looking over
the packaging the *tsanta* came in. Plus the beads and
other accouterments. Maybe there's something we
missed earlier."

"You got it," Nick said readily. Hair and fiber
analysis was his specialty. Grissom had already provided him with samples of the *tsanta*'s beads and
threads the night before.

"Catherine, Warrick." Grissom slid a folder across
a table to her. "Why don't you check out what the
market for shrunken heads is like these days? Find
out where one gets one's hands on an authentic
tsanta in this day and age."

Warrick saw where Grissom was going with this.
"Who's buying, who's selling . . . that sort of
thing?"

"Exactly," their supervisor said. "After all, we
don't know for sure that the individual who mailed
the head to UNLV is the same person who harvested
the head. Maybe the mailer bought the head online
or from a local dealer."

"Always possible, I suppose," Catherine said. At
this point in her life, it took a lot to surprise her. She
started flicking through the folder, which seemed
discouragingly thin. Hopefully, they'd be able to
flesh out the case file soon. "Remember that moron
who tried to get rid of the murder weapon in a yard
sale?"

Grissom chuckled. "How could I forget? I managed to pick up the bloodstained hatchet, and a used ant farm, for just $1.75. Sadly, I don't think we can count on this case to be wrapped up quite so easily." His voice took on a more solemn tone. "Somebody put a lot of time, study, and concentration into shrinking this head. I suspect we're going to need to do the same to catch him."

"Okay," Warrick said. His chiseled features displayed his resolve as he spoke for everyone in the room. "Then let's do it."

4

GRISSOM FOUND JIM BRASS waiting for him in the CSI supervisor's office. The cop was admiring, if that was the right word for it, a partially desiccated *tsanta* that Grissom kept preserved in a jar of formaldehyde. The relic, which Grissom had inherited from a deceased colleague, shared shelf space with a two-headed scorpion, pickled rat fetuses, and other oddities. Mounted butterflies, moths, spiders, and other insects were displayed on the wall behind Grissom's desk, above rows of well-thumbed tomes on every conceivable subject. Although most of the animals and insects on exhibit were long dead, he also maintained a small menagerie of living specimens, including ants, cockroaches, and a pet tarantula, all kept safely behind glass, much to the relief of his coworkers and jittery visitors. Every exhibit was meticulously labeled, often in Grissom's own handwriting. A miniature refrigerator hummed softly in the background. No one was quite sure what Grissom kept there.

"You know, that DB from the university does look a whole lot fresher than this guy," Brass commented as Grissom entered the office. He shot Grissom an apologetic look. "No offense."

"None taken." Grissom sat down behind his cluttered desk, which was canted at a forty-five-degree angle to the door. Stacks of unwelcome paperwork awaited his attention. "The *tsanta* under investigation is a beautiful specimen, in near-perfect condition. It's almost a shame it's locked up in the morgue for the time being."

Robbins and David had done first-rate work reassembling the *tsanta* following the autopsy, refilling the empty skin with all but a small sample of the original sand. The shrunken head was once again ready to star as Exhibit A in court, assuming the case ever went to trial. *First we have to find out who he is and where he came from,* Grissom thought. *As well as who is responsible for the unusual condition of the remains.*

"Well, I'm not sure 'beautiful' is quite the right word I'd use to describe it," Brass replied, "but to each his own." He made himself at home in one of the vinyl-covered metal chairs facing the desk. This office had once belonged to Brass, in fact, during the cop's short-lived stint as supervisor of the crime lab. The political fallout from a young CSI's death several years ago had sent Brass back to Homicide, but he had never given Grissom any grief for replacing him. Although he'd never said as much, Brass seemed happier chasing down leads and interrogating suspects than riding herd on a bunch of brainy science whizzes. "Anyway, I got some info for you on where that lovely specimen *didn't* come from."

Grissom leaned forward. "Which is?"

"The Marjorie Barrick Museum at the University of Nevada, Las Vegas." Brass consulted his notebook. "I finally tracked down the curator, who informed me in no uncertain terms that they had no shrunken heads in their collection, missing or otherwise. Ditto for the Anthropology and Archeology Departments." He rubbed his eyes, worn out from running into dead ends all day. "I admit I haven't checked out the frat houses or sororities yet."

"I'm sure the university officials appreciate that," Grissom said dryly. In his experience, the heads of the college could be skittish when it came to alarming students and their parents. News of a possible headhunter on the loose would probably not go over well with the Alumni Association. "Thanks for looking into that, Jim, but I was afraid it wasn't going to be that easy. And UNLV isn't a medical college, so we can probably rule out any anatomy class hijinks."

Brass glanced over at the head in the jar. "Any progress ID'ing our vic?"

"Not yet," Grissom admitted, "although I've got the whole team working on it." Although they hadn't yet proven conclusively that this was a murder case, the ominous message still haunted him. *Tumashi akerkama.* Blood-guilt. Unscientific though it was, he couldn't help sensing that the elusive headhunter was just getting warmed up. Avenging past wrongs had been more than just a hobby for the Jivaro of old; it had been a way of life.

What if our modern-day headhunter feels the same way?

"Sounds good," Brass said. "Keep me posted." He heaved himself to his feet and headed for the exit. A thought occurred to him and he paused before the door. "That reminds me. You all set for the O'Malley trial next week?"

Richard O'Malley had killed his son-in-law, Don Cook, by sabotaging Cook's car so that it caught fire on the highway. O'Malley tried to pin the blame for the murder on a Vegas street gang, but Grissom had determined the real killer by linking a phony bit of gang-inspired graffiti to a paintbrush in O'Malley's garage. Although the crime had been solved months ago, the case was only just now going to court. Testifying and explaining often highly technical evidence to juries was a crucial part of every CSI's job.

"My presentation is all set," Grissom assured Brass. "The evidence is sound. The case is airtight. I'm not anticipating any surprises during the defense's cross-examination."

"Glad to hear it," Brass said. "At least that's one less murdering SOB on the streets."

"Yes." Grissom's gaze was drawn to a bulletin board mounted to the left of his desk. Faded mug shots and yellowing newspaper clippings served as a constant reminder of various criminals who had managed either to beat the rap or to evade capture. Such as Dr. Vincent Lurie, Claudia Gibson, Julia Fairmont, and even thirteen-year-old Hannah West. Grissom kept the discouraging display on hand so that he would always remember that cases were never closed until justice was finally served . . .

no matter how long it took. "Too bad someone else always comes along to maintain the murder rate."

Nick Stokes peered through the dual eyepieces of a comparative microscope at the bisected image before him. On the left was a magnified view of a small clay bead from the *tsanta*'s beard. On the right was a similar-looking bead Nick had picked up at a Michaels crafts-supply store earlier that evening, before reporting into work. He suppressed a yawn; one of the drawbacks of working the graveyard shift was that, even in a 24/7 city like Vegas, certain lines of investigation needed to be conducted during regular business hours. *Should I put in for the overtime, or is that not worth the hassle?* A receipt for the cost of the beads was tucked away in his wallet. Hopefully, he could get reimbursed for the out-of-pocket expense, at least.

Just have to make sure I don't lose the receipt before I get around to filing the paperwork.

He carefully examined the two beads under the microscope, adjusting the lenses to bring the divided image more clearly into focus. Each bead was a carved wooden sphere, about the size of a pea, with a hole drilled through the middle. To his disappointment, they were more or less identical.

Damn.

He leaned back and gave his tired eyes a break. Glass doors and walls sealed off the Trace lab from the gentle hubbub of the corridor outside. An AFIS computer terminal hummed on a metal desk nearby, next to a battered set of filing cabinets. Test tubes, pipettes, and other glassware occupied shelves and counters. A miniature refrigerator and oven were on hand to cool and heat samples, respectively. The air-conditioned atmosphere smelled faintly of chemicals. On the counter before him, carefully arrayed in clear plastic trays, were bead and thread samples from the shrunken head. A separate tray held a variety of commercially sold beads from the Michaels on South Decatur Boulevard.

Nick sighed and rubbed his eyes. *Another strike-out.* He had been at this for over an hour now, without any luck. He had been hoping that one or more of the beads from the *tsanta* would turn out to be made from some exotic bone or other material that was only available from a few specialized dealers, who might have records of recent sales or regular buyers. Unfortunately, he had already matched six of the original beads to ones found in an economy pack of "Jewelry Essentials Natural Beads," which had been on sale in quantity at the very first store he had checked.

So much for a hot lead. A frown marred his usually affable features. A former jock from Texas A&M University, the clean-cut, square-jawed criminalist was an easygoing guy under most circumstances. At the moment, though, he didn't even want to think about how many arts-and-crafts shops carried this brand of beads. To his knowledge, there were at least eight Michaels chain stores in Vegas alone. They even sold the same kind of coarse hemp thread. *One-stop shopping for your friendly neighborhood headhunter. . . .*

Nick tried not to let lack of progress get to him. Patience was essential when it came to forensics. *To go fast, go slow,* Grissom liked to say.

Still, whoever had prepared the *tsanta* certainly wasn't making Nick's life easy. The seeds beneath the eyes had turned out to be ordinary watermelon seeds, like what you'd find in the produce section of any grocery store. And so far, they hadn't found anything particularly distinctive about the sand inside the head, either. Nick wondered if the head-hunter had deliberately employed common materials to evade detection, or if he'd just shopped for something close and convenient. Every part of the *tsanta* could have come straight from any neighborhood mall.

Aside from the severed human head, that is.

He glanced over at the lab's large central table. Spread out on it was the packaging the *tsanta* had come in, which he had already determined to be just ordinary brown paper, cardboard, and Kleenex. A thorough examination had turned up neither fingerprints nor epithelials on the papers, which suggested that whoever had packed the head had been using gloves. Likewise, ALS had detected no traces of blood or any other bodily fluids. In fact, all he'd found so far was a grayish-black smudge on one of the tissues used to cushion the *tsanta* during its trip through the mail. According to Grissom, the Jivaro had darkened the skin of their trophies by rubbing them with ash, so as to keep the trapped soul of their victims from seeping out.

Maybe some of that ash had rubbed off on the Kleenex? That might be another indicator that the shrunken head had been prepared fairly recently.

Little John might very well have been alive only a week or so ago.

A labeled paper bag, stowed away under the table, held the contents of Vivian McQueen's wastebasket. Nick had sifted through the trash carefully, but found only discarded junk mail, trashed memos and correspondence, a greasy fast-food wrapper, a Styrofoam coffee cup, and exactly seventeen foil candy wrappers. Aside from revealing that the middle-aged office manager liked junk food and apparently recycled all bottles and cans, the collection had not yielded much. He glanced impatiently at his watch, wishing he had more to show for his efforts.

"Getting nowhere?" a voice asked him.

David Hodges smirked at Nick from the other side of the lab. The lanky Trace technician was perched on a stool in front of a light-transmission microscope and infrared spectrometer. His ID badge was pinned to the lapel of his blue lab jacket. Limp brown hair was combed away from his high forehead. His lean face bore a typically smug expression.

"I'm making progress," Nick insisted. He bristled slightly at Hodges's tone, but kept his cool. He reminded himself that Hodges had literally saved his life on at least one occasion. When Nick had been buried alive five years ago, it was Hodges who had figured out that Nick's acrylic glass coffin was booby-trapped—and had stopped Grissom and the other CSIs from accidentally blowing Nick to pieces. "Just working the evidence."

"Really?" Hodges eyed Nick's collection of beads and thread. "'Cause from here, it looks like you're assembling the pieces of a lovely bracelet."

Nick gave Hodges the benefit of the doubt and assumed that was an attempt at humor. He didn't

laugh. "And what exactly have you managed to ac-
complish lately?"

"Well, I've analyzed those smears you found on
that Kleenex," he stated smugly. "It's indeed wood
ash. Probably from burnt *Yucca brevifolia*."

"Joshua trees?"

"Um, yes." Hodges looked disappointed that Nick
had recognized the Latin name for the local desert
flora. No doubt he had been looking forward to
showing off his erudition. He recovered quickly,
though, and preened as though he had just broken
the case wide open. "Sounds like Grissom's favorite
new trophy was prepared using local materials. It
should have a tag, 'Made in America.'"

That's something, Nick admitted. Joshua trees were
ubiquitous in the deserts surrounding Las Vegas.
The region's early Mormon settlers had often used
them for fencing and firewood. "You know," he
pointed out, just to keep Hodges's ego in check,
"that doesn't exactly narrow our search much."

Hodges shrugged. "Hey, I can't solve all your
cases for you."

Technically, it was illegal to sell human body parts
over the Internet, but that didn't stop people from
trying. Catherine recalled an instance a few years
ago when a guy tried to hawk his wife's kidneys via
e-mail—without her knowledge or consent. Was it
possible to order a shrunken head online nowadays?

Why not? she thought. *Lord knows you can find
pretty much anything else. . . .*

She sat before the glow of a flat-screen computer
monitor in the corner office she shared with the

day-shift supervisor. Warrick stood behind her, leaning over her shoulder, as they shopped online together. Although she kept her cool on the outside,
she privately found his close proximity slightly distracting; there had always been an unspoken
"thing" between them, even though they had never
done anything about it. She thought she had put
that fantasy to bed for good when the good-looking
CSI got married a few years back. Then again, he
was divorced now. . . .

Watch it, she warned herself. Fishing off the company pier was never a good idea. *Look at how well
that worked out for Grissom and Sara.*

"I gotta admit, this beats digging through Dump-
sters," he commented, practically in her ear. Like
most CSIs, he wore no cologne on the job.

"Tell me about it," she agreed. Not that she objected terribly to getting her hands dirty; prowling
through messy crime scenes was part of the job.
Still, it was nice to be able to do some investigating
in air-conditioned comfort for once. Although it was
only about sixty degrees outside at this time of
night, it had been raining heavily on her way in.
Catherine was glad to be indoors. And to be using a
mouse instead of a shovel.

She typed "shrunken heads" into a box on the
screen and clicked the SEARCH tab. "Okay, here
goes." EBay immediately presented her with dozens
of offerings:

A "museum-quality" replica boasting "smoked
balsa wood ash skin tones and natural textures,"
cast in oven-fired polymer clay.

A variety of cheap rubber knockoffs.

Pirates of the Caribbean action figures and accessories.

Circus posters. ("Shocking! Bizarre!")

A vintage sideshow counterfeit or "gaff."

A "Shrunken Head Apple Sculpture Kit" from the 1970s, featuring a sinister portrait of Vincent Price on the packaging. The late horror-movie actor posed as a mad scientist while he held up a pair of homemade shrunken heads with shaggy Troll hair and wizened features.

That dopey movie Greg had mentioned, available only on VHS.

An academic textbook on Jivaro culture.

An R. L. Stine novel.

A punk-rock album.

Miscellaneous T-shirts, jewelry, postcards, toys, props, and Halloween masks.

But no actual shrunken heads. Catherine scanned down through the listings, just in case she had missed something, but found only plenty of imitations and novelty items. "No luck. This stuff is all pretty innocent, if occasionally overpriced."

"Looks like it," Warrick agreed. "Well, at least we know where to go Christmas shopping for Grissom now."

"Or Greg," she said wryly. "You just know he'd love that Vincent Price toy."

For herself, Catherine wasn't remotely tempted by any of the items up for sale. Giving up on eBay, she tried Craigslist instead, but struck out entirely there. Apparently, nobody had posted any ads for shrunken heads lately. Warrick sat down in the spare chair and flipped through the phone book. "You'll be shocked to learn," he stated after a few minutes of fruitless searching, "that there are no listings for Shrunken Heads or *Tsantas* in the Yellow Pages."

"Imagine that." She was starting to wonder if they were on a wild-goose chase. *Wouldn't be the first time.*

Warrick put the phone book aside. "So, where *does* one get a genuine shrunken head these days?"

"Besides making your own?" She continued surfing the Net, trying out various search engines and combinations of words until she finally clicked on a link that caused her to sit up straight in her chair. A grin lifted the corners of her lips. "Hang on. Check this out."

Jungle drums pounded from the computer's speakers. Animated Tiki torches crackled along the borders of a website advertising "AUTHENTIC SHRUNKEN HEADZ!!!" Lurid color photos of convincing-looking *tsantas* cycled against a black background. A cartoon witch doctor, with a bone through his nose, capered along the bottom of the screen. "The finest replicas made in the USA," a block of much smaller type proclaimed, "crafted using traditional South American techniques!"

"So?" Warrick didn't get it. "These are just more fakes. Pretty good ones, but still . . ."

She turned down the volume on the drums. "Take a look at this." Clicking on the contact information brought up a mailing address for a "Red Noir Studios" on Charleston Boulevard. "Looks like we've got at least one professional shrunken head manufacturer in town."

"Why am I not surprised?" he said. A lifelong native of Las Vegas, he had a jaded appreciation for the city's eccentricities. "Wanna go looking for a little head?"

Catherine smirked. "I'm not touching that." She rolled her chair back from the computer and stretched her legs. "Sounds like it might be worth a visit." Her wristwatch informed her that it was nearly five in the morning. She wondered what time Red Noir Studios opened. *I don't suppose they're running twenty-four hours a day.*

They headed for the door.

So much for our cozy desk job. Oh, well. At least we drew a more interesting assignment than poor Greg.

Vampire Weekend played over Greg's iPod as he sifted through the missing-persons case files on a computer in the DNA lab. The music did little to relieve his boredom; although he wouldn't dream of complaining to Grissom, the young CSI found his latest assignment both tedious and depressing.

There's just so many of them, he thought. Enough missing men, women, and children to fill up an entire dairy section's worth of milk cartons. Husbands, wives, sons, daughters, fiancées, roommates, girlfriends, and coworkers. Deadbeat dads and teenage runaways. Senile seniors and kidnapped children. Most of the lost kids could be chalked up to ugly custody battles, with the loser taking it on the lam with the offspring, but there were plenty of other cases where people, both young and old, just seemed to drop off the face of the earth.

Until their bodies turn up in the desert someday, or float to the surface of a lake.

He felt a sudden urge to call his own folks, just to connect. An only child, he was still close to his parents, especially his slightly overprotective mom. Calling California would have to wait until after the graveyard shift, however; not even his mom would appreciate a phone call at six in the morning.

A color photo of the mystery *tsanta* was pinned to the bulletin board next to the computer. Greg squinted at the monitor as he compared portraits of various missing adult white males to the grotesque specimen. This was trickier than it sounded. As feared, it was hard to relate the distorted features of the shrunken head to an actual living person. The prognathous jaw, for one thing, made Little John look more like a goateed caveman than a modern-day *Homo sapiens*. And who knew how much the contours of the face had shifted due to the absence of the skull?

Still, he was diligently compiling a list of possible candidates based on age, race, and hair color. The printer beneath the desk spit out color copies of the files on the top contenders, which he added to a steadily growing pile of papers. He was starting to think that there were more people missing in Las Vegas than inhabited some small towns.

The latest photo on the screen belonged to one Christopher Allen Marst, a thirty-eight-year-old bartender at the Luxor who had failed to report to work three weeks ago and hadn't been seen since. Greg examined the man's driver's-license photo. The bartender's beard was more blond than red, and his face looked a little meatier, but he might be Little John. Maybe he dyed his beard before he was murdered or lost some weight first? Or perhaps the headhunter just scraped too much fat off the inside of his skin?

Greg debated whether to add Marst's file to his stack of potential leads. He didn't want to risk missing a vital clue, but he didn't want to bury any leads beneath a heap of red herrings either. His foot tapped rhythmically against the floor, in sync with the music pouring from the iPod, as he weighed his options. His tired eyes glanced back and forth between the photos of the grisly *tsanta* and the AWOL bartender.

Aw, what the heck. Playing it safe, he hit the PRINT command. Several seconds later, he introduced Christopher Marst to the other "maybes" in the pile. *That's three weeks' worth of files down, with hundreds more to go.*

Faced with the daunting prospect of calling up yet another missing-persons case, Greg found himself pining for the good old days when he ruled the DNA lab. At the moment, untangling the knotty mysteries of the genetic code struck him as infinitely more appealing than reading up on another lost or kidnapped teenager.

But hey, he reminded himself, *you're the one who wanted the glamour and excitement of field work. . . .*

He switched to The Kills on his iPod and called up the next file.

In the past, when the lab needed a facial reconstruction done, Gil Grissom had called upon Teri Melvoy. An expert forensic anthropologist, Teri had assisted his team on several previous investigations, which was why he was so disappointed to read the e-mail that had just popped up on the screen of his laptop. Sitting behind his cluttered desk, he quickly scanned the message:

> *Gil,*
> *Thanks for thinking of me. This sounds like a fascinating case, but I'm afraid the FBI has dibs on me for the time being. I've been drafted to help them out regarding this mass grave that just turned up in rural Pennsylvania, which they suspect is the dumping ground for a prolific serial killer. It's a huge job that's probably going to keep me tied up for weeks to come.*
>
> *Since I'm guessing that your shrunken head can't wait, let me recommend an alternative. Constance Molinez at UCLA is something of a protégé of mine and a real up-and-comer when it comes to computerizing the entire facial-reconstruction process. She's energetic, imaginative, and, thanks to her computer skills, likely to put me out of work one of these days. I've attached her contact information. Feel free to drop her a line.*
>
> *Give my regards to Catherine and the rest of the gang.*
>
> *Best,*
> *T.*

Sighing, Grissom started to tap out a polite reply, thanking Teri for the suggestion. There was a knock at his door. He looked up to see Wendy Simms, the late-night DNA tech, standing in the doorway. An attractive brunette in her mid-thirties, whose dark hair was currently tied up in a ponytail, she usually kept to her lab down the hall. A blue lab coat was draped over her shapely figure, which had once earned her a bit part in a slasher movie. "Got a minute?" she asked.

"By all means." He closed the laptop in order to give Wendy his full attention. "Come on in."

She stumbled slightly as she entered the office, bumping into a shelf of bottled reptile fetuses. Grissom's eyes widened in alarm as his best Gila monster specimen tottered precariously for a moment, but Wendy caught the jar before it fell and carefully replaced it on the shelf. "Oops," she murmured, blushing in embarrassment. Around the lab, Wendy had something of a reputation for clumsiness, although her lack of coordination had thankfully never affected her work. "Sorry about that."

"No harm done," Grissom said, repressing a sigh of relief as she successfully made it to one of the metal chairs facing his desk. "How can I help you?"

"It's about running the mitochondrial DNA from the shrunken head," she admitted. "I confess that I haven't had a whole lot of experience with mtDNA—that's more of an archeological thing than a CSI thing—and we aren't really set up for it."

Grissom frowned, but was not too surprised. Wendy was right that mtDNA testing was hardly standard procedure. *I was afraid of this.*

"Don't get me wrong," she hastened to add. "I'm all up for a challenge, but don't want to compromise our investigation by doing a half-assed job with the equipment at hand."

"Agreed," Grissom said. "So what do you suggest?"

Wendy leaned forward. "Well, I could send the sample to the FBI like we've done before, but that can take forever. I don't think shrunken heads rate high on the Bureau's priorities, unless, of course, we thought the head belonged to Osama Bin Laden." She caught herself rambling, and got back on track. "But I may have a better idea. I've been reading up on mtDNA testing and there's this amazing new gadget, the Genome Sequencer FLX, that's supposed to speed up the process considerably. It can identify millions of base pairs an hour."

"And you would like the lab to acquire this technology?" Grissom said skeptically. He had no idea how much this new equipment would cost, but he guessed it wouldn't be cheap. And Conrad Ecklie, the lab's reigning assistant director, was not exactly known for his generous purse strings. In fact, his latest memo on cost cutting and "unnecessary expenditures" was currently buried somewhere on Grissom's desk.

"Someday, sure," Wendy enthused. "When you can squeeze it into the budget. But in the meantime, guess who already has one?"

Grissom wasn't sure if that question was supposed to be rhetorical or not. "The FBI?"

"Nope. Even closer to home." She paused for dramatic effect. "The Anthropology Department at UNLV."

Grissom instantly saw where she was going. "Professor Kim, the head of the department, did offer his full cooperation with our investigation. I wonder if that extends to lending us access to their equipment." Glancing at his watch, he saw that it was only six A.M. "I'll give Kim a call first thing this morning."

"Great," Wendy said. "I'm definitely available to make a field trip to the campus as soon as you can set something up."

"I'll see what I can do." He was impressed by her initiative and creative thinking. Rumor had it that Wendy was thinking of following Greg's lead and becoming a full CSI. Perhaps that wasn't such a bad idea? He gave her a nod of encouragement. "Good idea, by the way."

5

RED NOIR STUDIOS WAS situated in the Arts District south of Fremont Street. Although it wasn't even noon yet, the temperature was already in the eighties. Glaring sunlight beat down on a horse-drawn carriage that was giving tourists a tour of the neighborhood. Instead of the usual graffiti, elaborate murals and colorful portraits, many worthy of framing, were painted on the sides of buildings and undefended billboards. Abstract sculptures adorned the sidewalks. Hip-looking posters advertised the District's monthly "First Fridays" arts festivals.

Warrick and Catherine pulled up in front of a former slaughterhouse that now held an eclectic collection of galleries, boutiques, and studios. The stockyard had been paved over to form a spacious parking lot. Warrick squeezed their black Denali into a convenient space near the entrance to the building. As this was strictly a fact-finding expedition, they left their field kits locked up in the back of the SUV, along with their telltale FORENSICS vests and jackets. *No need to alarm the neighborhood,* Warrick thought, *by making them think there's a crime scene nearby.*

An enticing aroma wafted from the open door of a coffee shop on the corner. Warrick was tempted to take a detour for a quick cup of java. Upon arriving earlier that morning, he and Catherine had discovered that Red Noir didn't open for business until eleven A.M. He had squeezed in a catnap back at his apartment (while Catherine went home to see her daughter off to school), before rendezvousing with Catherine back at HQ, but he could have still used a few more hours of sleep before reporting back to work at midnight. That coffee was sounding better and better.

Maybe after our Q&A with the chief headhunter.

The studio turned out to be on the second floor of the converted slaughterhouse. The building looked as if it had been completely gutted and rebuilt on the inside, but the veteran CSI couldn't help wondering if the walls would still glow blue if he sprayed them with Luminol. Spilled blood tended to outlast even the most determined efforts to erase it, as any number of murderers had learned to their chagrin.

"Welcome to Shrunken Heads R Us," Catherine said in anticipation. "Wonder what kind of place this is."

"Don't ask me," Warrick replied. "Kind of artsy and boho, maybe?"

They climbed a steep flight of stairs before reaching the entrance to the studio. The door was locked, so they had to wait to be buzzed in. "Come on in!" a female voice called from inside.

The lobby beyond the door was clearly intended to be dramatic. Black walls and dim lighting left the corners of the room shrouded in murky shadows. A large framed poster extolled the spine-tingling virtues of some old B-movie titled *The Four Skulls of Jonathan Drake.* Coarse threads dangled from the sewn lips of a shaggy-haired headhunter with lurid green skin and fiendish yellow eyes. A smaller insert depicted a mad scientist dangling a shrunken head over a bubbling cauldron. Warrick thought he vaguely remembered watching the black-and-white flick on *Nightmare Theater* as a kid. Spotlights mounted in the ceiling lit up a trio of glass display cases that showcased approximately a half-dozen shrunken heads. A pair of low leather couches faced a chrome-and-glass coffee table. Magazines and cat-alogs were spread out on top of the table. Bauhaus played over the Muzak system.

"Hello? Can I help you?" a receptionist greeted them from behind the front desk. A slightly anorexic-looking goth girl, she fit the studio's macabre decor perfectly. Her braided red hair would surely have tested positive for henna. Wide green eyes peered out through stylish cat-eye glasses. A frilly black bustier and matching choker contrasted sharply with her pale white skin, which looked as if it seldom felt the touch of the sun. A silver ankh rested above her meager cleavage. The dim lighting made it difficult to discern her age, but Warrick put her in her mid-twenties.

She seemed puzzled, and mildly disoriented, by

their arrival. Noting the conspicuous absence of a
cash register, Warrick guessed that the studio didn't
get a lot of drop-in visitors. *Probably do most of their
business by mail or online.*

Catherine presented the younger woman with
her laminated ID badge. "Catherine Willows, LVPD
Crime Lab. And this is my associate, Warrick
Brown."

"Crime lab?" The girl's eyes widened in alarm.
She glanced guiltily at a closed drawer behind the
counter. "Wh-what do you want?"

Warrick spotted an empty ashtray by the phone.
Sniffing discreetly, he caught a distinct whiff of
cannabis in the air. He figured the girl had been enjoying a controlled substance when the two CSIs
had arrived and had ditched the joint before buzzing
them in. *Talk about a relaxed work environment,* he
thought. *Wonder what the health plan is like?*

"Stay cool," he assured her quickly. He flashed
her a smile to put her at ease. "We're just here looking for some info on, well, shrunken heads." He gestured at the nearest display case. "Seems like you
folks might have some expertise in that area."

The girl's tense body language softened. "Oh,
you've definitely come to the right place then." She
automatically went into sales mode. "We produce
the finest imitation *tsantas* available, at a competitive
price."

"So we've heard," Catherine said. "And you are?"

"Karla. Karla Tinges." She came out from behind
the counter to greet them. Beneath the bustier, she
wore a black leather miniskirt and boots. Curiosity
replaced anxiety in her eyes. "So, I just have to ask:

How come the police are interested in shrunken heads? Did somebody get their noggin sliced off . . . for real?"

That's what we're trying to find out, Warrick thought. "I'm afraid we're not at liberty to discuss the details of our investigation." The press was bound to get wind of this story eventually, with all of the complications and pressure that was likely to entail, but there was no need to spill the beans just yet. "We'd really appreciate your cooperation, though."

"Oh. Right." Although visibly disappointed by their reticence, Karla seemed amenable to assisting them. She shrugged and leaned back against the front of her desk. "Sure. Whatever we can do."

A closed door beyond the reception area presumably led to the rest of the studio. "Like my associate said," Catherine stated, "we're looking for info on shrunken heads in general. Who would be the best person to talk to here?"

"That would be El Jaguar, my boyfriend," Karla volunteered. "Basically, it's just the two of us. He's the artist—and a brilliant one, as you can see— while I take care of the business end of things. You know, billing, marketing, that kind of thing."

"Sounds like a workable arrangement," Warrick said. He wished his ex-wife, Tina, had been as supportive of his career. Maybe they'd still be together. "Can we speak with El Jaguar?"

"No problem."

She scurried off to fetch her partner, leaving the two CSIs alone in the showroom. Amusingly, she took her trashcan with her, no doubt to dispose of any illicit substances contained therein. A toilet flushed somewhere behind the door.

"There goes our leverage," Catherine observed. Apparently, the pungent atmosphere had not escaped her notice, either. "Right down the drain."

"Maybe we won't need it," Warrick said hopefully.

He took a moment to admire the shrunken heads on display, many of which he recognized from the studio's website. Variations in size, coloring, facial hair, and other characteristics distinguished the *tsanta* from each other. Apparently, you could get blond, brunette, redheaded, or even white-haired heads, depending on your tastes. Most of the phony heads were male—intended to represent Jivaro warriors fallen in combat—but there were a couple of female faces, too. Bones, beads, feathers, and other bangles adorned the replicas, which looked pretty convincing to the naked eye. "El Jaguar" did good work.

Little John would have fit right in.

Catherine eyed the replicas dubiously. "Okay, I don't want to be all judgmental here, but who exactly would want to buy one of these?"

"Besides Grissom?" Warrick replied. "Just about any ten-year-old boy."

Catherine shook her head. "Why am I suddenly glad that Lindsey is a girl?" She peered through the glass at what, rather bizarrely, appeared to be the shrunken head of a giant sloth. "Anyway, I doubt that most ten-year-olds could afford these prices." According to the website, the cost of the replica heads went from around fifty to eighty-five dollars. "Wonder how much the real thing goes for?"

"Let's hope El Jaguar can tell us that," Warrick replied. "And who is willing to pay that much."

As if on cue, the door to the back of the studio swung open, and the artist emerged, trailed by his girlfriend, who looked positively mundane by comparison. El Jaguar was a portly white dude, clad in a king-sized black T-shirt, shorts, and sandals, who had gone out of his way to look as much like one of his artworks as possible. Bogus stitch marks were tattooed above and below his lips and eyes. Greasy brown hair hung past his shoulders. Novelty contact lenses gave him blood-red eyes. His face was deeply tanned. A bone necklace rattled around his neck. Another bone was thrust through his nose.

"Oh my," Catherine murmured. A bemused expression briefly passed over her face. "El Jaguar, I presume?"

"Call me Tyrone," he insisted. His gravelly voice hinted at a nicotine habit. A metallic-gold portrait of a snarling wildcat was emblazoned on his voluminous T-shirt. "El Jaguar is my public persona, but I figure you folks just want the facts, ma'am." He chuckled amiably. "The name on my birth certificate is Tyrone Coghlan, but what kind of moniker is that for a headhunter? It's all about the image, you know. Better for business."

"Understood," Warrick said, suppressing a grin. The man was a walking advertisement for his wares. "Art doesn't sell itself."

"You got it." Tyrone settled himself onto one of the couches facing the coffee table. "Please make yourself comfortable." The man's cooperative attitude belied his intimidating appearance. Karla perched on the arm of the couch beside him. "So, how can I be of assistance to the LVPD?"

The CSIs sat down opposite the bohemian pair. Warrick let Catherine take the lead. "What can you tell us about the market for shrunken human heads?" she asked. "Especially real ones."

"Well, it used to be a thriving business," Tyrone said. "American and European traders would provide the Jivaro with guns and ammunition in exchange for genuine human heads. This was a great arrangement for the Jivaro; they could kill their enemies more efficiently and make a profit doing so. Unfortunately, it also gave them a real incentive to stage more raids and capture more heads, which caused a serious escalation in hostilities along the Amazon. It also backfired on the traders sometimes. There's a famous story, which may or may not be true, about a greedy Dutch explorer who trekked into the jungle in hopes of making a killing in the shrunken head business—only to end up as a *tsanta* himself."

Warrick smirked. "Served him right, I guess."

"Pure poetic justice," Tyrone agreed. "The trade in human heads pretty much dried up, however, after the governments in Peru and Ecuador banned the practice. These days, most genuine *tsantas* are in museums or private collections."

Warrick recalled that UNLV claimed not to have any shrunken heads in its possession. "So how would one go about obtaining a genuine specimen these days?"

"It wouldn't be easy," Tyrone informed him. "Or cheap. Christie's had an actual *tsanta* up for auction a few years back. It sold for over $10,000."

"Whoa." Warrick whistled in appreciation. He hoped that Doc Robbins had Little John securely locked up in the morgue. "That's serious coin."

Tyrone nodded. "It would probably be cheaper to steal one. Which has been known to happen."

"Really?" Catherine asked.

"Oh yeah," Karla piped up. "Someone snatched a shrunken head from the Ripley's Believe It or Not Museum in Niagara Falls a couple of years ago. And one is supposed to have disappeared from the Smithsonian under suspicious circumstances." She fidgeted on the arm of the couch, anxious to take part in the interview. "The Ripley's people offered a reward for their head, but I don't think they ever got it back."

Catherine glanced briefly at Warrick before making a decision. She removed a manila envelope from her purse and extracted a color photo of Little John. She handed the photo over to Tyrone and Karla. "Have either of you ever seen this head before?"

The artist's crimson eyes practically bugged out as he squinted enthusiastically at the *tsanta*. Karla shifted her position to try to get a better look. "Move your head," she complained. "I can't see."

Tyrone ignored his girlfriend's complaints. "What a beauty!" he exclaimed. "Is this for real? Where'd you find it?"

"It just sort of turned up," Catherine explained vaguely. "We're trying to determine its origins now. I take it this isn't one of yours? From your private collection, maybe?"

Tyrone snorted. "I wish!"

"So do I," Catherine said. That would have made

their job a whole lot easier. "Do either of you recognize it?"

Karla tugged on the photo until Tyrone reluctantly surrendered it. He shook his head. "Sorry. I've spent a lot of time looking at antique specimens, both at museums and online, and this one's not ringing any bells. I'm pretty sure I've never seen it before. Marvelous craftsmanship, though. Look at the elegant crudity of the stitching. You can spot a lot of fakes because the sewing is too good. The Jivaro didn't have modern sewing machines or equipment, so the real *tsantas* look a little rougher along the seams."

Warrick was disappointed that Tyrone couldn't identify the head. *Guess it couldn't be that easy.* "What about you, Karla?"

"Nope." She handed the photo back. "Tyrone's the expert, not me." She beamed at her boyfriend. "We've got some good books on this subject if you want to borrow them, though."

Warrick suspected that Grissom probably had his own copies of the books, but he appreciated the offer. "'Thanks. We might take you up on that."

"Just to be clear," Catherine pressed. "You folks just make imitations, right?" She shrugged apologetically. "No offense. I have to ask."

"Authentic museum-quality replicas," Karla corrected her. "But yeah, all our heads are made of boiled leather and wool. Goatskin, mostly. We press the skin over carved wooden busts, then shave the goat hair off to expose the faces. No actual human heads involved."

"A shame, really," Tyrone added. He sighed ruefully. "Do you know how much I could get for a real shrunken head?"

"Oh yeah?" Warrick saw an opportunity to cut to the chase. "Like from whom? Anyone in particular?"

Tyrone looked away uneasily. "Um, not really."

Warrick didn't buy it. "Are you certain of that? You must know who your best customers are. Who the big spenders are." He flipped through the catalogs on the table, which seemed to specialize in rather outré tastes. Besides shrunken heads, the catalogs also advertised skull jewelry, handcrafted vampire fangs, gothic candelabra, and other spooky accessories. "I mean, I imagine it's something of a niche market. There can't be that many people out there who are big-time shrunken head collectors."

"You did offer us your full cooperation," Catherine reminded him. "And we could really use your help here."

"I don't know," Tyrone said hesitantly. He exchanged a nervous glance with Karla. "There is this one guy, I suppose . . . but I'd hate to involve him in this."

Let alone piss off your best customer, Warrick thought. "This may well be a murder investigation, Mr. Coghlan, Ms. Tinges." He kept the pressure on both of them. "If there's any more information you can share with us, it's vitally important that you do so. Innocent lives may be at stake."

Warrick was laying it on pretty thick, but it seemed to do the trick. "Okay." Tyrone sighed in resignation. "I do have one steady customer who is into shrunken heads in a seriously big way, and,

boy, does he have money to burn. He's commissioned a number of specialty jobs from me over the
years, done exactly to his specifications. And he's
very picky about how realistic they look." Twisting
around on the couch, he pointed toward a display
case a few feet away. The harsh glare of the spotlight exposed a female head with platinum-blond
hair parted down the middle. Feathered darts
pierced the *tsanta*'s protruding lips. "See that head
there? Looks pretty good, doesn't it? I did that one
especially for this client, but he ended up rejecting it
just because he didn't think the ears were quite
right." He scowled at the memory. "I spent *hours* on
those ears."

"I know, honey," Karla cooed soothingly as she
massaged his shoulders. "Those ears are beautiful.
That jerk didn't know what he was talking about."
Her eyes suddenly lit up, and she turned toward the
CSIs in excitement. "Hey, if we help you catch the
killer, you think we could get some publicity out of
it? Maybe you can mention our name to the press?"
You could practically see the headlines flashing
across her brain. "The name of the studio, I mean,
and our Web address . . ."

Warrick stifled a laugh. Karla wasn't kidding
when she said she was in charge of marketing. *Hey,
anything that gets them to cough up the info we need.*

"I'll see what we can do," he said, "*if* there really
is a killer out there. We don't know that for sure
yet." Leaning forward until his face was only a few
inches away from Tyrone's tattooed countenance,
he asked the next logical question. "This finicky
client of yours, he ever express interest in obtaining

a real shrunken head? Maybe ask you for a lead in that direction?"

Tyrone winced slightly before answering. "Maybe."

"But we wouldn't have anything to do with that!" Karla took pains to point out. "We're perfectly legit, honest!"

"Of course you are." Catherine took out her notepad. "But we're going to need a name and an address."

6

"WHAT HAVE YOU GOT for me today, Nick?"

Ronnie Litra ran the Questionable Documents unit at the lab. He was a large, stocky man with frizzy brown hair and wire-framed glasses. His ID was pinned to the lapel of his blue lab jacket. Judging from his girth, you'd never guess that the forensic documents examiner was also an avid Jet Ski enthusiast. He was seated at a counter, examining some allegedly counterfeit stock certificates, when Nick walked in.

"I was hoping you could help me with this." Nick dropped a sealed plastic bag onto Ronnie's desk. Inside the bag was the cryptic note that had been enclosed with the shrunken head. Was the ominous inscription *tumashi akerkama* an explanation or a warning?

"No problem." Ronnie put the bogus certificates aside and picked up the note, which he inspected through the transparent plastic. "This came with Little John?"

Nick wasn't surprised that Ronnie was already familiar with the case. The shrunken head was still a
hot topic around the facility. "Bingo." He nodded at
the note. "Any chance you can tell me where it
came from?"

"Probably," Ronnie said confidently. Using latex
gloves, he carefully removed the note from the bag
and slid it under his magnifying glass. "Looks like
laser printing. Good. That gives a good chance of
identifying the printer." He extracted a blue LED
flashlight from a drawer beneath the desktop and
turned toward Nick. "Would you mind flicking off
the light?"

"Sure." Nick flipped the switch, casting the documents lab into relative darkness. Only the subdued
overhead lighting from the hall outside allowed him
to see his way around. He watched as Ronnie examined the note under the blue light of the flashlight.
"Any luck?"

"You bet," the other man said. "Come check this
out."

Nick came behind Ronnie, who stepped aside to
let the CSI look through the magnifying lens. He
was encouraged by the other's man cheerful expression.

"See the yellow dots?" Ronnie said triumphantly.
"Ever since at least 2005, most major manufacturers
have rigged their color laser printers to embed a pattern of tiny yellow dots on all printed pages. The
dots are practically invisible to the naked eye, but
can be exposed by a blue light and a microscope—if
you know what you're looking for."

Squinting, Nick could just make out the dots.

"The idea was to help track down counterfeiters, right?"

"Exactly. The manufacturers quietly started doing this at the request of the Treasury Department, but there have been accusations that the FBI has gotten in on the act, too, and might be using the codes to keep tabs on who is printing what for groups like the ACLU and Amnesty International. Some dissidents have even printed lists of which commercial printers are rigged and which ones aren't." Ronnie shrugged. "Guess your friend the headhunter missed those lists."

Lucky for us, Nick thought. He wasn't sure he entirely approved of the government being able to spy on people through their printers, but he wasn't about to turn down a viable law-enforcement technique, especially when there was a potential headhunter on the loose. "Good thing the perp decided to splurge on color printing, too." As he recalled, black-and-white lasers and inkjets did not produce the hidden dots. Nick nodded at the note. "Can you crack the code?"

"Just watch me." Ronnie took a digital photo of the note under the blue light, then asked Nick to turn the lights back on. Putting away the flashlight, he loaded the image from the camera into his computer and sat down at the keypad. Nick circled around to watch. After a few moments, the image appeared on the computer monitor. He zoomed in on a corner of the note. "The grid is repeated throughout the print job, so all we need is this one section."

To Nick's disappointment, the yellow dots were barely visible. "Can you actually read that?"

"Give me a minute." Ronnie tapped a few keys, and the computer software enlarged and brightened the faint yellow dots so that the pattern was more clearly confined. "See? That's more like it." He gave Nick a mischievous grin. "Now here's the sneaky part. These codes, which are unique to each printer, are *supposed* to be top-secret, which means that, in theory, we'd have to appeal to the FBI or the Treasury Department to find out what machine this note was printed on. Which can be a pain."

"No kidding," Nick agreed. The Feds were not always known for their swift and friendly cooperation with the LVPD; indeed, more than once, the crime lab and the FBI had found themselves at cross purposes. Nick wasn't looking forward to trying to pry the printer info from Washington. "You said 'in theory.'"

"So I did." He called up a menu of options on his screen. "In practice, the Electronic Freedom Foundation has already cracked the codes for most of the major printer manufacturers—Canon, Xerox, et cetera—and posted the info online. You can even download a program that automates the decoding procedure." He feigned an expression of total innocence. "I might just happen to have that program on my computer."

"All right then," Nick said enthusiastically. This was the best news he'd heard all night. "Let's get cracking . . . no pun intended."

"Okay, here's a question for you," Catherine said. "If genuine shrunken heads are such hot commodities, why just *give* one away to the local university?"

Warrick manned the wheel of the black Denali, while Catherine rode shotgun. The sun was high in the sky, a little after noon, as they cruised down West Charleston Boulevard. According to Tyrone Coghlan, a.k.a. El Jaguar, his number one customer, one Vincent Vonderlynn, resided in Summerside, a ritzy planned community in the southwest corner of the city. Catherine checked to make sure her seatbelt was fastened securely; Warrick had a well-deserved reputation for going heavy on the gas pedal.

"I don't know," he replied. "Didn't Grissom say that the Jivaro attach no importance to the heads once their rituals are complete, that they just discard them afterward?"

"Yeah," Catherine said. "But we aren't living in a small tribal village here. In twenty-first-century America, a real *tsanta* is worth thousands. Who throws away something that valuable?"

Warrick munched on a fast-food taco as he drove. "A killer who wants to dispose of the evidence?"

"By making an anonymous donation to the Anthropology Department?" Catherine finished off a cheese burrito. "That's not exactly the best way to cover your tracks."

"True enough." Warrick accelerated to pass a slow-moving van. "Unless the headhunter wants the world to know what he did. Shrinking your enemy's head is all about boasting rights, in a sense."

That's one way to look at it, she thought. *Although there have got to be easier ways to get back at somebody.*

Summerside was a sprawling community of luxury homes and condos, nestled within acres of parks, jogging trails, golf courses, and malls. Vonderlynn's address led them to an ostentatious mega-mansion complete with a three-car garage, palm trees, and a marble fountain out front. The grandiose architecture evoked a Spanish hacienda. Terra-cotta tiles were used in abundance. Towering columns supported the imposing front portico. An ornate balcony looked out over the street. A pair of stone lions guarded the landscaped grounds.

"Nice digs," Warrick commented as they parked the Denali in front of the mansion, which made Catherine's own home look like a Third World hovel by comparison. The heat and glare hit them as soon as they stepped out of the SUV. "Looks like this guy can afford an authentic shrunken head or two."

"And then some," Catherine agreed. They took the paved walkway up to the portico. A brass knocker cast in the face of a snarling *tsanta* greeted them. Catherine rang the doorbell instead.

A chime echoed loudly beyond the door, which was opened a few moments later by a slim blonde in a maid's uniform. "Hello?"

"Las Vegas Crime Lab," Catherine announced. "We're here to talk to Mr. Vonderlynn."

"The police?" She squinted anxiously at Catherine's ID. "Is something wrong?"

Catherine was accustomed to this reaction. People were seldom pleased to find the police at their doorstep. "Nothing you need to worry about. Is Mr. Vonderlynn at home?"

"Um, I think he's taking a nap," the maid said sheepishly.

Lucky him, Catherine thought. She and Warrick were well into a double shift, having headed straight from Red Noir Studios to Summerside, except for a quick detour past a drive-through window for lunch. They had flirted with the idea of calling it a day after they got Vonderlynn's name and address from Karla, but had ultimately decided that they might as well take advantage of the daylight hours to interview the wealthy *tsanta* enthusiast before the graveyard shift rolled around again. Otherwise, it would be another twenty-four hours before they could reasonably call on him again.

"Please wake him," she said with a certain lack of sympathy. According to Tyrone, Vonderlynn was a Microsoft millionaire from Seattle who had retired early at the age of thirty-five. Catherine still had decades to go before claiming her pension.

"All right," the maid agreed reluctantly. She left them waiting on the front porch while she fetched the master of the house. Removing her sunglasses, Catherine was grateful for the shade provided by the portico. The brass knocker, with its engraved stitched lips and sculpted mane, bore a slight familial resemblance to the replicas at Red Noir Studios. Catherine wondered if it had been custom-made by El Jaguar.

She fought a yawn and lost. "I hope this trip is worth the overtime." She reminded herself that Vincent Vonderlynn was not actually a suspect at this time, just a potential window into the world of black-market shrunken head trafficking, assuming such a world even existed. Her tired eyes burned with fatigue. The greasy burrito gurgled unhappily in her stomach. *Maybe this could have waited until to-morrow after all.*

The door soon swung open to reveal a rumpled-looking white male wearing a purple bathrobe. Alas, Vincent Vonderlynn was hardly attractive enough to make this a particularly titillating sight, at least as far as Catherine was concerned. A pudgy frame and sagging jowls suggested that he seldom took advantage of Summerside's community gyms, golf courses, and tennis courts. Mussed brown hair was receding into history, leaving the former computer whiz's youth behind. He looked flushed and disheveled. A cotton sash mercifully held the robe together. Catherine hoped to God he was wearing something underneath, but couldn't have sworn to that. His bare toenails needed trimming.

"All right." He looked annoyed at having been roused from his siesta. A slight British accent sounded more affected than genuine. "What's this all about?"

Catherine introduced herself and Warrick. "If you don't mind, we'd like to ask you questions about your shrunken head collection."

"My collection?" His jaw dropped in surprise. "How the devil do you know about that?"

"We hear it's the most impressive in Las Vegas," Catherine said, ducking the question. No need to incriminate Tyrone and Karla if they didn't have to. Catherine didn't want to penalize the artsy couple for their cooperation by souring things with their best customer. "And we could use your expert advice."

"Is that so?" He stepped back into the foyer to

look the two CSIs over. He seemed torn between curiosity and suspicion. "My collection is perfectly legal. There's no law against it."

"No one's saying there is," Warrick said. He wiped the sweat from his forehead. "Mind if we step inside?"

Vonderlynn blocked the doorway. "Do you have a warrant?"

"Do we need one?" Catherine replied with a bit of an edge to her voice. Lack of sleep wasn't helping her patience, but she tried to keep her irritation under control. "We just want your assistance, Mr. Vonderlynn. This isn't a raid."

"I suppose." He grudgingly stepped aside. "Come on in, then."

Air-conditioning came as a cool relief as they entered the mansion's luxurious foyer. Tapestries and oil paintings hung on lustrous oak-paneled walls. Marble tiles stretched across the floor to where a sweeping grand staircase rose majestically toward the upper reaches of the mansion. The maid hovered at the foot of the stairs, curious to find out what was up.

"That will be all, Stacy," Vonderlynn dismissed her. "Go vacuum the sunroom or something." He escorted them down a lengthy hall. "We can do this in my study, I guess."

A pair of sliding wooden doors admitted them to the study, which was furnished in a distinctly masculine style that reminded Catherine of the Explorer's Club at Disney World. Shrunken heads occupied stained mahogany bookshelves and trophy cases, alongside other exotic accouterments such as voodoo dolls, native fetishes, and Tiki idols. A pith helmet hung on an ornate iron coatrack, presumably for atmosphere. An elephant rifle was mounted above the fireplace, which was thankfully unlit; the fireplace itself was something of an unnecessary extravagance in Vegas. A shaggy lion-skin rug, complete with head, bared its fangs. Framed above the door was a bamboo blow pipe, with matching darts. A hollowed-out elephant's foot was being used as a wastebasket. A meerschaum pipe rested on an ashtray. The stuffy atmosphere was redolent of tobacco.

Vincent Vonderlynn clearly fancied himself a Great White Hunter, at least vicariously.

He deposited himself in a plum-colored wingback chair. "Please make yourselves at home," he said in a belated attempt at hospitality. The CSIs shared a chaise longue across from their host. The gaping jaws of the rug were within striking distance of Catherine's toes. "Can I get you anything? Coffee? Tea? A soda?"

"No, thank you," Catherine said automatically, then reconsidered. Maybe a little caffeine wasn't such a bad idea. "On second thought, maybe I'll take you up on that coffee."

Warrick assented as well. "Coffee would be great, thank you."

"No problem." Vonderlynn plucked an iPhone from the pocket of his robe and dialed the maid. "Stacy, two cups of coffee for our guests. And a *venti* soy chai for me." He tucked the phone back into his pocket. "Stacy was my favorite barista at the Venetian until I stole her away to work for me. Tripled her salary."

Catherine hoped the money was worth it. "That's very generous."

"I thought so." Vonderlynn settled back into his chair. "So, what brings you here, detectives?"

"Forensic investigators, actually," Catherine corrected him. Not wanting to waste time, she presented him with the photo of the shrunken head. "We'd like you to take a look at this."

The avid collector reacted much as El Jaguar had. His piggish eyes bugged from their sockets. "Is this authentic? Where did it come from?"

"Do you recognize this head?" Warrick asked. "Or can you tell who made it?"

Vonderlynn looked up from the photo. "No and no." He reached over and swung the arm of a standing floor lamp closer to the chair to give himself more light. "Can I keep this photo for my collection?"

"Not right now," she informed him. Besides the fact that they didn't want the picture leaked to the press, the dead man's friends and family might not appreciate having their loved one's grisly remains plastered all over the Internet. "Maybe we can get you a copy later."

"Uh-huh," he sulked, no doubt sensing that Catherine was blowing him off. His interest in the meeting curdled. "Is that it? Are we done?"

"Not exactly," Warrick said. "We'd still like some information on shrunken heads in general. As you can imagine, this is pretty new territory for us. We don't get a whole lot of unidentified *tsantas* floating around Vegas. Maybe you can tell us all about the market for shrunken heads?"

The CSI's appeal appeared to flatter Vonderlynn's ego. "That's quite a far-reaching topic, about which I am extremely well informed. What do you want to know?"

"Let's start with an easy one," Catherine suggested. "How did you get into shrunken heads?"

Vonderlynn shrugged. "Always have been. I think I read a *National Geographic* article at an impressionable age, and I've been obsessed ever since. It's just such an amazing and unique phenomenon. Lots of cultures have practiced headhunting over the years, from the Far East to the ancient Celts, but only the Shuar actually shrank their enemies' heads. It practically reeks of black magic, especially when you're a kid."

"The Shuar?" Warrick asked.

"The specific clan that did most of the headhunting back in the old days," Vonderlynn explained pedantically. "'Jivaro' is actually a western term that was applied to them by outsiders. Many modern-day Shuar reject the name."

"Good to know," Catherine said. She wouldn't want to accidentally offend any headhunters she ran into.

"Shrunken heads have fascinated people for generations," Vonderlynn went on. Now that they finally had him talking, he seemed to be enjoying the audience. Catherine guessed that he didn't have many opportunities to show off his vast knowledge on the subject. "Did you know that they're mentioned in *Moby-Dick*?"

"No, I didn't," she admitted. *But I'll bet Grissom can quote the relevant passages.* Before Vonderlynn could do the same, she gestured at the *tsantas* on display. "Are these all fakes?"

He frowned at her description of his collection. "High-quality reproductions and classic antique counterfeits," he asserted. "I'll have you know that original counterfeits from the glory days of the shrunken head trade are considered highly valuable collectibles these days."

A knock at the door heralded the return of Stacy, who brought in the beverages on a silver tray. Vonderlynn brazenly ogled the maid's shapely legs as she served the coffee to the CSIs. Warrick added milk and sugar to his mug, while Catherine took hers black. "Thanks," she said. "I needed this."

The curious maid tried to linger, but Vonderlynn waved her away. "Don't you have vacuuming to do?" He sighed in exasperation as Stacy departed the study, closing the doors behind her. Foam from his chai clung to his upper lip. "A bit of a snoop, that one."

Warrick picked up where they had left off. "You ever try to obtain a real *tsanta*?"

"Of course," the collector said. His brown ceramic mug had been fashioned to resemble a Tiki head. "I'm always on the lookout for an authentic specimen, but unfortunately, the genuine articles show up on the market very infrequently. I almost managed to snag one at an auction a few years ago, but some anonymous bastard outbid me at the last minute." He scowled at the memory. "I still regret not getting that one."

At least he was up front about his desire to obtain an honest-to-goodness shrunken head. Catherine wondered how far he would go to complete his collection. Far enough to try making his own—or to hire someone else to do so? *Maybe he has more than a pretty barista on his payroll?*

"I hear they get stolen sometimes," Warrick commented.

Vonderlynn nearly choked on his chai. "I-I wouldn't know anything about that."

"Are you sure?" Warrick pressed him, sensing blood.

"I'm positive." Vonderlynn squirmed uneasily in his chair. "I mean, naturally, I've heard of such things, but I've never had any personal experience along those lines. As a victim, that is," he added hastily. "Nobody has ever tried to steal my collection that I know of."

Warrick arched an eyebrow. "But I thought you didn't have any real shrunken heads to steal?"

"Huh?" It took Vonderlynn a second to catch up with Warrick's reasoning. "Oh, right. I meant nobody has ever tried to steal my rare antique replicas."

Is that so? Catherine thought skeptically. Vonderlynn was acting like a man with something to hide. *I wonder what that could be.*

The hot coffee gave the exhausted CSI a welcome boost of energy. Cup in hand, she got up and strolled around the study. A *tsanta* on a nearby bookshelf caught her eye. The female head, with its platinum-blond tresses, resembled the one that Tyrone had grumbled about before. Probably a replacement for the one Vonderlynn rejected the first time, she surmised. The ears didn't look all that much more realistic to her, but then again, she was no connoisseur.

"You like that one?" Vonderlynn sounded eager to change the subject from *tsanta*-rustling. "I had it commissioned specifically. It's the spitting image of my ex-girlfriend in Seattle."

Lovely, Catherine thought. Was it just her imagination, or did the female *tsanta* look a little like Stacy as well? *I wonder if there are any cute platinum blondes in the Anthropology Department at UNLV?*

Another head occupied a position of honor on the fireplace mantel. It rested on a velvet cushion beneath a domed glass cylinder. Its withered face was sewn into a perpetual grimace. Stringy black hair hung from its scalp. A small feathered arrow was thrust through its nose. More feathers dangled from its ears. Coiled cords hung from its lips like a second beard.

She gravitated over to the fireplace. "What's the story with this one?"

"Nothing really," he sputtered.

"Oh yeah?" She looked back at him. "So why the special treatment?"

Beads of perspiration began to form on Vonderlynn's forehead. "Just a sentimental favorite," he insisted. "It was the very first classic counterfeit I ever acquired, or maybe one of the first . . ." Heaving himself up from the chair, he tried to interest her in a miniature sloth head instead. "Have you seen this one? The Shuar actually believed that they were descended from the sloths of South America. The shrunken head of a sloth was considered to have many of the same mystical properties as the head of a human enemy, and they were sometimes used in rituals in place of a regular *tsanta*."

"Fascinating," Catherine lied. She peered through the transparent glass at the supposed counterfeit. The canister was free of dust, for which they probably had Stacy to thank. "Hey, Warrick. Come take a look at this."

Vonderlynn forgot all about the sloth head. "Look," he objected. "I think I've been very accommodating, but I really don't think there's much more to be gained here." He made a show of loudly sliding the wooden doors open. "Allow me to show you out."

"But we haven't finished our coffee yet," Warrick pointed out. He strolled over to join Catherine by the fireplace. "Find something interesting?"

She stepped aside to let him look at the head under glass. "Now I'm no expert, but I think I'm starting to be able to tell a replica from the real thing. Is it just me, or do those ears look just a little too realistic?"

The *tsanta*'s scraggly black mane had been combed back away from its ears, the better to expose the intricate convolutions and folds. Bright orange feathers dangled from the lobes. A minute patch of skin on the *tsanta*'s head appeared to have rotted away.

"You know," Warrick agreed, "you may be on to something here." He reached for the glass knob at the top of the canister. "Mind if we take a closer look?"

Vonderlynn lost his cool. "Get your hands away from that glass! That's an expensive collectible, very fragile!" He pointed at the door. "I think you need to leave now."

The CSIs didn't budge. "These look like suspicious human remains to me," Warrick declared. His shrewd green eyes scanned the cluttered chamber. "I think we need to confiscate all of these heads as evidence."

"Absolutely," Catherine agreed. If this creep was lying to them about not owning an actual human head, what else might he be concealing? If nothing else, Grissom would want to compare Arrow Nose to Little John, to see if there were any indications that they had been crafted by the same headhunter. "Better contact the coroner's office and get David here."

"You can't do this! This is harassment!" Vonder-lynn exclaimed, practically stomping his bare feet on the carpet. His florid expression turned beet red as he pulled out his iPhone once more. "I'm calling my lawyer!"

"Fine," Catherine answered, fishing her own cell phone from her pocket. "I'm calling a judge."

"And voilà! Here we go."

Ronnie Litra handed Nick a printout from his computer, while the same information scrolled across the monitor. As promised, the EFF's bootleg computer program had translated the microscopic yellow dots on the note into hard data regarding the printer that had produced the ominous missive. "Looks like we're talking a Hapka brand laser printer, Model TS-300X, serial number 31052875. And the print job in question took place at exactly eight forty-seven P.M. on Sunday, March 31."

About ten days ago, Nick realized. More than

enough time to turn a corpse into a bona fide shrunken head and still have time to pop it in the mail to the university. "Thanks, Ronnie. You're a wizard!"

"One of many around here," the man replied modestly. He looked pleased to have contributed to the case. "Now you just have to find out who that particular printer was sold to."

"I'm on that right now," Nick assured him, hoping that the manufacturer wouldn't put up too much of a fight before surrendering the information. He'd get a warrant if he had to, but it couldn't hurt to try a little charm first. Not to mention appealing to the company's sense of civic duty.

Yeah right, he thought. *Like that ever works.*

7

"GRISSOM? YOU HAVE COMPANY."

He looked up from his desk to see Greg standing in the doorway. He was accompanied by a small, round Filipino woman wearing a black leather jacket over a plain white T-shirt. A faint layer of stubble coated her shaved skull. Barely more than four feet tall, she made Greg look like a professional basketball player by comparison. Biker boots and acid-washed jeans completed her ensemble. She had the youthful face and radiant glow of a teenager. A wide grin linked her plump rosy cheeks.

"Hi there!" a chirpy voice greeted him. Large brown eyes looked him over. "So you're the famous Gilbert Grissom? Teri told me all about you."

"Constance Molinez?"

The forensic artist was not what Grissom was expecting—and almost the exact opposite of Teri Melvoy, who had recommended her. Whereas Teri was tall, blond, sophisticated, and thoroughly professional, her so-called protégé looked and acted like the world's bubbliest punk rocker. Grissom wondered if maybe he had made a mistake calling her in on this case.

"The one and only." She squeezed past Greg into the office, dragging a rolling suitcase behind her as though she had come straight from the airport. A *venti*-sized Starbucks coffee cup was clutched in her free hand. Her eyes widened at the sight of his various collections and menageries. "Wow. Cool office."

Grissom glanced at his watch. It was only nine-twenty P.M. "I wasn't expecting you so soon."

"I caught an early flight." She dropped into one of the chairs in front of Grissom's desk, then pivoted around to look at Greg, who was still poised in the doorway. "Thanks for the escort, dude. I think we're cool here. You can get back to catching the bad guys."

Greg hesitated, as if he was unsure whether he should leave his boss alone with the visitor. "You okay, Grissom?"

"I certainly hope so." He peered over the top of his reading glasses at Constance. "Excuse me for asking, but how old are you, exactly?"

"Hah!" she laughed. "Don't worry, I get that all the time. I'm twenty-four, actually, but nobody believes me." She threw up her hand to indicate that she was resigned to her fate. "Probably going to get carded until I'm forty!"

Grissom refrained from asking to see her driver's license. After all, despite her unnervingly immature affect, Constance Molinez *had* flown all the way in from L.A. to assist in their investigation—and on a moment's notice, no less. Indeed, he had first contacted her early this morning and here she was less than twelve hours later.

"Well, thank you for volunteering your expertise in this matter." He leaned across his desk to welcome her. "I appreciate your coming out here on such short notice."

"Are you kidding?" She shook his hand energetically. "Once you mentioned the shrunken head, I dropped everything and made tracks for the airport. Talk about a unique challenge! Besides, just between you and me"—she gave him a conspiratorial wink—"a case like this could really make my reputation."

Grissom hoped her ambition wouldn't compromise her efforts on their behalf. "I'm more concerned with putting a name to our victim."

"Well, sure! That goes without saying." She rubbed her palms together eagerly. "So, where's the infamous shrunken head? Let me at it!"

Grissom couldn't decide whether her hyperexcited state was encouraging or alarming. *Just how many of those large coffees has she had today?*

He pulled out one of his desk drawers, removed an airtight plastic container, and placed it on the desktop between them. The distorted profile of the *tsanta* was visible through the clear plastic. Grissom had borrowed the shrunken head from the morgue in anticipation of this meeting. Given the mummified state of the remains, refrigeration had not been an issue.

"Is that it?" The young woman's eyes bulged

from their sockets. "And you kept it in your desk? Wow. This is so wild. I mean, I've seen these things behind glass at museums before. They've got some great ones at the Ripley's Museum in L.A., but I've never actually examined one before."

She gleefully reached for the container, but Grissom held up his hand. "Gloves," he reminded her, offering her a box of latex gloves. "This may be evidence in a murder trial."

"Oh! Right." Her broad face reddened as she pulled on the gloves. Moving a tad less precipitously, she cautiously opened the container. A burp of trapped air escaped the canister as she lifted the lid. "Okay then. Let's take a look at you."

She held the *tsanta* up to the light of the desk lamp. Grissom ignored the head himself, choosing to examine his guest instead. Her lapse with the gloves had not instilled confidence, yet she seemed to be inspecting the head with a great deal of concentration. Maybe she knew what she was doing after all?

Teri *had* spoken highly of her. . . .

"Funny," she murmured, perhaps as much to herself as to Grissom, "the lips appear to have shrunken less than the rest of the face. Wonder what their original proportions were." She turned the specimen over in her hands. "There still seems to be some cartilage in the ears and in the tip of the nose, which may make things a little easier. Still, no skull, no teeth, no eyes . . ." She frowned and shook her head. "You're not giving me a lot to work with here, Gil."

Apparently, they were on a first-name basis now. "That's why these remains pose such a dilemma, Ms. Molinez," he said, choosing to overlook the familiarity. "Without a skull, a traditional facial reconstruction is impossible. And dental records—"

"Please, call me Connie," she interrupted. "'Ms. Molinez' makes me feel like I've been called to the principal's office." She placed the *tsanta* back in its container. "Anyway, you were saying?"

Grissom tried to reboard his train of thought. "Obviously, dental records will be of no use here. I've been thinking about the problem since we last spoke, however, and one possible solution came to mind. As you know, the American method of three-dimensional facial reconstruction relies on our knowledge of the tissue depths between the skin and the skull at numerous key landmarks on the face. By using markers of different depths, a skilled artist such as yourself or Teri Melvoy can reconstruct the face from the bone up."

"Right." Connie sipped on her coffee. "But we don't have a skull, just a dried-up bag of skin with some hair on it."

"True. But shouldn't the tissue depths be the same? Suppose we emptied the shrunken head and laid the face out upside down on a smooth surface. Adding depth markers of the appropriate size to the underside of the skin, then closing it up again, would theoretically create a void in the shape of the missing skull. Then we could use that void to create a replica of the skull, either physically or via computer, that you could employ as the basis for a more

conventional facial reconstruction." A note of intel-
lectual excitement entered his voice as he warmed
to his theory, which struck him as both elegant and
ingenious. "Of course, we'd have to compensate for
the shrinkage of the skin somehow, but perhaps you
can suggest the best way to—"

"Nah," she said bluntly. "That would never
work."

Grissom was taken aback by her brusque dis-
missal. "And why is that?" he asked, a bit more
testily than he intended. "It's just the reverse of the
usual process."

"Yeah, but skin isn't bone." She got up and borrowed a fossilized human skull from a shelf and carried it back to her seat. "And faces are all about the
underlying bony architecture. That's what gives
every face its unique proportional layout. The skin's
just like wallpaper; it shapes itself around the bone."
Snatching a random memo from Grissom's desk, she
pressed it against the contours of the skull to
demonstrate her point. The paper creased and
folded over the bony ridges. "Trust me on this. I've
been talking lately to some of the world's top vascu-
lar surgeons, the guys who are pioneering the new
technology of facial transplants, and the general
consensus is that it's the skull that truly forms the
face, not the flesh on top of it. Which is a good
thing, now that facial transplants are on the verge of
reality, 'cause otherwise we'd soon have a lot of
people walking around wearing dead people's faces.
And how creepy would that be?" She shuddered
theatrically. "Fortunately, that's not how it works. If

someone transplanted your face onto someone else's skull, your own mother wouldn't recognize you."

Despite the gruesome imagery, Grissom had to admit that she certainly sounded authoritative on the subject. He was aware that the first successful facial transplant had taken place in France a few years ago and that there were surely other surgeons looking into the technique, in hopes of helping patients whose faces had been destroyed by accidents or violence.

None of which, however, brought them any closer to identifying the shrunken head on his desk. "So what do you propose?"

She pulled a CD envelope from a zippered pocket on her leather jacket. Her grin resembled that of the skull in her lap. "You got a computer lab around here?"

Leaving the suitcase and *tsanta* behind, he led Connie down the hall and past the DNA lab, where he spied Wendy Simms hard at work, to the audio-visual lab next to Catherine's office. As usual, Archie Johnson was seated before one of the lab's many high-definition computer monitors. The lights in the room were dim, the better to increase the visibility of the screens. The young Asian A/V tech was busy increasing the resolution on some grainy security footage from a recent convenience-store robbery. His efforts reminded Grissom that the mystery of the shrunken head was hardly the only case on their docket; nevertheless, he found himself growing more uneasy with each day that passed without a breakthrough regarding the *tsanta*'s origins. The possibility that there was still a modern-day head-hunter at large in the city continued to trouble him.

What if he's just getting started?

"Nice setup!" Connie said, checking out the A/V lab. Her gaze fell on Archie. "Tasty eye candy, too."

Archie looked up from his screen. The slim twenty-five-year-old technician was arguably bet-ter-looking than the average lab rat. He seemed un-certain how to respond to the stranger's remark. "Um, hi?"

Grissom introduced their visitor to Archie. "Ms. Molinez . . . Connie is consulting with us regard-ing the shrunken head. I believe she requires access to our imaging programs."

"You bet!" She came up behind Archie and in-spected his equipment. "Verrry impressive. And the computer's not bad, either."

"Focus," Grissom admonished her.

"Okay, okay," she giggled. Connie then looked at Grissom with a more serious expression. "So . . . you said you did a scan of the shrunken head?"

"That's right," Grissom said, anxious to get back to business. "Both intact and flattened out."

She nodded approvingly. "You got those scans on file?"

"Hang on," Archie volunteered. A few rapid key-strokes saved what he was doing, then banished the incriminating security footage from the screen. He used his mouse to open another file. Within mo-ments, a three-dimensional scan of the *tsanta* ap-peared on the monitor. "This what you're looking for?"

"It'll do for now," she said with a sly wink in Archie's direction. She nudged him playfully with her elbow. "Scoot over, handsome."

Archie readily abandoned his seat to the intruder. "All yours."

He made a beeline for the door.

"Oh, he left," Connie remarked.

"Never mind that," Grissom said. "Now what?"

Grudgingly returning her attention to the computer, she removed a silver compact disc from its envelope and inserted it into the computer's CD drive. The drive hummed vigorously for a moment, and an icon in the shape of a human skull appeared on the screen. "Yo ho ho," she chirped. "You've been boarded, mateys."

Grissom was suddenly reminded of Greg Sanders back during his more sophomoric years. "And that is?" he asked patiently.

"My own personal brainchild," she said proudly. A click on the icon opened up a new window on the monitor. This one contained a menu of choices from ABO (F) to ZUNI (M), as well as a full palette of electronic imaging tools such as one might find in Photoshop or Z-Brush. "Meet FaceWrap 5.0, my own stab at computerizing the facial-reconstruction process. Which is not as easy as it sounds, I'll have you know. Plenty of people, including various law-enforcement agencies, have sunk a lot of time and money into developing software like this, but nobody has quite perfected their programs yet." She smiled benignly at the screen. "Still, I like to think my baby here comes pretty darn close."

Grissom recalled Teri mentioning Connie's computer prowess in her e-mail. "What can it do?"

"What can't it?" she bragged. "Seriously, among other things, FaceWrap contains three-dimensional scans of composite skulls for an ever-expanding menu of ages, ethnicities, and body types. Every individual skull is different, of course, but after scanning *waaay* too many grinning Jack Skellington wannabes, I've come up with, say, the average male Caucasoid skull."

She clicked on a choice labeled CAU (M), and a glowing green skull appeared on the monitor. Her fingers danced over the keyboard and the virtual skull rotated in three dimensions before coming to rest only a few inches away from the scan of the shrunken head. She shrank the skull until it was at the same scale as the image of the *tsanta*.

"Ordinarily," she explained, "I would use my program to shrink-wrap virtual skin around a scan of an unidentified real skull, but this time we'll use the same software to stretch your shrunken head's shriveled skin over a generic skull template."

She looked back over her shoulder at Grissom. "I'm guessing you don't want to try stretching the real skin over a physical skull model?"

"I think that would be unwise," he said. To be honest, he had considered soaking the *tsanta* in lanolin or some other solution in order to restore its elasticity, and perhaps stretch it back to its original proportions, but had ultimately decided against it. "Too much risk of tearing or otherwise damaging the evidence."

She nodded. "I figured as much. That's why I prefer computers. You always have a backup."

Grissom watched as she superimposed the flattened skin of the *tsanta* over the virtual skull. The fit was imperfect at first, the eye holes failing to match up with the empty sockets and the lips out of sync with the clenched teeth, among other problems, but as a grid pattern materialized over the merged images, FaceWrap went to work, methodically making minute adjustments to the digitized skin and cartilage in order to "shrink" it into place over the bony planes of the skull. He found the process compulsively viewable. Still, one thing bothered him.

"You said that this is an average skull. What if our John Doe had an atypical skull?"

"Always a danger," she admitted. "We're playing the odds here. But hey, this is Vegas, right? Maybe Lady Luck will smile on us."

Grissom had put himself through college playing poker for money. He didn't believe in luck. "Around here, that's the perennial refrain of suckers."

"Yeah, I guess it probably is," she said, picking up a little of his world-weary tone. Taking her hands away from the keyboard, she spun the chair around to face him. "But I promise I'm not hustling you here. It's not going to be a perfect likeness, but hopefully we can capture the basic gestalt of the face. Studies have shown that even though most of us *think* that we recognize other people because of their most distinctive features—their eyes, their nose, their smile, whatever—we're actually responding more to the overall array of the face. That's why you can spot a friend from a block or two away, even though you can't actually make out any details at that distance. It's all about the *gestalt*."

Grissom nodded. "The sum is greater than the whole of its parts."

"Or at least more recognizable," she said, "which is what we're going for here."

"Precisely." Even a crude approximation of Little John's original features might bring them one step closer to determining his identity—and the identity of the unknown individual who had mailed the severed head to UNLV. Grissom gestured at the screen, where the shrunken skin was still being slowly adjusted to conform with the skull underneath. "How long does this process take?"

A traditional facial reconstruction, of the sort performed by Teri Melvoy and others, was a time-consuming process, often taking many days.

"I'm not sure," Connie said. "I've never actually put the software to this particular purpose before, so it may take a couple of tries to get it right. That's probably three or four hours right there. Then the hard part starts."

"Which is?"

"The artistic part," she explained. "The computer can only do so much automatically. After it gets the basic parameters down, I still need to add a few tweaks to make the final product look more lifelike. Give it the human touch, you know? Facial reconstructions require both art and science. Lucky for you, I spent two summers studying life drawing and sculpting at the Art Institute in New York." She basked in the memory. "You should have seen some of my nudes. They were things of beauty."

A thought occurred to her, and she glanced over

at the doorway. "You think Archie would be interested in posing for me? For the sake of art?"

"Maybe you can ask him later," Grissom said diplomatically. He tried to steer the conversation back to the topic at hand. "Are there any other resources you require?"

She turned back to the developing image on the screen. "I don't suppose you know how fat or tall this guy was? That might have an effect on the shape of his skull. Were there any scraps of clothing with the head that might indicate whether he was fat or scrawny or what?"

"I'm afraid not," Grissom said. "All we've got is the head."

And a possibly threatening note.

"Too bad," she sighed. "Good thing for you guys that I love a challenge." The image froze and stuttered on the screen. She jiggled the mouse, but nothing happened. The digital reconstruction was halted in mid-progress. "Damn. I was afraid of this."

She cracked her knuckles over the keyboard, then rebooted the computer.

"Anything I can do to help?" Grissom asked.

She gulped down the last of her coffee and handed the cup to Grissom.

"I'm going to need a lot more caffeine."

8

UNLV'S SPRAWLING CAMPUS made a nice change from the sterile confines of the DNA lab. Wendy Simms enjoyed the fresh air and sunlight as she made her way to Wright Hall. College kids strolled past her on the way to classes or else killed time playing Frisbee on the greens. The sight of a diligent coed studying beneath the shade of a leafy tree raised pleasant memories of her own college days back in San Francisco. It was good to get out of the lab, even if it meant working a double shift. Not for the first time, she flirted with the idea of applying to become field agent. *Hey, if Greg Sanders can do it, why can't I?*

John S. Wright Hall turned out to be an imposing complex of modern-looking sandstone wings radiating outward from a central rotunda. An exterior atrium brought together two of the projecting wings under one roof. A desert garden, complete with palm trees, fronted the rotunda. Convenient signage directed her to the main offices of the

Anthropology Department, where Professor Malcolm Kim awaited her.

"Ms. Simms?" The head of the department was good-looking, in a tweedy, older man kind of way, with a firm handshake. He reminded her of a slightly more mature version of the Korean guy on *Lost,* not that she ever had time to watch TV anymore. "Right on time, I see. I hope you had no trouble navigating the campus."

"Not at all," she assured him. Eschewing her usual lab attire, she had dressed up in a pin-striped blazer, vest, and pants. "Thank you for taking time out of your busy schedule to meet with me." It had taken a day or two to set up this appointment, but she intended to make the most of it. "Dr. Grissom asked me to convey to you just how much we appreciate your extending this courtesy to us."

Kim waved away any thought that they were inconveniencing him. "Once Dr. Grissom explained your situation, I was happy to oblige." Despite his cordial tone, however, the friendly academic struck her as slightly on edge. He licked his lips nervously. "I don't suppose your colleagues on the police force have figured out who sent that shrunken head to us yet?"

Wendy couldn't blame Kim for being uncomfortable; in her experience, most people got nervous dealing with the criminal justice system, even if they were totally innocent. Heck, she automatically slowed down every time she spotted a patrol car on the freeway.

"I'm afraid that's not my department," she apologized. "I'm just trying to give the *tsanta* a name."

"Of course," Kim said. "Forgive me for prying." He gestured toward the bustling corridor before them. Glass windows in closed doors offered glimpses of crowded classrooms, lecture halls, and laboratories. Although it was midway through the hour and classes seemed to be in session, there was still plenty of activity in the hall. Students toted books and exchanged notes in the corridor. "Here. Let me show you the way to our Bioanthropology lab."

"I'm eager to see it." She walked beside him through the building. Strolling students and instructors cast curious looks in their direction. The youthful faces of the former made her feel older than her thirty-five years. "From what I've read online, I'm incredibly jealous of your new Genome Sequencer."

Kim chuckled. "Thank God for grant money and generous alumni. The Sequencer is proving to be an incredibly useful tool. Believe it or not, we've been able to track the tribal migration patterns of various prehistoric Native American communities by means of mitochondrial DNA extracted from two-thousand-year-old pieces of chewing gum."

"Really?" she asked, intrigued. "Dentyne or Doublemint?"

"More like wads of shredded yucca," Kim explained. "We call the dried-up remains 'quids' and they're spongy little reservoirs of prehistoric saliva. And that's not all. We've also managed to extract mtDNA from dried menstrual blood on aprons worn by cave-dwelling Native Americans who once lived in what is now Utah and Arizona."

"No kidding?" Wendy almost wished that Hodges, her on-again, off-again lab buddy, had come along on this excursion. He was nerdy enough to find all of this fascinating as well. Of course, he'd probably also make some tasteless joke about prehistoric tampons, but that was Hodges for you. "I hope we're not disrupting your research too much by hijacking your equipment."

"Don't worry about it," Kim insisted. "I think a modern-day criminal matter trumps any historical detective work, at least in the short term. Our fossils and artifacts have held their secrets for millennia. I think they can wait a few more days."

Good point, Wendy thought. "Still, once again, we really appreciate you going out of your way for us."

"It's the least we can do," he said. "Trust me, I want to get this . . . issue sorted out as much as anyone else." A troubled expression flickered across his face, and he muttered under his breath. "Maybe even more so."

Wendy wondered what he meant by that. *Am I missing something?*

Before she could formulate an appropriate reply, Kim came to a halt in front of a closed door. A sign on the adjacent wall warned of hazardous chemicals within. "Anyway, here we are." He opened the door and stepped aside chivalrously. "Ladies first."

The lab beyond was larger and had a lot more open space than the labs back at CSI HQ, no doubt to accommodate entire classes full of students. Wendy was suddenly thankful that she seldom had to carry out her procedures in front of an audience. Wooden cabinets held an impressive collection of human, primate, and fossil casts. Labeled drawers filled the spaces between counters long enough to prepare a five-course meal on, assuming you knew how to cook. Sinks, fume hoods, centrifuges, and the usual basics lined the counters.

Despite the ample space, however, the lab was currently occupied by only one researcher, a scruffy-looking young man who looked up from a microscope as Wendy and Kim entered the room. His unkempt ginger hair and stubble practically screamed grad student. Acid burns and chemical stains blotted his white lab coat, while his open-toed sandals tempted fate by defying conventional lab safety standards. Once again, Wendy was struck by just how fresh-faced and immature the student was, compared to her memories of herself as a sophisticated college student. *He's just a kid. . . .*

"Nathan . . ." the professor addressed the younger man, "this is Wendy Simms from the crime lab, as we discussed. Wendy, this is Nathan Hendros, our resident tech wizard. I confess he knows more about how the Genome Sequencer works than I do. I'm more of a libraries and microfiche kind of guy."

"Pleased to meet you," Nathan said. He stepped away from the counter to join them. Yellow stains on his fingertips testified to too much time handling chemical reagents. He smelled faintly of phenolphthalein. "You know, the professor didn't tell me that the cop lady was going to be a babe."

"Nathan," Kim said in a warning tone.

"It's okay," Wendy said. She was used to lab rats who didn't get out much. "I get that all the time . . . or so I like to think. But I'm not a cop. I'm a DNA technician employed by the Las Vegas Criminalistics Bureau."

"Wow," Nathan said. "That's so cool."

"In that case," Kim said, stepping away, "if you don't mind, I'll leave you in the capable hands of Mr. Hendros here." He headed for the door. "Please let me know if you need any further assistance . . . and Nathan, don't embarrass us. Ms. Simms is here on serious business."

"Don't I know it," Nathan said, sounding only mildly chastened. He waited until Kim closed the door behind him before winking at Wendy. "Like he's never hit on a hot coed when he thought no one was looking."

Wendy wasn't sure whether Nathan was kidding or not. In any event, that was more than she wanted to know. *I just analyze DNA. I don't worry about who is trading it.*

Thankfully, Nathan changed the subject. "So, you're here to borrow Genie, right?"

"Genie?"

"Short for Genome Sequencer FLX," he explained. "It's kind of my nickname for her."

"Cute," Wendy said. "And less of a mouthful, I guess." Looking around the lab, she spotted a device that resembled the apparatus she had seen online. "Is that her over there?"

The Genome Sequencer consisted of a white plastic box, about the size of a commercial laser printer, sitting on top of an upright gray computer tower. A keyboard and mouse occupied a sliding shelf between the upper unit and the hard drive. A six-inch LCD screen was mounted on a black plastic post rising from the Sequencer.

"Very good!" Nathan stated, clearly impressed. He

walked her over to the equipment. "Behold the love of my life, Genie herself. Taking the drudge work out of genetic sequencing at over twenty million bases per run."

"So I hear," Wendy said. "But how exactly does it work? I watched the instructional video at the manufacturer's website, but it was more hype than substance." She leaned over to take a closer look at the equipment. "Besides, a virtual experience is no substitute for the real thing."

Nathan snickered. "You clearly haven't played *Grand Theft Auto IV* yet. Seriously, though, let me demonstrate." He walked over to a nearby centrifuge and pulled out a shallow assay plate about the size of a compact disc. He held the plate carefully to avoid spilling its contents, which appeared to be suspended in some sort of oil-based emulsion. "This is a new batch of mtDNA, freshly harvested from a Paleolithic spit wad, that's all ready to run. The trick is that the genetic sample has already been broken into nebulized micro-fragments, each of which has been affixed to a separate tiny bead. The DNA capture beads are then centrifuged into individual wells on this PicoTiterPlate, which is basically one big fiber-optic chip." He held the plate up for her inspection. "Believe it or not, this plate alone contains approximately two hundred thousand wells, each of which also contains bioluminescent enzymes, which light up to varying degrees depending on how the genetic fragments react to different DNA bases, which are washed over the plate one at a time. Optical sensors measure the frequency and intensity of the flashes, and voilà! Since each plate holds two hundred thousand beads, ginormous amounts of DNA can be deciphered in record time. Then the computer links the fragments back together to get the entire sequence."

It sounded almost too good to be true. Wendy resisted the temptation to conk Nathan over the head and pirate the whole apparatus back to her lab. "And that's it? You make it sound so easy."

"Well, the hard part is preparing the plates," he admitted, "but here's where it gets really awesome." He lifted a lid on the left side of the Sequencer and slid the assay plate into a waiting slot, much as one might load a CD into a car stereo. "That's the optical subsystem." He then lifted a larger lid on the right side of the device, exposing rows of plastic vials and tubing. "Now I just have to refill the fluidic assembly with the sequencing reagents." He poured various colored solutions into matching colored reservoirs. "The nucleotides are flowed sequentially through the sample during the run. First the adenine, then the cytosine, guanine, and thymine."

Wendy recognized the four fundamental bases that made up all DNA. She winced slightly as Nathan was forced to open a fresh bottle of one solution; she knew from her research just how expensive those reagents were. *Maybe Grissom can talk Ecklie into reimbursing the university for their expenses?*

Once all four reservoirs were filled, Nathan closed the lid with a dramatic flourish. "Now all we need to do is press GO." He indicated a lighted button on the Sequencer. "Would you care to do the honors?"

"Can I?" Wendy felt like a kid riding an elevator for the very first time. She grinned at Nathan as she stepped forward and pressed firmly on the GO button. Genie instantly hummed to life. Within minutes, coded sequences, consisting of multiple permutations of A, C, G, and T, started flashing across the LCD screen above the Sequencer. "That's it?" she asked.

Nathan smiled proudly and gave his electronic girlfriend an affectionate pat. "That's it. Another four-point-five hours and we'll have the whole recipe."

Damn, Wendy thought. *I have got to get myself one of these things.*

"So," Nathan asked, "you bring me a sample from the famous shrunken head?"

Wendy nodded. "That's why I'm here." She fished a sealed test tube from the pocket of her blazer. It had taken her two days to extract a viable sample of mtDNA from the cellular debris in Little John's hair. The dead cells had resisted dissolving, but she had eventually managed to rupture the cell walls by treating them with detergents. Once the mitochondria were floating freely in a liquid solution, she had extracted the tiny sausage-shaped structures and ultracentrifuged them into layers in order to obtain the DNA fraction, which she had then replicated via PCR. It had been an exacting process, but she figured she had enough for Nathan to work with. "You need any help preparing the plate?"

"I was hoping you'd ask." He took the sample from her hand. "Between the two of us, we'll have this ready for Genie in no time."

Good, Wendy thought, despite the unsettling feeling that she had just entered some sort of analytical threesome. *Now the CSIs need to get me some samples to compare this mtDNA against, so we can figure out just whose head got mailed to this very building.* Unfortunately, there was no federal database for mtDNA, the way there was for regular DNA. *CODIS isn't going to do us any good here.*

The way Wendy saw it, she'd done her part. The rest was up to Grissom and the others.

"Mission accomplished, Commander!"

Connie Molinez marched into Grissom's office and dropped a color printout on his desk. It was nearly ten in the morning, but he wasn't even close to calling it a night yet. If nothing else, he hadn't wanted to head home while the visiting forensic artist was still slaving away on their behalf. He had checked in on her through the night, and occasionally found her dozing in Archie's chair while FaceWrap did its work, but he knew that she had also put in many long hours of work in front of the computer.

Certainly, she looked as if she had just pulled an all-nighter. Dark circles shadowed her droopy brown eyes. The stubble dotting her shaved skull looked a bit thicker than when she had first arrived from Los Angeles. Her pudgy fingers shook as they clung to her coffee cup like it was the Holy Grail. A manila envelope was tucked beneath one arm.

"You've finished the reconstruction?" Grissom asked.

"Yep," she said proudly. "Take a look."

He picked up the printout. The eight-by-ten piece of glossy paper featured a computer-generated portrait of a white adult male sporting a reddish beard and mustache. The face looked slightly generic, but it was undeniably more human in appearance than the *tsanta*'s grotesque visage. The lips, which were now back in proportion to the rest of the face, no longer protruded obscenely. Tapered temples no longer gave the head an unnatural pear-shaped contour. Computer artistry had erased the sooty brownish-black residue staining the *tsanta*'s skin, replacing it with ordinary Caucasian skin tones. The stitches binding the eyelids and lips together had been digitally removed, although the eyes remained shut.

A good call, he thought. In the absence of any hard evidence regarding the color or appearance of the victim's eyes, it was probably best not to make something up. A wrong guess might significantly alter the appearance of the face, reducing its resemblance to the real thing. *Closed eyes avoid confusion.*

"So," she prompted him. "Not bad, huh?"

"Not at all," he said sincerely. The funny thing was, despite all of Connie's digital manipulations, Grissom thought the image still bore an undefinable kinship to the shrunken head, which suggested that they hadn't completely distorted the evidence beyond recognition. Of course, they wouldn't know for sure how close they had gotten until they ultimately determined the identity of Little John and could compare the reconstruction to an actual picture of the deceased, but at least they had one more tool to work with now. "This is just what we were looking for."

"Cool!" She dropped into a chair, looking as if she had just run a marathon. Fatigue had muted her caffeinated ebullience from the night before. "I had to guess a little regarding his hairstyle, but I chose something fairly conventional so it wouldn't be too distracting if I got it wrong."

"That's the most we can do in these cases," he assured her. No artist's sketch or facial reconstruction ever got things completely right, but Grissom had seen plenty of victims and suspects identified on the basis of vaguer descriptions. "It's a starting point."

The next step would be to have multiple copies of the portrait made and distributed to Brass and the rest of the team. At some point, they might want to release the image to the press, but Grissom was inclined to hold off on that for now. The media was an uncontrollable entity that often generated more heat than light.

"But wait, there's more," she said, mimicking a late-night infomercial salesman. Grinning, she removed two more printouts from the manila envelope and slid them across the desk toward Grissom.

"What's this?" he asked.

"Two alternative versions, each slightly different from the first." She leaned forward to point out the changes. "Remember how we discussed that we didn't know what this guy's build was like? Well, just to play it safe, I gave you a couple of variations: one using a leaner skull, for a taller guy, and one using a wider skull, for someone more like me."

Grissom compared the three images to one another. He was surprised at how different the same skin looked when stretched over the three different skulls. *The skin's just wallpaper,* he remembered. *I see what she meant.*

"Maybe you can show all three of them around?" she suggested. "Odds are, one of them should look like your guy."

Grissom regarded the young woman with new respect. Despite his initial reservations, he was impressed by her hard work and diligence. How had Teri described her again? *Energetic and imaginative.* That had certainly proven to be the case.

"Thank you very much. I truly appreciate the extra effort you've put in here."

Despite her exhaustion, she beamed at his praise. "Hey, wait until you get my bill. And I'm expecting a glowing letter of recommendation, too."

"You'll get it," he promised. He was already anticipating a battle with Ecklie over the young woman's consulting fee, but he would get her compensated for her labors one way or another, even if it meant dipping into his discretionary fund. "And I'll tell Teri just how much help you were."

"Well, I hope you finally pin a name on Red here." She slurped down the last of her monster-sized cup of coffee. "Oh, one more thing. You think you can round up somebody to drive me to the nearest motel? I think I need to sleep for a week or two." Her eyes hopefully scanned the corridor outside. "Is Archie still around?"

9

Nick was sharing some leftover pepperoni pizza with Greg Sanders in the break room when his cell phone rang. Fumbling with greasy fingers, he managed to put down the pizza and retrieve the phone from his pocket without making too much of a mess. A quick glance at the phone's digital display confirmed that this was the call he had been waiting for. *About time*, he thought as he pressed the device to his ear.

"Hello? Yes, this is Nick Stokes from the crime lab."

Greg looked on curiously from the couch. Metal bookcases lined the walls of the break room. Louvered blinds spared them from the streetlights outside. A fresh pot of coffee was percolating over by the sink, while a soda vending machine hummed in the background.

"Hang on," Nick said to the voice at the other end of the line. "Let me write that down." He gestured toward a pen lying on the counter next to the microwave and Greg hastily handed it over to Nick, who scribbled an address on a paper napkin, then read it back over the phone just to make sure he had gotten it right. "That's it? Great. Thanks a lot. I really appreciate you getting back to me on this."

Ending the call, Nick tucked his phone back into his pocket. He waved the napkin like a victory flag. "Yee-hah. Now we're getting somewhere."

"Progress?" Greg asked. A gooey strand of melted cheese stretched from his lips to the drooping slice in his hand.

"Finally!" Nick gloated. "That was the company that manufactured the headhunter's laser printer. They've been giving me the runaround for over a day now, bouncing my calls from office to office, but I guess that warrant from Judge Hermosa finally got their attention. They just told me whom they sold that particular printer to." He glanced at the address on the napkin. "A psychiatric clinic over on Regatta Drive."

"Whoa!" Greg put down his pizza. "That sounds familiar." He jumped to his feet and dashed out of the break room. "Don't go anywhere. I'll be right back!"

Okay, Nick thought. *What's that all about?* He recalled that Greg had been scouring the missing-persons files for Little John's true identity. *Sounds like we might be on to something.* He wolfed down another slice of pizza while he waited impatiently for Greg's return. Maybe Little John wouldn't be a John Doe much longer?

Less than five minutes later, Greg came rushing back into the break room, brandishing a sheaf of stapled-together printouts. His blue eyes gleamed triumphantly. "I knew I remembered something about a psychiatrist on Regatta." He eagerly handed the file to Nick. "Guess all that grunt work paid off after all."

"It usually does," Nick said as he quickly scanned the documents.

The file concerned a missing person named James Arnold Zounek, a single fifty-one-year-old white psychiatrist who had apparently disappeared about twelve days ago. *Around the same time that the headhunter's note was printed,* Nick noted, *on the doctor's own printer?*

He double-checked the address of Zounek's clinic against the scribble on the napkin.

They were the same.

"Sure looks like him, doesn't it?" Greg commented.

A color Xerox of Zounek's face showed a smiling, somewhat smug-looking professional sporting a reddish mustache and goatee. He appeared a bit younger than his fifty-plus years, possibly due to plastic surgery and hair dye. Nick glanced around the break room. "Where are those facial reconstructions of the victim Connie Molinez whipped up?"

Greg was way ahead of him. He thrust three of the eight-by-ten glossies into Nick's hand. "Tell me we're not talking the same guy here."

Nick compared the photos, quickly focusing on the leanest of the three computer-generated portraits. It wasn't a perfect match—the real Zounek's hair was styled differently and his nose was fleshier—but he could definitely see a resemblance. "Let me get this straight," he said incredulously. "Our shrunken head is actually a shrink?"

* * *

The Grace Tranquillity Mental Health Clinic was located in an upscale neighborhood only a few miles from the Hill Haven Golf Club. The clinic was part of a high-end shopping village and office park, sharing its parking space with an orthodontist, an optician, a coffee shop, a children's bookstore, a gourmet chocolate shop, a stationery shop, and an Italian restaurant. An embossed brass placard outside the front entrance revealed that Dr. James Zounek was one of three mental-health professionals who practiced out of the clinic. The temperature was creeping toward the nineties as Grissom and Brass arrived early the next morning. It was supposed to be a scorcher of a day.

"Kind of a long way from the Amazon," Brass observed dryly. "Not exactly a happy hunting ground for heads."

"At least not in the literal sense," Grissom replied. "Figuratively, I'm not so sure." The possibility that Zounek had become the butt of a perverse, possibly homicidal joke had not escaped his mind. If they were indeed on the right track, the missing doctor had gone from head shrinker to shrunken head sometime over the past few weeks. *Does one of his patients have a twisted sense of humor?*

He followed Brass into a pristine waiting room, where about a half-dozen patients and hangers-on occupied padded metal seats in air-conditioned comfort. A large flat-screen television, tuned to a cable news channel, kept some of the visitors up-to-date on current events, while others preferred to leaf through the generous assortment of magazines on display, including *Time, Newsweek,* and *Psychology Today.* A discreet survey of the waiting room suggested that the clinic catered to a fairly affluent, genteel clientele. None of the patients looked particularly like a headhunter, but Grissom knew better than to rule any of them out on such a superficial analysis. Nevada's penitentiaries were full of unlikely-looking suspects who had ultimately been found guilty of heinous crimes. A sullen teenager, who was fidgeting next to his scowling mother, clearly wanted to be anywhere else, yet that hardly struck Grissom as a motive for murder, let alone decapitation. Easy-listening music added to the peaceful atmosphere. A security camera, inconspicuously installed in a corner of the ceiling, was monitoring the scene.

The television, whose volume had been muted in favor of closed captioning, was currently covering that gang shoot-out in Henderson that had the day shift occupied. Grissom was relieved that the mysterious shrunken head had not hit the news yet but feared that they were running out of time on that score. A story that sensational couldn't fly beneath the media's radar much longer.

I can just imagine the headlines.

"Good morning. Do you have an appointment?" the receptionist asked the men as they approached the front desk. She was an attractive woman in her early thirties whose auburn hair was cut just below her ears. A neatly pressed tan pantsuit served as professional attire, while a jade brooch provided a touch of glamor. Although she greeted them with a smile, her chestnut eyes held a slightly wary expression, as though sensing that they weren't here for the usual reasons.

"Captain Jim Brass, Homicide," the detective introduced himself, flashing his badge. "And this is Dr. Gil Grissom from our crime lab."

Grissom noted that Brass made a point of stressing the criminalist's academic credentials. Perhaps he thought Grissom's Ph.D. would carry a little extra weight in this environment. Grissom was neither flattered nor chagrined by the ploy. *Can't hurt, I suppose.*

The woman's eyes widened. "This is about Dr. Zounek, isn't it?"

"I'm afraid so," Grissom confirmed.

She glanced nervously at the people in the waiting room, who were starting to show a little too much interest in the proceedings. "Perhaps we should discuss this somewhere more private," she suggested, lowering her voice. "I wouldn't want to upset our patients or their families."

"Private works for me," Brass said gruffly. "Lead the way."

The woman guided them past the front desk and into the hallway beyond. Framed artwork, mostly of desert landscapes, decorated the pale green walls, whose color, Grissom assumed, had been deliberately selected for its soothing qualities. They soon found themselves inside a wood-paneled office furnished with a desk, a couch, and a couple of chairs. An hourglass and a memo pad rested on the tidy desk. A Persian carpet protected the floor. Bookshelves stacked with psychiatric texts and journals filled one wall, competing with an extensive display of diplomas, testimonials, and news clippings mounted around the room. Many of the clippings featured photos of Dr. Zounek himself. Grissom recognized the goateed psychiatrist from the missing-persons file Greg had extracted from the police database. The resemblance to the best facial reconstruction, not to mention the printer connection, encouraged Grissom to think that they were closing in on the *tsanta*'s true identity.

Unfortunately for Dr. Zounek and his loved ones.

"This was his office," the receptionist said unnecessarily. She closed the door behind them and stood in front of the doctor's desk as she faced them stiffly, her arms crossed over her chest. She looked understandably tense and uncomfortable. "What would you like to know?"

Brass took out his notebook. "Let's start with your name."

"Of course," she said apologetically. "Rudolph. Elizabeth Rudolph, although I mostly go by Liz." Her brow furrowed. "Excuse me, did you say you were from Homicide?"

"That's right," Brass confirmed.

She took a deep breath, as though bracing herself for the worst. "Does that mean you've . . . found . . . Dr. Zounek?"

"We're hoping you can help us with that." The cop produced a copy of a revised version of Connie Molinez's extrapolation of the shrunken head's features. The simulation now sported the same hairstyle worn by the missing doctor. "This is a facial reconstruction of a dead body that turned up recently. Would you say that this looks like Dr. Zounek?"

The computer-generated portrait provoked a less horrified response than a picture of the *tsanta* probably would have, but Liz Rudolph still gasped at the sight. "Oh my God. It's him. At least I think so. It's hard to be certain. . . ."

We're going to need something more definitive than that, Grissom thought. "Do you know if Dr. Zounek had recently undergone plastic surgery?"

"Why, yes!" Rudolph confirmed. "Over his vacation last year. He denied it at first, but he fessed up eventually." She sounded puzzled by the question. "Is that important?"

"Possibly," Grissom said. Their theory concerning the *tsanta*'s identity was growing stronger by the minute. He roamed the office while Brass interviewed the anxious receptionist. There were no obvious signs of violence, just as the initial missing-persons investigators had reported. He spotted a small portable refrigerator, similar to the one in his own office. "Excuse me," he interrupted. "Do you mind if I look inside here?"

Rudolph looked puzzled by the request. "No. Not at all. But I'm not sure what you're expecting to find. . . ."

Inside the fridge was some bottled water, a moldy-looking salad in a plastic container, a six-pack of Coke, a couple cartons of yogurt, an ice-cube tray, and an unopened bottle of a microbrewery beer he'd never heard of. Grissom's eyes immediately zeroed in on a half-finished bottle of Perrier. "Does anybody else use this fridge?"

"Not really," Rudolph said. "Sometimes he offered a fresh bottle of water to his patients, but his personal stuff was strictly off-limits." She smiled rue-fully. "A college intern caught hell once for 'borrow-ing' one of the doctor's sodas without permission."

Brass raised an eyebrow. "Ran a tight ship, did he?"

"He could be . . . demanding," Rudolph con-ceded. "Dr. Zounek insisted on excellence and had little patience with anything that fell short of his standards."

"Or anyone?" Brass asked.

"Sometimes," she admitted. "He had his good days and his bad days, just like anyone else."

Grissom was intrigued by these insights into the doctor's personality, but verifying the *tsanta*'s iden-tity was still his top priority. "I'd like to confiscate the contents of this fridge," he declared. "For pur-poses of DNA identification."

The unfinished Perrier bottle looked particularly promising. With luck, there were still traces of Zounek's saliva on the lip of the bottle. *Nice of him to keep it refrigerated for us.* They could also check the salad and the utensils for samples. And if that didn't work out, there was always Zounek's private resi-dence a few miles away. According to his file, the doc-tor's condo apartment had already been searched by the missing-persons squad, but it probably couldn't hurt to have a couple CSIs give the place another once-over. Nick, maybe, or Greg. If nothing else, there was sure to be more samples of Zounek's DNA avail-able at the condo.

"Go ahead," Rudolph agreed. "I probably should have cleaned it out weeks ago."

"I'm glad you didn't," Grissom said. He placed the

Perrier bottle in an evidence bag and made a mental note to box up the rest of the fridge's contents later, after he retrieved his field kit from the Taurus parked outside. "In fact, I would appreciate it if you could instruct the clinic's staff to leave this office untouched from now on."

"I can do that." The disposition of Zounek's snacks seemed to be the last thing on the receptionist's mind. "I'm sorry, but I have to ask. What do you think happened to Dr. Zounek?"

"We're still investigating the circumstances," Brass informed her, "but we obviously haven't ruled out homicide."

"Oh God," she whispered. Visibly shaken by the possibility, she teetered unsteadily on her feet and grabbed the desk to steady herself. "I don't believe this. How is it possible . . . ?"

"Perhaps you should sit down," Brass suggested.

Grissom was briefly tempted to offer the woman a bottle of water from the fridge, but he was reluctant to contaminate the evidence. What if the headhunter had left his fingerprints on one of the bottles?

"Yes, thank you." She started to sit down on the couch, then reconsidered and settled into one of the chairs instead. Grissom guessed that she wanted to be viewed more as a professional than a patient. She took a couple of deep breaths to regain her composure. "This whole experience has been very stressful for us, as you can imagine."

"Naturally," Brass replied. "Still, I need to ask you some more questions. For starters, how many people work at this clinic?"

"Five, minus Dr. Zounek, that is." She counted them off on her fingers. "Drs. Vanderos and Okata, myself, two more clerical workers." Her gaze turned inward momentarily as she conducted a quick mental inventory. "Plus the janitorial staff, I guess. They usually come on after hours."

"I'm going to need a complete list of names," Brass said. "We'll probably be interviewing each of you if our subject does turn out to be Dr. Zounek."

"All right," Rudolph said. "I can get that list for you before you leave."

Grissom hoped she would use the office printer to produce the list. He needed to acquire a sample document from the printer to confirm Nick's analysis of the headhunter's note. "You mentioned a college intern before." His brain noted a possible connection to the university. "Do you have any students working here now?"

"Not at the moment," she said. "That's mostly a summer thing."

"I see," Brass said. Grissom figured he was probably thinking along the same line. "Well, we're going to want names and addresses for them, too."

Rudolph frowned slightly at the prospect. "That's going to take a bit more digging, but I'll see what I can do."

"Thank you." Grissom encouraged her. "It could be very helpful to our investigation." A question occurred to him. "I don't suppose you recall if any of those interns were majoring in anthropology?"

She blinked in surprise. "No, I don't think so. Most of our interns are interested in psychology or social services."

"Not exactly the same thing," Grissom admitted. Although college students had been known to change their majors.

"Let's get back to Dr. Zounek," Brass said. "When was the last time you saw him?"

She glanced fretfully at the door, no doubt worried about leaving the front desk unattended for too long. "I already went over this with the other officer."

Lieutenant Dawson in Missing Persons, Grissom thought. Dawson and her colleagues had investigated the psychiatrist's disappearance earlier but failed to turn up any major leads. According to the file, Dr. Zounek had been a law-abiding citizen with no criminal record or connections or any obvious enemies, a bachelor with no family in the area. No hits had been registered on his credit cards or bank accounts since he went missing. His absence had been reported by one of his professional colleagues after he failed to report to work two days in a row.

"Think of us as a fresh pair of ears," he told her. "Sometimes it helps to go over these things one more time, just in case something got overlooked the first time around." He reached for a psychiatric analogy. "In therapy, crucial information and memories seldom surface in the very first sessions. Insight comes with time and reflection, as you're surely aware."

"I suppose," Rudolph conceded. "Anyway, as I told the other officer, that would have been Friday the twenty-eighth. Dr. Zounek was working late that evening, catching up with his paperwork, when

I left for the day. When we came back to work the next Monday, his car was still parked out front, but he was nowhere around. Nobody's seen him since."

A search of the doctor's home had turned up no evidence of violence. The doctor's automobile—a red 2006 Ferrari—had been impounded by the LVPD. A more thorough forensic examination of the vehicle was clearly on the agenda.

"Was anyone else working late that night?" Brass asked.

"No, I don't think so." She searched her memory. "Dr. Vanderos had taken the day off to attend a wedding, and everybody else left about five. At Dr. Zounek's request, I stayed for a few more hours to assist with the paperwork, but called it a day around seven."

Brass jotted the hours in his notebook. "So you were possibly the last person to see him?"

"I guess so." Rudolph shivered at the thought. "You mean the last person to see him *alive*, don't you?"

"Not necessarily," Grissom said. "We don't know where he went or whom he might have met after you left him."

Plus, of course, there was always the killer.

"What did you do after you left work?" Brass said.

She saw where he was going. "You're wondering if I have an alibi for that night, aren't you?" She smiled sadly. "Honestly, I'm afraid I went straight home, took a long bath, and went to bed. Not exactly the most exciting way to spend a Friday night, but it had been a long week."

"Did you see or talk to anyone at home?"

"Just myself." Rudolph's voice faltered. "My husband died eight months ago, in a traffic accident."

Grissom could tell the death still grieved her. "My condolences."

"Thank you," she replied. "Sometimes I still find it hard to believe he's gone."

"Let's get back to the office then," Brass said. "What about the cleaning crew? Had they come on yet before you left?"

She shook her head. "No. Not at all."

"You seem pretty certain about that," Grissom noted.

"Well . . ." She hesitated. Picking up the hourglass from Zounek's desk, she toyed nervously with the timepiece. "I probably shouldn't say anything. I wouldn't want you to get the wrong idea."

"The wrong idea about what?" Brass pressed her.

Grissom played the good cop. "If there's anything more to tell us, even if you think it doesn't matter, we really need you to share it with us."

Silence ensued as the troubled receptionist appeared to wrestle with her conscience. Grissom wondered how often this room had borne witness to similar moments, as Dr. Zounek waited patiently for his patients to unburden themselves. He hoped that Liz Rudolph would be equally forthcoming.

Finally, Liz Rudolph seemed to come to a decision. "I guess it would look worse if I tried to hide it," she rationalized aloud. "But, to be honest, I think Carlos—the night janitor—was kind of avoiding Dr. Zounek. I suspect he would have stayed away from the office until after he was sure the doctor had left for the day."

"And why is that?" Brass asked.

"It's no big deal," she insisted, "but there had been some unpleasantness a few weeks earlier, when Dr. Zounek had tried to get Carlos fired. But it had all blown over by the time Dr. Zounek went missing. I'm sure that Carlos didn't have anything to do with his disappearance."

Grissom's ears perked up. None of this had made it into the case file.

"Why did Dr. Zounek want Carlos fired?" Brass inquired.

She tried to make light of the matter. "It was nothing, like I said. Dr. Zounek came back to the office one night and caught Carlos watching TV in the waiting room when he was supposed to be working. Carlos insisted that he was just taking a break, but the doctor felt he was loafing on the job. Frankly, this was something of a sore spot where Dr. Zounek was concerned. He liked to get his money's worth out of his employees and resented it if he thought he was being ripped off."

Grissom wondered just how hard he worked Liz Rudolph and his other employees. Zounek was starting to sound like someone who rubbed people the wrong way sometimes. Enough to inspire someone to slice off his head?

"Personally, I think the whole thing got blown out of proportion," Rudolph divulged. "As long as the offices got cleaned, who cared if he took time out to watch his favorite show or a game or whatever? As it happened, Drs. Okata and Vanderos calmed Dr. Zounek down eventually, and Carlos got off with a warning. But I think I would have remembered if I had left the two of them alone in the building together." She shook her head emphatically. "Trust me, Carlos Vallejo was nowhere around when I left the office that night."

Which doesn't mean he didn't show up later on, Grissom reasoned, *or that he wasn't waiting to ambush Dr. Zounek outside by his car.*

Grissom hated to indulge in ethnic profiling, but an obvious question presented itself. "Do you happen to know if Mr. Vallejo is of Peruvian or Ecuadorian descent?"

Rudolph was taken aback by the question. "Why do you ask?"

"Just trying to get a fuller picture of the people involved," Grissom said mildly. The possibility that the janitor might have cultural ties to the Jivaro could not be discounted. "What do you know about his background?"

"Not much," she admitted. "We never spoke much." She put down the hourglass. "How well do you know the janitor at your office?"

Not well enough, Grissom thought. The fact that Natalie Davis, the obsessed serial killer otherwise known as the Miniature Killer, had worked on the cleaning crew at CSI headquarters, right under their very noses, still rankled him. Sara Sidle had almost died because he and the other CSIs had never given the mousy young cleaning woman a second look. "Touché."

Her point made, Rudolph stood up and headed for the door. "Now, if you don't mind, I've been away from my desk for far too long, and there are patients waiting."

Brass blocked her path. "I understand, but we're not done here yet. Can you think of anyone who might want to harm Dr. Zounek?"

"I already told the police everything I know," she protested. "Dr. Zounek had a very well-ordered life. As far as I know, he had no drinking or drug problems, no gambling debts, no angry exes, no malpractice suits, nothing. I can't think of any reason why anyone would want to kill him."

"Girlfriends?" Brass asked. "Boyfriends?"

She sighed in exasperation. "Nothing serious. And he wasn't gay, just single. I'm sure he dated occasionally, but I can't remember any important women in his life." She shrugged. "My impression was that he liked to keep things casual."

Grissom noted the conspicuous absence of any family photos in the office. If Zounek had a significant other, her photo was not on display. He wondered if the same could be said of the doctor's apartment. Certainly, Zounek wouldn't be the first person to hide his personal life from his coworkers and subordinates. *Look at me and Sara.*

Brass doggedly continued to question the increasingly restive receptionist. "And how long have you worked for Dr. Zounek?"

"About five years." She tapped her foot against the carpet. "Now, is that all?"

"Not exactly," Brass said. "What about his patients?"

She bristled noticeably. "You must know I can't discuss them with you. Patient-doctor confidentiality and all that."

"But you're not their doctor," Grissom pointed

out. "And we're not asking you to surrender any patient's confidential files, at least not yet." He held up his hand to fend off any more protests. "You're certainly at liberty to reveal any sort of suspicious interactions you might have observed between Dr. Zounek and a patient outside their private sessions. Perhaps in the waiting room or in the hall?"

"You're splitting hairs," she accused him. "Our patients still expect—and deserve—their privacy. And I take that very seriously, even if I don't have a medical degree, thank you for pointing that out."

"I'm sorry," Grissom apologized. "I didn't mean to offend you or denigrate your position here. I was simply trying to point out that you're not entirely constrained by the obligations of the doctor-patient relationship. You're free to help us find Dr. Zounek's killer, if indeed he was murdered. I'm sure that's an outcome we all hope to achieve here."

Her feathers unruffled a bit. "Of course. I want to assist you in your investigation if I can. But I'm just not comfortable discussing our patients and their problems."

Grissom got the impression that she was stonewalling them. Was she protecting one patient in particular or just the entire practice?

"Look, Ms. Rudolph," Brass confronted her. "You're a busy person and so are we, so let's not waste any more time here. Let me show you what we think happened to your boss." He handed her a pocket-sized snapshot of the *tsanta*. "I ought to warn you, it isn't pretty."

The woman's face went pale as she dropped back into her seat. She stared numbly at the photo for a long moment before finally averting her eyes. Her voice faltered. "Is that . . . a shrunken head?"

"Dr. Zounek's head, it's looking like." Brass retrieved the photo from her trembling fingers. "So maybe you can understand why we're not kidding around here. Now tell me straight: Did the doctor have any patients who might do something like this?"

Brass's approach was more direct, and brutal, than Grissom would have preferred, but it seemed to yield the desired results. Liz Rudolph buried her face in her hands.

"Danny," she whispered. "Danny Skiller. He's one of Dr. Zounek's more volatile patients. A very troubled young man."

"How troubled?" Brass demanded.

She lifted her head and looked the detective squarely in the eye.

"He threatened to cut Dr. Zounek's head off."

10

THE INTERROGATION SUITE at police headquarters, one block from the crime lab, was a far cry from the sumptuous clutter of Vonderlynn's private study at Summerside. Soundproof ceramic tiles cut the room off from the outside world, isolating the suspect. The bare walls and floor were starkly neutral. A large horizontal mirror reflected the chamber's Spartan furnishings, while allowing outside observers to watch the interrogation via a one-way window. A closed-circuit camera monitored the proceedings.

Let's get on with this, Warrick thought.

A glass-covered metal tabletop divided Warrick and Catherine from Vonderlynn, who sat opposite them alongside his attorney, an impeccably groomed black woman named Yvonne Waverly. Ms. Waverly was a full partner in a prestigious local law firm and clearly not to be underestimated. When it came to lawyers, Vonderlynn could afford the best.

"So, just to be clear," she began, "my client is not yet charged with anything?"

"That remains to be determined," Detective Sofia Curtis confirmed, "pending the results of this interview."

The female police officer, who was seated between Warrick and Catherine, had once been a CSI herself before deciding to pursue her original ambition of becoming a detective. She continued to work closely with Grissom and his team on certain investigations. With Brass busy searching for Daniel Skiller, she had agreed to assist in this interrogation. A tall blonde with long straight hair and blue eyes, Sofia wore a white dress shirt with slacks. Warrick found her much easier on the eyes than, say, Brass or Detective O'Riley.

"Understood." Waverly scribbled a note onto the legal pad in front of her. "I want it noted for the record that my client is voluntarily cooperating with this investigation, in the interests of clearing this matter up and having his property restored to him in a timely manner."

Vonderlynn's entire collection, including the arrow-nosed *tsanta* with the suspiciously realistic ears, was currently residing in the evidence lockers at CSI headquarters. The colorful trophies had created quite a stir at the lab when Warrick and Catherine had carted them all in two days ago. Greg, in particular, had looked like a kid in a candy store.

"You'd better not have damaged any of my heads," Vonderlynn groused, glowering across the table at the two CSIs. A plus-size gray business suit had replaced the voluminous robe he was wearing when they first met. "If there's so much as a scratch on any of my valuable collectibles, I'll sue this entire department!"

His attorney placed a restraining hand on his arm. "Let me handle this, Vincent." She fixed her steely eyes on Warrick and the others. "Precisely what evidence do you have against my client?"

Sounds like my cue, Warrick thought. He slid a photo of the confiscated *tsanta*, which Catherine had dubbed "Arrow Nose," across the table. Warrick had taken the photo himself as soon as they had gotten the warrant. "A forensic examination has concluded that this is an actual human head, or at least the skin and hair from one."

Although he had once been a canny card player, before his gambling habit got the best of him, Warrick wasn't bluffing this time. Besides those telltale ears, Doc Robbins had found nasal hairs in the *tsanta*'s miniature nostrils. In addition, microscopic analysis had confirmed that hair and tissue samples taken from the *tsanta* were one-hundred-percent human. Sofia handed the official report over to the lawyer, who quickly reviewed its contents.

"That's not what you told us before," Catherine reminded Vonderlynn. "You insisted this head was a fake."

The millionaire's indignant bluster deserted him. "I guess I was mistaken." An unconvincing grin failed to conceal his obvious anxiety. "How about that?"

"Come on, Vincent," Catherine said. "You seriously expect us to believe that a serious collector like yourself can't tell a fake from the real thing?

Even I spotted the difference, and I've been on this case for less than a week." She rolled her eyes. "Who do you think you're fooling here?"

He tried to brazen it out, despite the CSI's skepticism. "Actually, there are some very good reproductions out there. Anyone could get fooled sometimes."

"But why would any savvy dealer try to pass off a real *tsanta* as a fake?" Warrick asked. "Where's the upside in that? Unscrupulous types profit by selling counterfeits as the real thing, not the other way around."

"Well . . . um . . ." Vonderlynn was at a loss for an explanation. "Maybe the dealer didn't know it was real, either. . . ."

"Cut the crap, Mr. Vonderlynn," Sofia said, taking off the kid gloves. "Where did you get the head?"

Waverly interrupted before the squirming collector could say anything more. "I'm advising my client not to answer any further questions." Gathering her notes and tucking them into an attaché case, she stood up and gestured for Vonderlynn to do the same. "Unless you intend to hold my client, this interview is over."

"That's your prerogative," Sofia conceded. "But I doubt that Mr. Vonderlynn wants to remain under suspicion of murder."

"Murder!" Vonderlynn reacted as though he had been punched in the gut. His florid complexion went pale. "What the hell are you talking about? I never killed anybody."

Yvonne Waverly also looked taken aback. "I don't understand. I was under the impression that we were talking about a historical relic." She sat back down at the table. "Maybe a distasteful one, but still . . ."

Sofia presented them with a color photo of the original shrunken head. "Meet Dr. James Zounek, a prominent local psychiatrist. We have reason to suspect that Dr. Zounek was murdered sometime in the last few weeks by someone who obviously has a thing about shrunken heads." Sofia looked pointedly at the flummoxed millionaire, who was sweating visibly. "Now another severed head has turned up in Mr. Vonderlynn's possession, something he lied about to these CSIs." She paused to let the damning facts sink in. "You can see how this looks bad for your client."

"All right, all right!" Vonderlynn blurted. "I lied, okay? But I didn't kill anybody. I bought that head on the black market and lied because I knew it was stolen."

His lawyer tried to caution him. "Vincent . . ."

"No!" he insisted, ignoring his counsel's advice. "I want to get this cleared up, now!" He stared in horror at the photo of the murdered shrink. "Jesus, you people don't really think I chopped this guy's head off, do you? I've never even heard of this Dr. Zoonik or whoever!"

So you say, Warrick thought. The doctor's associates would have to be questioned regarding Vonderlynn, to see if there was any connection between the missing psychiatrist and the retired computer whiz. Or between Vonderlynn and the university, for that matter. "You didn't happen to attend UNLV, did you?"

"What?" The collector looked puzzled by the question. "What's that got to do with anything?"

"Just asking," Warrick said. "Are you connected to the university in any way?"

"Do I look like a college kid?" Vonderlynn replied sarcastically. "No, I never went to UNLV. I only moved to Vegas a few years ago, after I hit it big in Seattle."

Another thing we need to verify, Warrick thought. He dropped the topic for now and tapped the photo of Arrow Nose. "Okay. So where did this head come from?"

Vonderlynn hesitated for a moment before committing himself. "The Smithsonian," he confessed finally. "In Washington, D.C."

"We know where the Smithsonian is," Sofia said impatiently. "Go on."

Defeated, he slumped in his seat. "They've got plenty of *tsantas* that are just packed away in the back, because Native American remains aren't allowed to be put on display in publicly funded museums anymore. Hell, they've even got two entire shrunken *bodies* locked away out of sight, where no one can admire them." He shook his head in disgust. "What a waste."

"How did you get your hands on this particular head?" Sofia asked.

He dabbed at his sweaty brow with a monogrammed handkerchief. "A couple of years ago, back in 2006, I was contacted by this guy who works in the archives at the Smithsonian. He figured no would ever notice if a *tsanta* or two went missing. Called himself 'Tsanta Claus.'"

Ouch, Warrick thought.

"Let me guess," Catherine said. "You jumped at

the chance to get your hands on a genuine specimen."

"Sure. Why not?" he said defensively. "This beauty was just gathering dust anyway, not doing anyone any good. I *rescued* it from obscurity. And I even arranged to have the original replaced by a replica, so that no one would be the wiser."

Warrick wondered if that replica had been commissioned from Red Noir Studios. *Sounds like we might need to call on Tyrone and Karla again.*

A tape recorder preserved Vonderlynn's confession. "It's not like anyone got hurt or anything," he insisted. "It was a victimless crime."

His lawyer intervened before he got himself in any deeper. "I think you've said enough, Vincent." She looked hopefully at Sofia and the CSIs. "Perhaps we can work out some sort of deal here? If my client agrees to make restitution and perhaps volunteer the name of his contact at the Smithsonian?" Warrick was impressed with how quickly Ms. Waverly had adjusted her strategy. "Surely it's in the public interest to expose the individual who is abusing the trust of one of our national institutions?"

"That's not my call," Sofia said tersely. "To be honest, my primary focus is our murder investigation."

"But I just told you," Vonderlynn exclaimed, "I had nothing to do with that!"

Unfortunately, at least as far as this case was concerned, Warrick was starting to believe him. His story sounded plausible enough. Plus, as it happened, Trace had yet to establish a positive link between the two shrunken heads. The dyes and fibers found in Arrow Nose had failed to match those used in the late Dr. Zounek's remains. Furthermore, Doc Robbins's initial finding suggested that the *tsanta* confiscated from Vincent Vonderlynn's study was older and more deteriorated than the one sent to UNLV . . . as though Arrow Nose had been sitting on a shelf in the back of a museum for years.

They'd have to confirm Vonderlynn's story with the Smithsonian, of course, but it was beginning to look like their search for the Vegas headhunter had taken a wrong turn. The sleazy collector was apparently guilty of conspiring to steal a shrunken head, but maybe he really didn't have anything to do with the disappearance, death, and subsequent mutilation of James Zounek. *We nabbed the wrong bad guy.*

Which put them right back where they started.

"What about that murder investigation?" Waverly asked.

Sofia shrugged. "We can't rule out your client as a suspect just yet, but for now he's free to go while we check out his story. I wouldn't recommend that he leave the county, however, until this matter is fully resolved." Her stern voice dared Vonderlynn to cross her. "In addition, I'll be notifying the authorities in D.C. about the alleged theft of the head as soon as this interview is concluded."

"Do you have to?" Vonderlynn whimpered. His piggish eyes searched for mercy, but found it in short supply. He slunk toward the exit after his attorney, then hesitated in the doorway. "I don't suppose there's any chance I can get my collection back in the meantime?"

"Don't press your luck," Catherine told him.

The black-and-white security footage played out on the screen of Grissom's laptop. There was no audio, but he followed the narrative easily enough:

A heated confrontation transpired in the waiting room of the Grace Tranquillity Mental Health Clinic. Dr. James Zounek, his head still firmly attached to his shoulders, offered a plastic prescription bottle to an upset young man who had apparently just stormed out of the psychiatrist's private office without the pills. The patient, whom Liz Rudolph had identified as Daniel Skiller, age twenty-two, angrily swatted the pill bottle from the doctor's hand. The plastic vial bounced across the floor, and its cap came loose, spilling tiny white capsules all over the waiting room. His lean face contorted with rage, Skiller ranted at the startled psychiatrist before exiting the clinic. He slammed the door behind him.

Embarrassed by the ugly scene, Zounek avoided the shocked eyes of the other patients as he disappeared back into his office with as much dignity as he could muster, but not before barking some instructions at Liz Rudolph. The disgruntled-looking receptionist scurried out from behind the front desk to clean up the mess made by the fallen pill container. She shot a dirty look at the doctor's back.

Grissom rewound the footage to get another look at the irate patient. Daniel Skiller was a lanky Caucasian youth wearing a ragged army-surplus jacket, jeans, and sneakers. Bangs of greasy brown hair hung before his eyes. A scraggly beard failed to conceal his pimply complexion. His wild eyes bulged from their sockets.

Was this the face of a headhunter? According to Liz Rudolph, the younger man suffered from paranoid delusions and, at the behest of his family, had been under Zounek's care for years.

Grissom couldn't quite read Skiller's lips, but the receptionist had vividly recalled the youth's parting words: *"You try to poison me again and I'll cut your head off!"*

Brass leaned over to take in the video footage as well. The rumpled detective was sitting next to Grissom in the front seat of his Taurus, which was parked across the street from the suspect's apartment. "Gotta wonder why Ms. Rudolph didn't mention this altercation to the missing-persons unit?"

"Well, in her defense," Grissom observed, "she didn't know that Dr. Zounek had been decapitated at the time. Plus, I imagine that outbursts from agitated patients are not uncommon in her line of work. She may not have made the connection until you showed her that picture of the shrunken head."

"I suppose," Brass muttered doubtfully. "Seems to me she could have saved us a whole lot of running around if she'd been a little faster on the uptake."

Looking away from Grissom's laptop, he contemplated Daniel Skiller's run-down apartment, which was located above a liquor store in a seamy part of downtown off Fremont Street. Drawn curtains overlooked a small parking lot jammed between a tattoo parlor and a plasma-collection center. Winos, drifters, and other hard-luck cases were lined up outside the latter, waiting to exchange their blood for ready cash. Cigarette butts, fast-food wrappers, and discarded bandages littered the pavement; bloodstained cotton balls clung to the bandages. A used condom lay in the gutters. There was enough random DNA scattered around that Grissom hoped they would never have to process this block as a crime scene.

"Nice neighborhood," Brass said. "I thought this kid's family had money."

Grissom had to admit that this impoverished environment clashed with the genteel clientele that Dr. Zounek's clinic appeared to cater to; apparently, Daniel Skiller's father owned a profitable chain of drugstores. "They can pay for his treatment, but they can't control where he lives. Sometimes young people reject their backgrounds and end up in places like this, just to assert their independence."

"Don't I know it," Brass said glumly.

Grissom instantly regretted his words. Brass's own daughter, Ellie, had turned to drugs and prostitution. Father and daughter remained estranged to this day. "My apologies. I didn't mean to evoke painful memories."

"Forget it." Brass nodded stoically at the unsavory milieu surrounding them. "Just don't say I never take you anywhere nice."

Tracking down Daniel Skiller was turning out to be a challenge. Unemployed and on disability, the suspect had no fixed schedule and only this one address. Brass and Grissom had already come by once looking for him, but no one had opened the door, nor were there any signs of life within the apartment: no lights, no music, no TV. Phone calls to Skiller's home and cell-phone numbers had gone unanswered. An unmarked LVPD patrol car had staked out the apartment overnight, but no one saw Skiller come or go. It was now ten in the morning the following day and Brass's patience was clearly wearing thin.

"So where do you think this kid is?" he groused. "He's got to come home sometime, doesn't he?"

"One would think," Grissom agreed, "but this *is* Las Vegas." The city's hedonistic lifestyle, where the action never stopped, practically encouraged people to stay out all night. Twenty-four-hour casinos, diners, bars, and clubs offered plenty of tempting alternatives to one's own bed. "For all we know, Daniel Skiller could be on a gambling spree, staying over at a friend's house, or out of town. It's even conceivable that he's left Vegas for good."

Perhaps after disposing of Dr. Zounek?

"Yeah," Brass admitted. "Hell, maybe he just got lucky." He glanced at the ranting mental patient on Grissom's screen. "Stranger things have happened."

"Every day."

Grissom's cell phone rang, interrupting the discussion. He answered it promptly.

"Grissom here."

Greg Sanders's voice issued from the phone. "Sorry to barge in on your stakeout, but I thought you should hear this. Wendy just called from the lab at the university. Seems the mitochondrial DNA from the shrunken head is a match for Dr. Zounek's."

"Really?" Grissom asked, as Brass looked on curiously. "Is Wendy certain of that? The results have been verified?"

"You bet," Greg said. "You should hear Wendy rave about this high-powered Sequencer they're using at UNLV. I think she's in love."

Grissom nodded in satisfaction. "Good work. Compliment Wendy for me."

He ended the call and informed Brass of the DNA match. "Or, to be more precise, the victim and Dr. Zounek had the same mother at least." MtDNA was passed along unchanged along maternal lines, so, technically, it could only be used to trace family relationships on the mother's side. Still, the evidence pointed strongly to one conclusion: the shrunken head belonged to the missing psychiatrist. "Looks like we definitely have a murder on our hands . . . and a headhunter on the loose."

"Great," Brass said sourly. He massaged his forehead, as though he felt a headache coming on. "You're the expert here. Any chance you can give me some sort of psychological profile of this nutjob?"

Grissom frowned. Ordinarily, he preferred hard evidence to vague theoretical abstractions. "That's not exactly my specialty. I'm a forensic scientist, not a profiler."

"Take a stab at it anyway," Brass urged him. "Indulge me."

Grissom sighed and lowered the lid of his laptop. "I'm reluctant to speculate too much about the 'why' behind the murder, at least at this early stage of the investigation, but traditionally, headhunting is all about claiming the power of your enemies. Perhaps the killer is someone who feels powerless or put-upon in real life?"

"Like a paranoid mental patient?" Brass suggested.

"Or a janitor," Grissom pointed out. Although Daniel Skiller was their prime suspect at the moment, due to his threat against Dr. Zounek, they couldn't rule out Carlos Vallejo, either. Vallejo, whom they had yet to interview, also had a possible grudge against the murdered psychiatrist, not to mention better access to the clinic's laser printer. Political correctness aside, Grissom was still curious as to Vallejo's ethnic background.

Threat or no threat, we can't leap to the assumption that Daniel Skiller is our killer.

A patrol car pulled up behind the Taurus. A pair of uniformed officers emerged from the vehicle. Grissom recognized them as Susan Muckerheide and Duane Parks. Brass rolled down the window on the driver's side as the officers approached. "You got my warrant?"

"Signed, sealed, and delivered," Parks assured him. He was a burly dark-haired man with a slight Texan accent.

"About time." It had taken a bit of effort to persuade Judge Cushman to let them break into Skiller's apartment, but taken together, the shrunken head and the death-threat video had presented a compelling argument for not waiting any longer to search the premises. Brass looked over the warrant to make sure everything was in order, then tucked it into the pocket of his sportcoat. Parks stepped aside as the detective got out of the car. "The ram's in the back," he instructed the other two officers. "Let's get this over with before I'm eligible for my pension."

Grissom stowed his laptop beneath the seat and exited the Taurus from the other side. After staking out the apartment for the last hour or so, it felt good to stretch his legs. He retrieved his field kit from the rear of the vehicle before making sure that the Taurus's doors were thoroughly locked. This wasn't the sort of neighborhood where you left your car behind without a qualm.

The line in front of the plasma center thinned out as the party of police officers crossed the street toward the parking lot. Shifty-looking individuals rapidly made themselves scarce. Grissom had on his blue FORENSICS windbreaker and baseball cap. Sunglasses protected his eyes from the afternoon glare. Muckerheide carried the battering ram. The thirty-five-pound metal ram had a black rubber grip. High-strength plastic coated the impact area.

"Over here," Brass instructed the other cops. "Muckerheide, you're with me. Parks, keep an eye out for our suspect." He handed the hefty officer a blowup of Skiller's driver's license photo. "I don't want him walking in on us unannounced."

"Will do," Parks said. He scanned the photo, committing it to memory. "I'll watch from the car."

The smell of urine emanated from behind the stairs leading up to Daniel Skiller's apartment. More DNA, Grissom noted out of habit. "You wait here," Brass cautioned, "just in case there's somebody lurking inside." He eyed Grissom warily. "Please tell me you're carrying."

CSIs were required by protocol to carry their weapons while in the field, as well as to pass regular firearms proficiency exams. It wasn't Grissom's favorite part of the job, but he recognized the necessity of the policy; despite all attempts at caution, CSIs sometimes found themselves in hazardous situations where they were called upon to defend themselves or others, occasionally with lethal force. "Naturally." He opened his jacket to reveal the sidearm holstered against his hip. "Let's hope I won't need it."

"Yeah," Brass grunted. He had been shot in the line of duty before, nearly losing his life on at least one occasion. "Wouldn't that be great?"

The detective climbed the stairs to a small landing outside the door of the apartment. Muckerheide toted the ram behind him. A stuffed mailbox, overflowing with junk mail and circulars, suggested that Skiller had not been home for days. Brass rapped on the door anyway.

"Daniel Skiller? Open up, please. It's the police."

As before, there was no response. Watching from below, Grissom didn't even see the drapes stir. If Skiller was at home, he was either ignoring them or oblivious.

"The hell with it," Brass declared. He backed up to give Muckerheide room to position the ram. "Give it all you've got."

Holding on to the ram by its handle, the beefy uniform swung it against the flimsy wooden door. One good slam was all it took to shatter the lock, sending the door flying inward. Brass peered cautiously around the doorframe before, gun in hand, stepping into the apartment. "Watch yourselves," he urged the other officers. "And don't lose your heads, in more ways than one."

Minutes passed as Grissom waited downstairs for the police to conduct a preliminary sweep of the premises. Curiosity, as well as the pervasive urine smell, made the interval seem even longer. The silver field kit rested on the blacktop beside him. A narrow alley separated the rear of the liquor store from the back of the building behind it. A Dumpster and a loading dock took up much of the available space. Glancing around, Grissom didn't see any obvious places to bury a headless corpse, although he made a mental note to have the Dumpster searched should any evidence within the apartment point toward foul play. He listened intently, concerned that at any moment, he might hear shouting—or even gunshots—from the residence above. His sidearm weighed heavily against his hip.

He admitted to mixed feelings. Finding Daniel Skiller inside could lead to a violent confrontation, but at least they would know where he was. An ambush or a waste of time? Neither prospect was appealing.

Finally, after about ten minutes, Brass emerged from the open doorway at the top of the stairs. "All clear," he pronounced. "Come on up."

Hefting his kit, Grissom accepted the invitation.

An overall impression of squalor and neglect struck Grissom as soon as he entered the low-rent apartment. The police had already flicked on the overhead lights, exposing cracked stucco plaster and peeling yellow trim. Cobwebs gathered in the cor-

ners of the ceiling. Thrift-store furniture, patched
with liberal applications of duct tape, rested on
dingy brown carpeting. Aluminum foil was taped
over the windows, on the other side of the heavy
curtains. A couple of unframed posters were tacked
to the walls. The most disturbing was a large black-
and-white photo of a thalidomide child from the
1960s, with flippers where its hands and feet should
have been. "NEVER FORGET!" read the stark cap-
tions above and below the tragic portrait. "NEVER
AGAIN!" A second poster featured the Periodic
Table of Elements with a lurid red X slashed across
it. "CHEMICALS SUCK!" warned the defaced chart.
"CHEMICALS KILL!"

Grissom thought he detected a theme. Apparently, Daniel Skiller had strong opinions regarding
the pharmaceutical industry. No wonder he reacted
so negatively to the prescription Dr. Zounek had
tried to press on him. The only question was
whether his objections to the medication stemmed
from paranoia or personal experience. Possibly a little bit of both.

"Charming taste in art," Brass said. He met Grissom just inside the door. He grimaced at the de-
formed child on the thalidomide poster. "How'd you
like to look at that every day?"

"Not exactly Renoir," Grissom admitted. His
own apartment was decorated with mounted but-
terfly displays and modern art. Removing his sunglasses, he glanced around the living room.
"Nothing concerning shrunken heads or the Jivaro,
however." A quick survey revealed a short hallway
leading to what looked like a coat closet. Open

doors faced each other across the corridor. "What's the layout?"

Brass gestured around the apartment like a particularly unenthusiastic realtor. "Living room, attached kitchenette, bedroom, bathroom." He grimaced in disgust. "All the comforts of home, if you don't mind living like a pig."

"Actually, pigs are very clean animals," Grissom said. "If left to their own devices, they take great care not to soil their eating and sleeping areas."

Brass appeared strangely underwhelmed by this information. "I'll keep that in mind."

The atmosphere within the apartment was uncomfortably warm and stuffy; if not for the risk of alerting Skiller to their presence, he would have been tempted to open a window. Grissom sniffed the air but failed to detect the distinctive aroma of rotting flesh. He took this as a strong, if not necessarily conclusive, indication that James Zounek's remains were nowhere in the vicinity.

"No headless bodies in the tub, I take it?" he asked Brass.

"Not that I noticed." The detective dispatched Muckerheide to keep watch with Parks, while Grissom got to work. He decided to start with the kitchen, on the grounds that it was the most likely place to prepare a shrunken head. The compact cooking area, which was only about the size of a canoe, was separated from the living room by a partition with a cutout window in it. Dirty dishes were piled up in the sink. Empty cardboard pizza boxes were stacked on top of the oven range, suggesting that Skiller didn't do a whole lot of cooking. An open box of granola rested on the counter next to the microwave, alongside a roll of Saran Wrap that also needed to be put away. He caught sight of a mouse as it scurried behind the refrigerator.

Grissom pulled on a pair of latex gloves. Lifting the pizza boxes, he found a thin layer of dust coating the range's heating elements. Evidence that the oven had not been used to simmer a human head lately? He checked the kitchen cabinets and drawers, but found nothing incriminating. None of the materials used to prepare the *tsanta*—beads, hemp cords, watermelon seeds—was present. Neither was the skull of James Zounek.

Magnets pinned coupons and family photos to the fridge, implying that Daniel Skiller was not entirely at odds with his concerned family. The smiling snapshots offered a different perspective on the troubled young man from that of the damning security footage. Grissom resolved to remember that while Skiller might be a deranged headhunter, he was also someone's son or brother. Once again, Grissom found himself faced with ambivalent feelings. Proving Skiller's guilt would solve their case, but break his family's heart.

Just concentrate on the evidence, he told himself. Tragedy was a daily part of his profession, but the scientific method would lead him to the truth—and perhaps to a degree of closure for all concerned. *Sometimes that's the best we can hope for.*

He opened the fridge. In the past, he had made some gruesome discoveries in refrigerators, including stolen organs, murdered infants, and severed body parts, but the contents of Skiller's fridge were not nearly so dramatic. Only bottled water, fresh produce, and leftovers greeted his eyes. The interior lightbulb had gone out at some point, forcing Grissom to rely on a pen-sized flashlight. ALS revealed no suspicious bloodstains.

More interesting was the wastebasket under the sink, where Grissom found several unopened letters from Dr. Zounek's office. The letters had been torn in half before being tossed in the trash, but the return address on the envelopes was still readable. He carefully bagged the mutilated correspondence for closer inspection later.

"Any luck so far?" Brass asked. He had peeled away part of the aluminum foil covering one window in order to spy furtively on the parking lot below. There was always a chance that Skiller might return at any minute.

Grissom shook his head. "No smoking guns or blow pipes."

Moving on to the bedroom, he found a single-sized futon buried beneath a heap of disordered sheets and comforters that smelled as though they were badly in need of washing. Dirty laundry was strewn about the floor. An unmoving ceiling fan failed to disperse the rank atmosphere. A stack of men's magazines, of the heterosexual variety, rested on the floor near the bed. Plastic milk crates held a small library of paperback books. Scanning the titles, Grissom encountered mostly Dean Koontz novels, biographies, and erotica. Nothing on shrunken heads, the Jivaro, or anthropology. A quote from Rachel Carson had been painted, with surprisingly graceful calligraphy, on the wall of the bedroom: "*As*

*crude a weapon as the cave man's club, the chemical bar-
rage has been hurled at the fabric of life."*

Grissom recognized the quote as a line from *Silent
Spring*. It was difficult to consider that book an in-
citement to murder, but who knew what leaps
Daniel Skiller's troubled imagination had taken?
Had he felt himself under assault, perhaps by Dr.
Zounek?

Brass appeared in the doorway. He sniffed disap-
provingly at the mess. "You know, I don't think he
entertains much."

"A reasonable assumption." Grissom sorted through
the clean clothes hanging in the bedroom closet.
"He appears to live alone as well."

The tiny bathroom boasted just a shower, no tub,
and offered only a few more insights into Skiller's
personality. Peeling back the scummy shower cur-
tain, Grissom found only a single bar of unscented
soap. No shampoos or conditioners. Likewise, the
medicine cabinet held only a single toothbrush,
dental floss, and a tube of baking-powder tooth-
paste. Skiller's aversion to chemicals clearly extended to his personal hygiene. No prescriptions
lurked in the cabinet, not even so much as a bottle
of aspirin. A cockroach bolted across the cracked
porcelain sink before escaping down the drain.

Grissom considered checking the sink and
shower drains for blood residue, but decided to hold
off on that for now. At present, there was no evidence that a crime had been committed here.

He saved the living room for last. The modest furnishings consisted of a patched vinyl easy chair, a

rickety card table, and a pair of folding metal chairs. The foil over the windows cut down on the lighting, so Grissom supplemented the flickering overhead lamp with his own flashlight. He found the window coverings a disturbing sign; Skiller clearly valued his privacy, perhaps to an excessive degree. Who exactly did he think was spying on him? A TV set perched atop another plastic milk crate. Cardboard boxes, filled to the brim with papers, surrounded the easy chair.

"Get a load of his reading material," Brass advised.

The papers turned out to be stacks and stacks of computer printouts, downloaded from various websites. Skimming through them, Grissom found multiple articles, essays, and exposés denouncing the pharmaceutical industry. Reports on the Vioxx controversy, polemics against the Food and Drug Administration, studies attempting to link autism to various vaccines. Although some of the articles had been lifted from mainstream news sites, others flirted with fringier sources. Conspiracy theories and ecological manifestos abounded.

Brass read some of the printouts over Grissom's shoulder. "Looks like our friend here was a full-time crackpot."

"Well, he clearly spent a lot of time researching the subject." Grissom contemplated the reams of printouts, all carefully filed and stapled. He counted at least seven boxes. "Which raises an interesting question: Where is the computer?"

Brass looked around, his eyes widening in realization. "There isn't one."

"My point exactly." Grissom considered the problem. Skiller was unemployed, but he obviously had access to a computer somewhere. One solution instantly came to mind. "Where's the nearest public library?"

11

"YEAH, I DID A HEAD like that," El Jaguar admitted. "Vinnie told me he wanted a copy for his own collection."

Catherine and Warrick had returned to Red Noir Studios to wrap up the loose ends of the Vonderlynn investigation, mostly as a favor to the cops in D.C. The Smithsonian had confirmed that the arrow-nosed *tsanta* belonged to them; now the Feds wanted to know the origin of the replica that had been left in its place. At this point, Catherine suspected that this entire sideshow had nothing to do with James Zounek's murder, but she didn't want to compromise the investigation by getting sloppy. *Besides,* she thought, *it can't hurt to have the Smithsonian, of all places, owe us a favor.*

"You sure about that?" Warrick asked. They were back in the studio's spookily appointed lobby, but Catherine barely noticed the macabre curiosities on display. By now, shrunken heads were nothing new to her.

Tyrone took another look at the photo of Vincent Vonderlynn's favorite *tsanta*. "Positive. I'd recognize that arrow anywhere." He handed the picture over to Karla. "You remember this job, babe?"

"Oh sure," the goth girl chirped. She glanced over at her desk. "If you want, I'm sure there must be a picture of Tyrone's version in his portfolio. Would you like me to find it for you?"

"That would be great," Catherine told her.

While Karla scurried off to check her files, Warrick continued to grill El Jaguar. "And you had no idea why Mr. Vonderlynn wanted this replica?"

"Not a clue, I swear!" the artist exclaimed. "I thought it was just another custom job!"

Catherine wasn't entirely sure she believed him. As she recalled, both Tyrone and Karla had needed some prodding to surrender Vonderlynn's name and address before. Maybe they'd suspected that their number one client wasn't entirely on the up and up?

Not that it really matters, she thought. The Smithsonian had their head back, Vincent Vonderlynn was in big trouble, and none of this was bringing them any closer to finding Zounek's murderer. *I just hope Grissom and the others are making more progress than we are.*

"So what's going to happen to Vinnie now?" Tyrone asked.

"That's out of our hands," Warrick said. "But if I were you, I'd start rounding up some new customers. I think most of Mr. Vonderlynn's money will be going to his lawyers for the time being."

Tyrone's tattooed face fell.

"Bummer."

Gelson Community Library was a short bus ride away from Daniel Skiller's squalid apartment. Grissom and Brass drove there instead, but as they walked toward the front door of the modest suburban library, Grissom was troubled by the sight of a young mother exiting the building with her toddlers. Brass held open the door for the kids, each of whom was clutching a picture book or a DVD or two. Announcements taped to the swinging glass door touted children's story-time sessions, elementary-school book clubs, and English-as-a-Second-Language classes. This month's "Movie Night" feature was a G-rated animated film titled *Space Chimps*. All in all, the family-friendly environment struck Grissom as a bad place to attempt to apprehend a possibly crazed murder suspect. He found himself hoping that his hunch was wrong.

"Quite a change from the previous stop on our tour," Brass said. "Less winos, more rugrats."

Grissom wondered if the detective was equally apprehensive about the setting. "But possibly one individual in common?"

"That's the idea," Brass said. "Let's find out."

An absence of metal detectors testified to the relative safety of the neighborhood. Grissom's immediate impression upon entering was of a pleasant and inviting location that seemed to be doing a fair amount of business this sunny afternoon. New hardcovers were displayed face-out on metal book-shelves just past the entrance. A spin rack held a generous assortment of paperback romance novels. Returned books and videos were piled in a collection bin to the right. Posters featuring popular cartoon characters and TV stars extolled the joys of reading. A pair of librarians manned the checkout counter, while a third employee, who looked young enough to be a high school intern, was busy reshelving books in the mystery section. Men, women, and children of assorted ages roamed the stacks. Their voices were suitably hushed.

Ordinarily, Grissom would have enjoyed browsing the library's selections, but today he immediately zeroed in on the facility's free computers. Two rows of Macs, back to back, occupied a long horizontal table in the center of the ground floor, within easy view of the librarians' counter. All six computer stations were occupied. A placard at the end of the table reminded patrons to sign up at the front desk before using the computers.

"Don't look now," Brass said, "but there's our boy."

Hunched over the keyboard in front of the middle computer on the right was Daniel Skiller, wearing the same olive-green army jacket he had sported in the death-threat video. His oily hair looked as if it hadn't been washed in weeks; Grissom recalled the conspicuous lack of shampoo in his bathroom. His sloppy hygiene attracted an annoyed look from the gray-haired retiree sitting to his right. The teenage boy on his left was too busy watching hip-hop videos with the sound off to notice.

Grissom frowned. Although the subdued hubbub spoke well of the community's literacy rate, the crowded library was too busy for his liking. Counting the librarians, there were more than a dozen civilians on hand, including several children. He hoped that Skiller would come with them easily but feared the worst. Liz Rudolph had described the paranoid young man as "volatile"—and possibly dangerous.

He and Brass exchanged worried looks. "Perhaps we should wait for him outside?" Grissom whispered.

Brass shook his head. He nodded at a clock on the wall. It wasn't even noon yet. The library wouldn't be closing for another eight hours. "We could be waiting a long time."

They approached him quietly from behind. Intent on his research, he appeared oblivious to their presence. Grissom glimpsed an exposé on industrial pesticides on the screen. Skiller clicked repeatedly on the print command. Pages and pages of documentation were spit out by the printer at the far end of the table. At ten cents a page, Skiller was racking up quite a bill.

"Excuse me." Brass kept his voice low as he addressed the distracted suspect. "Daniel Skiller?"

The youth looked up irritably. Dark circles under bloodshot eyes hinted at serious sleep deprivation. His scraggly beard needed trimming. He hastily closed the window he was looking at. "What? What do you want?" he demanded, loud enough to draw the attention of both scowling librarians and his fellow patrons. "Oh, did someone complain about me again? I have just as much right to be here as anyone else. You can't discriminate against me just because I refuse to poison myself with chemical perfumes and shampoos!"

Alarmed by Skiller's outburst, nearby patrons backed away. The retiree got out of his chair with surprising speed. The hip-hop fan seemed hesitant to abandon his videos, but was dragged away by a worried friend. People watched tensely from a safe distance.

"That's right. Go ahead," Skiller accused them. "Don't get involved! Just let the Smell Police harass a law-abiding citizen!"

Brass tried to calm the angry suspect. "Perhaps we can talk about this outside?"

"Excuse me, what's going on here?" The head librarian, a slightly hippyish-looking older man whose gray hair was bound in a ponytail, stepped out from behind the checkout counter. A name badge on his sweater vest identified him as Mr. Strode. He hurried toward the computer stations. "Is there a problem?"

Grissom grabbed hold of Strode's arm before he could get too close to Brass or Skiller. "LVPD," he explained, showing the confused librarian his ID. "Please let us handle this."

"Talk about what?" Skiller challenged Brass. "About how you want to silence the truth, maybe drug me into submission? Screw that!" Without warning, he snatched the keyboard off the table and whacked Brass across the face with it. The smack of the keyboard against the cop's skull echoed across the library, eliciting anxious gasps and exclamations from shocked witnesses. Brass staggered backward, while Skiller vaulted onto the table, knocking over his chair in the process. He ran down the length of the table. Pandemonium erupted as panicked patrons dashed for the exits or ducked behind the stacks.

"Jim?" Grissom called out to his colleague.

"I'm all right!" Brass insisted. Dazed, he clutched his head in pain. "Get that sonofabitch!"

Skiller trampled over the printer, which was still spewing out his selections, as he leaped from the end of the table back onto the floor. He shot a hurried glance at the front entrance, only to spot Grissom between him and the door. Changing his mind, he darted toward the rear of the library. A middle-aged black woman, petrified with fright, inadvertently blocked his path. Swearing loudly, he hurled her aside. "Outta my way!"

Where's he heading? Grissom fretted. A FIRE EXIT sign pointed to the northwest corner of the library. Several rows of tall metal bookcases obstructed Grissom's view of the exit, which he guessed to be Skiller's destination. Rapidly taking in the geography, Grissom took a shortcut through the science fiction section in hopes of heading Skiller off at the pass. The tactic worked as the fleeing suspect tripped over a dropped stuffed animal and momentarily lost his balance. He sideswiped a display of the week's *New York Times* bestsellers, sending the stacked books spilling onto the floor. By the time Skiller regained his footing, Grissom had managed to stake out a position in front of the fire exit.

"That's enough, Daniel!" He kept his gun holstered, fearing that the sight of the weapon would agitate Skiller further. He held up his empty hands. "We just want to talk to you."

The two men faced each other at opposite ends of a narrow corridor lined on both sides with book-shelves. Grissom spotted a pair of restroom doors to Skiller's right. He hoped the fugitive wouldn't try to barricade himself in one of the lavatories. Out of the corner of his eye, he glimpsed Brass closing on Skiller's left side. The cop had his gun drawn, but, like Grissom, appeared unwilling to employ lethal force just yet. Or maybe he was worried that there might be innocent civilians hiding in the restrooms? Brass had once killed a fellow cop in a tragic case of friendly fire. Grissom knew he wouldn't risk shoot-ing an unseen library patron by mistake.

"Forget it!" Skiller ranted. "I'm not falling for your lies!" Grabbing thick hardcover books off the shelves, he started hurling them at Grissom, who had to raise his arms to defend himself. The heavy tomes bounced painfully against Grissom's forearms, driving him backward. Spittle sprayed from Skiller's lips. "You want to lock me away because I know the truth!"

The barrage of books put Grissom on the defen-sive, but he tried to keep Daniel talking. "And what truth is that, Daniel?"

"That our brains are steeped in chemicals every day, in the air and the water and everything we eat and drink. Even our tap water is polluted with pre-scription drugs, warping our minds, mutating our bodies! Can't you taste them in your mouth? I can. Every minute of every day!"

Before he could rant any further, the door to the restroom swung open, and a little Asian girl, no more than four years old, emerged directly in front of Skiller. *No!* Grissom thought, but it was already too late. Tossing his latest missile away, Skiller seized the child and lifted her off her feet. His right arm wrapped tightly around her waist, holding her in front of him like a human shield, he yanked a pencil from his back pocket and pressed its sharpened tip against the girl's vulnerable throat. "Leave me alone," he threatened, "or I'll kill her, I swear I will!"

Grissom's heart sank. The situation was rapidly spiraling out of control.

"Jodi!" An anguished cry came from a terrified young woman Grissom guessed to be the toddler's mother. Mr. Strode, the librarian, was holding her back over by the fallen bestsellers. The mother's ashen face was contorted with fear. Tears streamed from her eyes. "Oh my God! Please, let go of my baby!"

"Shut up!" Skiller yelled. He guiltily avoided the mother's eyes. "Somebody make her shut up!"

Brass called out to Skiller. "All right, Daniel. We're listening to you. Please don't do anything you'll regret later." He held a handkerchief to his bleeding forehead. The beginnings of a black eye purpled his face. His bottom lip was split. "Work with me here. I just want to make sure that nobody gets hurt."

"No!" Skiller shouted. "I know what you're planning, but it's not going to work. You're not going to lock me up, drug me, fry my brain with electricity!"

Grissom kept quiet, letting Brass take charge of the situation. The cop's experience and training made him better equipped to negotiate with the unhinged young man. Grissom called for backup on his cell phone. "We have a hostage situation at the Mesquite Community Library on Seventh Street," he tersely informed the dispatcher. "Immediate assistance is required."

He prayed that help would arrive before any innocent blood was spilled. Looking around, he was relieved to see that the other librarians were hustling the remaining patrons out the front door. *Good,* he thought. The less random variables in this equation, the better. Jodi's mother refused to join the exodus, however. She clung to Mr. Strode for support as she anxiously watched her child squirm helplessly in Skiller's grip. The frightened toddler was crying frantically now, adding to the chaos. Her tiny feet dangled in the air as she cried out in fear. "Mommy! MOMMY!"

"Hold still!" Skiller struggled to hang on to the thrashing child. White knuckles tightened around the wooden shaft of the pencil. The lead tip pricked Jodi's neck, and she whimpered fearfully. Skiller's cheek twitched erratically. "Don't make me hurt you!"

"Easy," Brass urged him. "Nobody is going to make you do anything. Look, I'm putting away my gun." Slowly and deliberately, the cop put the weapon down on top of an empty table. He took a cautious step forward.

Skiller spun around so that he was facing Brass. "Stay away from me!"

"Okay, okay." Brass backed off, holding up his hands. "No problem. You're in charge here." He tried another tack. "Listen to me, Daniel. This isn't you. I know what kind of man you are. You care about the world, about saving the planet from chemicals. You don't want to hurt that little girl. Little Jodi." He stressed the toddler's name in order to impress her humanity upon her captor. "C'mon, Daniel."

Skiller swallowed hard. "But you're going to lobotomize me! Stick needles in my veins. Pump me full of chemicals . . . just like my doctor tried to!"

Dr. Zounek? Grissom assumed. Despite the dire circumstances, he found Skiller's reference to the late psychiatrist provocative. Perhaps Skiller was indeed responsible for Zounek's murder? *He certainly seems unstable enough.*

Brass wisely avoided bringing up the doctor's disappearance and subsequent decapitation. Skiller was worked up enough as it was. "Nothing's set in stone," he promised. "We can work this out. Just let Jodi go."

"No way! Not until you leave me alone!" His back up against the reference shelves, Skiller began to edge toward the fire exit. He glared at Grissom. "Tell him to get out of my way!"

Brass nodded, and Grissom took a few steps to the side. Would they have to let Skiller leave the building with the child? Grissom was reluctant to attempt any last-minute heroics while Jodi's life was at stake. But could they truly trust Skiller to let the child go once he made his escape?

"This isn't a good idea," Brass advised the suspect.

Grissom hadn't heard any sirens, but he guessed that the library was already surrounded by police cars. "You know we can't let you leave with that little girl. We'll all be better off if we just talk this out."

"I'm not talking to you!" He sidled toward the door, stepping carefully through an obstacle course composed of all the books he'd tossed at Grissom. His eyes darted fearfully back and forth between Grissom and Brass. "Or my father or my doctor or . . . !"

Skiller's tirade was interrupted by a harsh cough from his hostage. No longer crying, Jodi was gasping now. "Help me, Mommy," she wheezed. "Can't breathe . . ."

"Oh God," the mother whispered. "It's her asthma." She started digging desperately through her purse. "She needs her inhaler!"

Skiller froze, uncertain what to do. "Crap," he muttered. The air whistled from Jodi's straining lungs as he stared down at the wheezing child in dismay. The pencil trembled in his grip. "Crap, crap, crap . . ."

The mother extracted the inhaler from her purse and started to come forward. "Stop! Don't come any closer!" Skiller ordered, his arm locked around Jodi's waist. Conflicted emotions showed on his tormented face. "Just let me think, will you?"

"Give me that." Brass took the inhaler from the white-faced mom. Kneeling down, he rolled it across the carpet toward Skiller. "All right, Daniel. Here it is. You know what you have to do. Little Jodi is depending on you."

The girl was visibly struggling to breathe. Her pale face had a bluish cast. Grissom prayed that

Skiller's antipathy to chemicals wouldn't extend to Jodi's asthma medication. *He must realize that she's in serious jeopardy.*

"Goddammit," the agonized youth moaned. His red-rimmed eyes teared up. His shoulders sagged in defeat. "This isn't fair. . . ."

He dropped the pencil and offered the inhaler to Jodi, who eagerly snatched it from his fingers and sucked deeply on the mouthpiece. Grissom held his own breath until he heard the toddler take a few deep breaths of air . . . and saw her color start to improve. He rushed forward, kicking the pencil out of Skiller's reach, and lifted Jodi into his own arms. An overwhelming sense of relief washed over Grissom.

Jodi would not be visiting the morgue today.

Giving up at last, Skiller slumped against the encyclopedias. Brass moved in and briskly shoved him down into a prone position on the floor. Skiller didn't resist as the bleeding cop cuffed and Mirandized him. "Daniel Skiller, you have the right to remain silent. . . ."

"Thank you, thank you!" Jodi's mother sobbed as Grissom handed the girl over. The crying woman hugged the toddler as though she never intended to let her go. Grissom hoped their ordeal wouldn't put mother or daughter off libraries permanently. "Are you all right, baby? My brave little girl!"

Mr. Strode took Grissom aside. The librarian looked both grateful and perturbed. "All right. What the hell was that all about?"

"I apologize for the disturbance," Grissom said, "but we have reason to suspect that Daniel Skiller poses a threat to the community."

"I see." Strode sounded only partially mollified. Grissom didn't blame him; no doubt, he would have preferred Skiller's capture to have transpired at another venue. "Can't say I'm too surprised," the librarian said. "He's here most every day. He gets upset sometimes if he has to wait too long for a computer." He sighed in relief as Brass escorted the prisoner out of the library. "So what happens to him now?"

Grissom took a moment to take in the mess left behind by Skiller's rampage. Ill-used hardcovers and paperbacks were strewn over the floor. His arms stung where Skiller had pelted him with atlases and dictionaries; he figured he'd have some bruises to show for this experience. The trampled printer looked liked a goner.

"Oh, I imagine we'll throw the book at him."

12

"OKAY. LET'S GO OVER this one more time. When was the last time you saw Dr. Zounek?"

Daniel Skiller had waived his right to an attorney, so he was all alone in the interrogation suite with Brass and Grissom. His left wrist was cuffed to the arm of his chair, while a guard stood posted outside just in case he got violent again. Several hours had passed since the altercation at the library, and Skiller had already been charged with resisting arrest, assaulting a police officer, and attempting to kidnap a child. Now they just needed to find out if he was guilty of Dr. Zounek's murder as well.

"I keep telling you, I don't know," the suspect muttered sullenly. "A couple months ago, maybe. I threw his goddamn pills in his face and haven't been back since." He hunched over the table, his fingers tapping restlessly on the glass. "I'm never setting foot in that snake pit again."

Grissom listened intently as Brass interrogated

Skiller. The youth's testimony was consistent with
the narrative the CSIs had gleaned from the torn
correspondence he had found in the wastebasket at
Skiller's apartment; apparently, the rebellious patient had missed a couple of scheduled appoint-
ments and ignored repeated requests to resume his
therapy. Liz Rudolph and the other employees at
the clinic had also confirmed that the death-threat
footage coincided with Skiller's last known encounter with the doctor.

Which didn't mean, however, that Skiller hadn't
ambushed Zounek at some later date. Perhaps in the
parking lot outside the clinic?

Brass glowered at Skiller. A swollen black eye
and a bruised face served as souvenirs of the
hostage crisis at the library. A Band-Aid was stuck
to his forehead over the injured eye. "So you don't
know anything about Dr. Zounek's disappearance?"

"Not a thing!" Skiller insisted. "I couldn't care
less what happened to that poison-pushing bastard!"

The cop deliberately pushed Skiller's buttons.
"You don't much like your doctor, do you?"

"He's not my doctor!" Skiller said. His cuffs jan-
gled as he lurched in his seat. "My family forced
him on me. He's got them all hooked on his pills:
tranquilizers and antidepressants and Viagra. He
and my dad are making a fortune selling toxins to
unsuspecting people. They all deserve to rot in
hell!"

Grissom noticed that Skiller kept referring to
Zounek in the present tense. Did he genuinely not

know that Zounek had been murdered, or was he just faking it? *It's also possible,* Grissom thought, *that he's in extreme denial.* According to Skiller, he hadn't slept in days, riding buses and walking the Strip all night, "working" in the library every day. If he had an alibi for the night Zounek was last seen, he was in no state to recall it. Skiller's days and nights had long since blurred into a bizarre nomadic routine.

"You ever tempted to speed that process along?" Brass inquired. "Maybe dispose of the good doctor once and for all?"

"I wouldn't do that!" he protested. He looked offended by the suggestion. "I'm not a murderer!"

"Oh yeah," Brass said sarcastically. "You're a real pacifist."

"What happened at the library wasn't my fault!" He stared guiltily at the tabletop. "I panicked! I was just defending myself."

Brass snorted. "You need to defend yourself from Dr. Zounek, too?"

"Maybe," Skiller hedged.

"Don't play games with me," Brass growled. "We know you threatened Dr. Zounek. Said you'd cut his head off ."

Skiller murmured evasively. "Did I? I don't remember."

"Maybe this will jog your memory." Brass opened a cardboard folder and took out the photo of Dr. Zounek's shrunken head. He slid the portrait over to Skiller. "Look familiar?"

The young man's reaction to the photo was peculiar. Instead of gasping in shock, he gazed at the pic-

ture as though hypnotized. His face went blank, almost devoid of emotion. His unblinking eyes were
transfixed. Tentatively, he reached out to touch the
photo with his free hand. His finger traced the outline
of the *tsanta* while he hummed quietly to himself.

"Daniel?"

For a moment, Grissom feared that Skiller had
slipped into some sort of catatonic state, as the
Miniature Killer had after she was captured, but
then the young man startled both him and Brass by
laughing uproariously.

"Hah! Look at him! Can you believe it?" Giggling
hysterically, he spat onto the photo. "Take that, you
smooth-talking, know-it-all snake. Guess the joke's
on you now!"

Grissom flinched, taken aback by the suspect's
drastic mood swing. It was as if a switch had
abruptly flipped inside the disturbed young's man
skull. Grissom was suddenly very grateful that
Skiller was shackled to his chair.

What triggered this transformation? Repressed
guilt? Elation?

Brass took advantage of Skiller's sudden eupho-
ria. He held up the spit-stained photo. "You have
something to do with this?"

The sight of the shrunken head provoked another
fit of giggles. A manic grin spread across Skiller's
face. "Sure. Why not? I killed him, all right. I murdered his sorry ass, then shrunk the hell out of his
thick skull. It was just what he had coming!" He
tried to snatch the photo from Brass, but his cuffs
restrained him. "You know what? They should hang
this artistic masterpiece in every pharmacy in the

country, as a warning to every other greedy pill pusher out there. I wish I had cut all of their heads off!"

He started rocking back and forth in his seat while singing off-key. "Plink, plunk, the shrink is shrunk. Yo, ho, ho, the shrink is shrunk . . . !"

"You killed Zounek?" Brass interrupted. "Give me details. When, where, how?"

Skiller seemed eager to reveal all. "You want it? You got it." His eyes rolled upward as he visualized the scene. "I nabbed the mad scientist outside his diabolical headquarters one night when nobody was looking. He begged and pleaded for mercy, but I knew I couldn't believe a word out of his mouth, so I dragged him into the shrubbery and lopped off his head!"

"With what?" Brass asked.

"A hatchet! A real sharp one I bought at the hardware store." Raising his right arm, he pantomimed bringing the handheld axe down like a tomahawk. "Splat!"

Grissom frowned. "We didn't find any blood splatter outside the clinic."

"Well, maybe you didn't look hard enough," Skiller said. "Or maybe the rain washed it away. Remember that big rainstorm last week?"

"Uh-huh," Brass said. His battered face held a neutral expression. "And where did you dispose of the body?"

"In the desert somewhere," Skiller claimed. "I buried the hatchet there, too." He laughed at his own words. "Ha! Get that, I buried the hatchet . . . for real!"

"Hilarious." Brass kept the interrogation on course. "How'd you get the body out there? According to the DMV, you don't have a car."

"I borrowed the doctor's snazzy sports car," the suspect explained. "Man, what a smooth ride. Have you seen that car? What a chick magnet!" He crowed in triumph, puffing out his scrawny chest. "I dumped Zounek's body outside town—minus the head, of course—then put the car back where I found it."

Grissom considered Skiller's confession. The basic scenario fit the facts of the case, but the details didn't add up. Nick had thoroughly searched Zounek's Ferrari without finding anything more incriminating than traces of semen in the backseat. Grissom found it hard to believe that Skiller could have transported a decapitated body—*and* a severed head—in the vehicle without leaving some bloodstains behind. Unless Skiller was lying and he had actually beheaded Zounek in the desert instead of behind the clinic. But why would he get a detail like that wrong—unless he was just making this "confession" up on the spot?

"Tell me, Daniel," he said. "How exactly did you shrink Dr. Zounek's head?"

Skiller's grin faltered a bit. "Why'd you want to know?"

"I'm a forensic scientist," Grissom said amiably. "Naturally, I'm fascinated." He nodded at the photo. "You did quite an impressive job."

"Hell, yes!" the youth agreed. "You should have seen me, shrinking Zounek's brains just like a witch doctor. I boiled his head for hours in this great big pot, using a secret potion I found on the Internet. Lots of rare African herbs you've probably never heard of. All natural, though. Nothing artificial."

"And that shrank the skull?" Grissom asked.

"Like magic!" Skiller said proudly. "The whole head shriveled up like a raisin."

Grissom sighed. "Thank you, Daniel. That was very informative." He turned toward Brass. "A moment of your time?"

A guard escorted Skiller back to his cell, leaving Brass and Grissom alone in the interrogation room. The cop's weathered face was glum, like that of a patient expecting an unfavorable diagnosis from his physician. "Let me guess," he said sourly. "That confession isn't worth the tape it's recorded on."

"I'm afraid not," Grissom confirmed. "Daniel Skiller doesn't have the slightest idea how to shrink a human head. He doesn't even know you have to remove the skull first."

Brass rubbed the bandage on his brow. "I was afraid of that. My aching head really wants to pin this murder on that punk, but there was something fishy about that whole confession." He gingerly lifted the spit-smeared photo from the table and chucked it into the trash. "Looks like he's nutty enough to fess up to a murder he didn't commit, but not crazy enough to actually be our headhunter."

"Unless it was all an act to throw us off," Grissom pointed out. It wasn't common for a guilty felon to volunteer a deliberately erroneous confession to divert suspicion from himself, but Grissom had encountered some very devious criminals over the years. Paul Millander. Kevin Greer, "the Blue Paint Killer." Walter Gordon. Natalie Davis. "We can't rule him out entirely."

Brass shrugged. "Anything's possible, I guess, although this loony-toon doesn't exactly strike me as a criminal mastermind. The good news is, he's not getting out of here anytime soon, not after that stunt he pulled at the library. One way or another, he's on ice for the duration."

True enough, Grissom thought. He wondered if Skiller's eventual attorney would attempt an insanity plea. The disturbed young man might very well end up hospitalized instead of incarcerated, which was fine with Grissom. That was a decision for a judge to make, not him. It was ironic, though; Skiller's paranoid rampage would no doubt cause him to be medicated exactly as he feared. *Or is it truly paranoia when you know that a certain destiny awaits you no matter what you do?* Grissom spared a moment to sympathize with the suspect's plight, before getting back to business. "In the meantime, perhaps we should focus our attention on Carlos Vallejo."

"I was just thinking that myself," Brass thought. "Too bad we haven't been able to track him down yet." It had been slightly less than forty-eight hours since their first visit to the mental health clinic, and they'd managed to get statements from every other employee there, but the janitor was proving elusive. "He didn't show up for work on Thursday or Friday, and we haven't been able to contact him at home either. I'm not sure, but I think he might be ducking us."

Perhaps for good reason, Grissom thought. "We still haven't figured out who used the clinic's laser printer to produce that note," he reminded Brass. Fingerprinting had proven inconclusive; pretty much every staff member at the clinic had used the printer since Dr. Zounek had disappeared. If the janitor's prints had been on the machine as well, they had long since been obscured by those of the other staffers. To complicate matters further, the hidden code on the note indicated that it had been printed on a Sunday afternoon, when the clinic had been closed for business, and whoever had dropped by the office that day had done a good job of avoiding the security camera in the waiting room. Reviewing the footage, Grissom had been frustrated to discover that the printer itself was not within view of the camera. "Vallejo has the keys to the clinic. He could have let himself in via the back door and used the printer when no one was around."

"As opposed to Skiller breaking in somehow," Brass said. "You know, I'm going to feel really stupid if it turns out that we should have been working harder on finding Vallejo instead of wasting time chasing after Skiller."

"Don't be too hard on yourself," Grissom said. "Skiller had the strongest motive. And there are only so many hours in a day."

"Well, maybe you scientists should do something about that," Brass quipped. "With all that high-powered DNA gear in the lab, why not whip up a clone of me so that I can follow two leads at once?"

Grissom smiled at the prospect of identical Brasses. "The problem with cloning is that pretty soon, we'd have twice as many criminals as well—and no way to tell their DNA apart."

"Hmph," Brass grunted. "Should've known there'd be a hitch."

His cell phone rang. "Hang on," he excused himself as he took the call. "Brass here. What's that? Oh, hell." His expression darkened at the news, whatever it was. Grissom wondered what was up. "Understood. We'll be right there."

Grissom watched as the detective wrapped up the call. "Bad news?"

"I'll say," Brass reported. "That was the sheriff. He wants to see both of us, right away."

13

SHERIFF BURDICK'S PRIVATE OFFICE, several floors above the interrogation suites, was larger and more opulent than Grissom's. Trophies and commendations lined the walls, along with photos of Burdick posing with everyone from Bill Clinton to Siegfried and Roy. Sunlight poured through the large corner windows, which offered spectacular views of the Las Vegas Strip and the rose-colored mountains beyond. Although it was six-thirty on a Friday, his personal secretary, Mrs. Mathis, was still posted outside the door. Mathis was a holdover from the previous administrations and was likely to outlast them all.

Grissom was not surprised to find Conrad Ecklie waiting inside the office with the sheriff. As assistant director of the crime lab, and Grissom's immediate supervisor, Ecklie was bound to take an interest in any high-profile case—which is what the Zounek murder had just become.

"Sheriff, Conrad," Grissom greeted the men politely

as he and Brass entered the office. Ecklie moved
quickly to close the door behind them.

"Thank you for coming, gentlemen," the sheriff
replied gravely. Burdick was a distinguished-looking
man in his mid-forties, with features lending themselves well to campaign posters and press confer-
ences. His tailored suit was neatly pressed. Shrewd
eyes looked Brass and Grissom over. He rose from
his chair, but did not come out from behind his desk.
"It seems that we have a situation on our hands."

"So I understand," Grissom said. Brass had
briefed him on the particulars on their way up.
"How bad is it?"

"Take a look for yourself." Burdick lifted a remote
from the desktop and aimed it at the large television
set installed in the dark wooden bookshelf that
dominated one wall of the office. A few clicks of the
remote called up a prerecorded news broadcast.
Grissom recognized the familiar face of Paula Francis, the local Eyewitness News anchor.

"The shrunken head of Dr. James Zounek, a respected Las Vegas psychiatrist, was delivered anony-
mously to the Anthropology Department of the
University of Nevada, Las Vegas," Francis intoned
grimly. A crime lab photo of the *tsanta* was superimposed on the upper right-hand corner of the screen.
"The LVPD is investigating this case as a homicide,
and reliable sources inform Eyewitness News that a
note enclosed with the severed head threatened future killings. For more on this shocking story, we
turn to . . ."

Burdick clicked off the TV. "The story broke an
hour ago," he informed them somberly, "and it's al-

ready all over the local and national news. It's the lead story on CNN, MSNBC, Fox News, and the bloody BBC for all I know. They've already dubbed the perp 'the Vegas Headhunter.' How catchy is that?" He shook his head unhappily. "I don't need to remind you gentlemen that this city depends on tourism. We can't afford this kind of publicity."

But you reminded us anyway, Grissom thought. He sympathized with the sheriff's concerns, but didn't want his investigation compromised by political concerns. "I have my entire team working on this case."

"But are you doing enough?" Ecklie asked. With his dark suit, bald pate, and saturnine expression, the assistant director looked more like an undertaker than a working CSI. Grissom guessed that Ecklie, who was essentially a bureaucrat at heart, was anxious to dissociate himself from any perceived failures on Grissom's part. "You've had the head in your possession for a week now."

"Five days," Grissom corrected him. "And in that time we've managed to identify the victim and open several lines of investigation." He refused to be intimidated by Ecklie's tactics. "Frankly, I think it's a testament to the professionalism of the entire lab that we've kept the story quiet this long."

The sheriff looked less than impressed by this accomplishment. "I understand we have a suspect in custody? And a confession?"

Brass shook his head. "There's a confession all right, but it doesn't hold water. To be honest, I think this suspect would confess to axing Lizzie Borden's mom and pop if we put enough pressure on him."

"Damn." Burdick glared at Grissom. "Is this true?"

"I'm afraid so," Grissom confirmed. "We have strong reason to believe that the confession is fabricated. Daniel Skiller is a disturbed and possibly dangerous individual, but I don't believe he had anything to do with the death of James Zounek."

This was *not* what the sheriff wanted to hear. "Well, I certainly hope you haven't wasted too much time on this nutjob. I want a *real* suspect behind bars, before this 'Vegas Headhunter' business gets even more out of hand. People come to Vegas to lose their cares and their inhibitions, for God's sake, not their skulls."

"We're working on it," Brass said. "We still have some promising leads to pursue. Plus, maybe all this publicity will work in our favor. It might drag a witness or two out of the woodwork."

Burdick slumped back into his chair. "Might as well get some benefit out of it." He looked at Grissom. "Is there anything your people need to solve this thing?"

"Funny you should mention that." Grissom turned toward Ecklie. "Conrad, I understand you've had some objections to recent expenditures on this case. Specifically, the 'excessive' cost of the mtDNA testing on the shrunken head and Constance Molinez's consulting fee?" The anthropologist's invoice had already been bounced back to Grissom's desk at least twice. "Not to mention all the overtime my people have been putting in."

Ecklie tugged uncomfortably on his collar. "I was just trying to maintain a degree of fiscal responsibility over the budget. You should have checked with me before promising to reimburse the university for that DNA testing. "

"Forget the penny-pinching," the sheriff scolded Ecklie. "Our tax revenues won't be looking so good if the tourists start staying home or going to Reno instead. Then where will your budget be?" He laid his hands down on the desk as he swept his gaze over his subordinates. "Get this straight, all of you. I don't care what you have to do or how much over-time you have to put in. Get this maniac and get him soon."

A knock on the door punctuated his marching orders. "Yes?" he demanded impatiently.

Sofia Curtis stuck her head in the doorway. "Sorry to interrupt, but there's something you need to know."

Grissom wondered what could be so important that Sofia would barge in on a meeting like this. Judging from her gloomy expression, it wasn't good news.

"It's the Headhunter," she said. "He's struck again."

14

THE CRIME SCENE WAS a Tudor-style house in an upscale suburban neighborhood near the university. A
fashionably xeriscaped front yard was already cor-
doned off with yellow police tape by the time Grissom and the other CSIs arrived, shortly before seven
P.M. As he got out of the Denali, Grissom was unhappy to see that a full-fledged media circus was
under way. News vans were parked down the block,
beyond a barricade set up by the uniformed police
officers who were first on the scene. TV news
copters hovered overhead. Anxious neighbors
watched the spectacle from their own front yards.
Unlike the avid reporters swarming the area, the lo-
cals seemed happy to keep their distance. Dogs
barked at the hordes of strangers encroaching on
their territory. An ambulance was parked in the
driveway.

"Dr. Grissom!" a reporter shouted at him from
the other side of the barricade. He recognized

Natalie Corville from the Ten O'Clock News. "Is it true that the Vegas Headhunter has claimed another victim?" Microphones and cameras were thrust in his direction. More voices clamored for answers. "Do you believe we have a serial killer on the loose? What progress is being made in this investigation? Do you have any suspects?"

Grissom ignored the insistent queries. Even at the best of times, he disliked dealing with the press. Besides, he didn't have any answers for them.

At least not yet. Perhaps the crime scene would provide them with the clues they needed? He had brought three of his best people—Catherine, Warrick, and Nick—in hopes of finding something that would uncover the true identity of the Headhunter at last. *Four CSIs should be enough to handle this job,* he thought. *At least we have a crime scene to process this time, not just a shrunken head in a box.*

A uniform lifted the crime tape to let the CSIs through. As they carted their field kits toward the front door of the house, which was being guarded by yet another uni, Grissom checked out the ambulance in the driveway. A distraught-looking woman was seated in the rear of the ambulance, being questioned by officers and paramedics. A blanket was draped over the woman's shoulders. Tears streaked her face.

The grieving widow, he assumed.

Brass was waiting for them in the living room, which was just off the front foyer. The detective had beaten them to the site by heading straight from the sheriff's office while Grissom was still rounding up his team. Brass held a somber expression as he presided over a grisly tableau.

A headless body, wearing a UNLV T-shirt and blue sweat pants, was propped up against the back of a black faux-leather sofa. It was facing backward on the couch, like a decapitated felon kneeling before the chopping block. A pool of clotted blood had collected on the gore-soaked carpet behind the sofa. The degree of clotting suggested that the body had been leaning there for at least a couple of hours, which placed the time of death sometime earlier that afternoon. A golden wedding band gleamed on the ring finger of the corpse's left hand. David Phillips squatted by the body. A quick glance around revealed no sign of the missing head, shrunken or otherwise.

I was afraid of this, Grissom thought. He took no comfort in the fact that his previous apprehensions regarding the case had proven correct. Part of him had been expecting a second head to be harvested ever since the first *tsanta* had showed up in the mail. *For once, I would have liked to be wrong.*

"You made good time," Brass said by way of greeting. He looked at Grissom as he stood a few feet away from the truncated corpse. "You remember Professor Malcolm Kim from the university? He was a little taller the last time we saw him."

By about seven inches, Grissom estimated. He recalled meeting Kim when he and Brass visited the Anthropology Department only days ago, when the *tsanta* had first showed up at the university, and he had spoken with Kim even more recently, when they'd arranged for Wendy Simms to make use of the department's Genome Sequencer. Staring over at the mutilated corpse, he couldn't help feeling that he had let Kim down by not catching the Headhunter before now. Apparently the cryptic message enclosed with the shrunken head, *tumashi akerkama*, had been a threat after all.

But what had Malcolm Kim done to incur the headhunter's wrath?

If indeed the body before them belonged to Kim. The general build looked about right, and apparently this was Kim's home address, but the absence of the head obviously raised some doubts as to the identity of the victim. "Are we sure it's him?" Grissom asked Brass.

"The wife thinks so. Says she recognized his clothes." Brass glanced in the direction of the front door, toward the driveway outside. "'Course she's pretty hysterical right now, so I suppose we should take that with a grain of salt."

And then some, Grissom thought. Although he was willing to tentatively identify the victim as Kim for the moment, they would need to verify that assumption by means of DNA, fingerprints, blood type, past injuries, and other indicators. He turned toward Warrick. "Make sure we get DNA and fingerprint samples from upstairs."

"You got it," Warrick promised. The younger CSI shook his head at the bloody crime scene. "So, the wife found the body?"

"Yep," Brass confirmed. "She was teaching a seminar at the university all day. Seems she's a professor, too. English literature or something. Got back home around six, only to find this waiting for her. Pretty much freaked out, no surprise. A neighbor called 911."

"That poor woman," Catherine said. "Any kids?"

Brass shook his head. "No, thank God. It was just the two of them. Not even a cat." The detective sounded as though he was relieved that they didn't have an agitated pet to deal with on top of everything else. "No sign of forced entry, by the way. So it's possible he knew the killer."

"Or else he simply left a door unlocked." Grissom worried about the sanctity of the crime scene. "You mentioned a neighbor. Did he or she enter the living room?"

"I'm afraid so," Brass reported. "The neighbor, one Paulette Cowan, found Ms. Kim screaming in the front yard, then came inside to investigate." He checked his notes. "She swears she didn't touch anything."

Grissom scowled. "Unfortunately, I don't think we can take that for granted. We're going to need DNA and fingerprint samples from Ms. Cowan, for elimination purposes."

"Assuming she's not the perp," Catherine pointed out.

"You think?" Nick asked. "It seems like a nice neighborhood."

Catherine snorted. "Like that means anything. For all we know, the friendly neighbor was having an affair with the husband—or the wife, for that matter. I'm guessing the Headhunter knew that Kim's wife was going to be away all afternoon. Probably been stalking the professor from day one."

Tumashi akerkama, Grissom thought. *Blood-guilt.* "The mailing of the *tsanta* certainly implies premeditation," he agreed, "but it may be too early to start speculating about the neighbors. At the moment, let's see where the evidence leads us." He looked over at David Phillips. "Time of death?"

The assistant coroner withdrew a spiked thermometer from the corpse's abdomen. Body fluids glistened on the metal spike. "Liver temperature's ninety-two-point-six. Rigor mortis is only a few hours along. I'd say death occurred around four hours ago." He peeked at his wristwatch. "Maybe around three P.M.?"

Grissom nodded. That meshed with the coagulated blood pool, which had already separated into solid purple clots and yellowish serum. He wondered when exactly Ms. Kim's seminar had taken place. If she was conducting the discussion at around three, she would have a convincing alibi.

"Lividity?" he asked.

"Just what you'd expect," David reported. "No indication that the body has been moved postmortem."

Catherine shook her head. "In other words, he was beheaded in his own living room."

"Or at least his body was," Grissom said. Turning his attention from the corpse to the setting, he scanned the room, which had a tasteful, scholarly feel, befitting its owners' academic backgrounds. Wooden bookshelves covered much of the wall space, while the TV and DVR were housed in a stained walnut wardrobe. Venetian blinds kept out the fading sunlight. Kachina dolls and tribal masks advertised Malcolm Kim's interest in anthropology.

An overturned reading lamp, lying broken on the floor near the doorway, indicated a struggle or perhaps a chase. Fragments of the shattered bulb littered the carpet. A plush burgundy sofa pillow looked out of place on the floor by the couch. An unfinished crossword puzzle, sitting on the coffee table in front of a comfortable-looking easy chair, suggested that Kim had been enjoying a leisurely afternoon before death came calling. A crossword fan himself, Grissom found the abandoned puzzle strangely poignant. How many other aspects of Kim's life would now be left undone? What other dreams and goals would he never fulfill?

He was almost tempted to finish the crossword on Kim's behalf, even as he realized that the dead professor had left them a bigger and more important puzzle to solve: the mystery of his murder.

"I guess we can rule out suicide," Nick commented. "I don't see a murder weapon, either."

Catherine took a closer look at the sticky puddle beneath the corpse's gaping throat. Blood-spatter analysis was her specialty. "No big bloodstains on the walls," she observed. "Just a sprinkling around the impact site. Judging from the lack of arterial spray, I'm guessing that Kim was killed before his head was chopped off. Otherwise, this scene would be a lot messier than it already is."

"That would be consistent with the killer's apparent MO," Grissom concurred. "Doc Robbins believed that the first head was also harvested postmortem."

"Harvest," Warrick echoed. "That's the right word, all right. This poor guy looks like he literally ran afoul of the Grim Reaper."

"Then perhaps we should look for a scythe instead of a machete," Grissom quipped.

Flashbulbs went off as the CSIs photographed the
crime scene from every angle, while David did the
same for the body itself before securing it for transport. Nick helped the young pathologist load the
headless corpse into a body bag and onto a gurney. A
hubbub of excited voices greeted the body as it was
wheeled outside. Grissom closed the front door to cut
down on the noise. He didn't want any distractions to
interfere with his concentration. "All right," he instructed his team. "Let's start with the living room
and work our way outward. You know the drill."

Catherine smirked at Grissom. "What? No *Sleepy
Hollow* reference? No historical allusions to Anne
Boleyn?"

"I try not to be predictable," he replied.

Brass stepped out of the room to let the CSIs
work. They cracked open their field kits in the foyer,
then fanned out across the crime scene, being careful not to step in the dried blood or broken glass.
The beams of their Maglites swept over the living
room as they moved methodically around the violated chamber. Grissom was disappointed not to see
any bloody footprints on the carpet. "How'd our
killer manage to decapitate a corpse without getting
any blood on his feet?"

"I think that's what the couch was for," Catherine
theorized. "He positioned the body that way on the
couch, with Kim's head facing away from him, so
that he could use the top of the couch as a chopping
block. In theory, the couch itself would have
shielded the perp from most of the spatter."

Grissom thought her scenario had the ring of plausibility. If the killer had positioned the body immediately after the victim's death, the lividity would not have set in yet. "How fastidious."

"Hey, I think I've got something!" Nick blurted. He was kneeling by the doorway, collecting glass fragments from the shattered floor lamp. The beam from his flashlight explored a narrow crack between the back of the nearest bookcase and the wall. He extracted a pair of tweezers from his vest and strained to reach behind the bookcase. A grunt escaped his lips, and he grimaced as he struggled with the tight squeeze and the awkward angle, but finally he caught hold of his target. "Holy cow. Take a look at this!"

Trapped between the prongs of the tweezers was a tiny clay dart, about half an inch in length. The fired clay was a dark brownish-gray. The sharpened tip of the dart tapered to a point, so that it resembled a large thorn.

"Careful," Grissom warned. "The Jivaro dipped their darts in poison."

"Will do," Nick promised. He laid the dart down on a piece of tissue and carefully dusted it for prints. "Looks like we've got a partial here." Being careful not to smear the print, he swabbed the tip of the dart, then tested the swab with phenolpthalein. The cotton swab turned pink a moment later. "Positive for blood."

Looks like our headhunter really is a traditionalist, Grissom thought. He would have to alert Doc Robbins to look for a puncture wound during the autopsy. Assuming, of course, that the wound was not to the head or the upper throat.

"Way to go," Warrick congratulated his friend from across the room. His gloved hands lifted the out-of-place sofa pillow from the floor. "I may have something, too." He turned over the pillow to reveal a slick whitish-green smear on the velvety red fabric. "Looks like dried saliva and mucus to me. Like maybe it was pressed down on top of the victim's face until he suffocated."

That struck Grissom as a reasonable hypothesis. "Perhaps the headhunter wasn't willing to wait for the dart to take effect," he speculated. "Or maybe the poison was simply intended to immobilize the victim long enough for the killer to finish the job?"

Catherine worked out the sequence aloud. "So he was drugged, suffocated, and decapitated—in that order."

"All in a matter of minutes," Grissom guessed. *Wonder if Dr. Zounek was dealt with as efficiently?*

The front door opened, and a police officer entered from outside. "Sorry to interrupt," he said to Brass in the foyer, "but we've been canvassing the neighborhood and we think we've found a possible witness."

"Great," Brass said. "I'll be right there." He stuck his head into the living room. "Grissom, you free to take part in this?"

Grissom thought it over. Eyewitness testimony was notoriously less reliable than physical evidence; still, he was curious to hear what this alleged witness had to say. "You okay here?" he asked Catherine and the others.

"I think we can manage on our own," she said wryly. "Go get the scoop for us."

Confident that his people had the situation in hand, and encouraged by the progress they seemed to be making, Grissom followed Brass and the uniform out the door, where the men were forced to run a gauntlet of determined reporters. If anything, the crowd surrounding the Kims' home was even larger than before. Grissom raised his hand to shield his eyes from the bright lights of the camera crews. Overworked cops held back the surging tide of reporters and their microphones.

"Dr. Grissom! What was it like in there?"

"Did you find another shrunken head?"

"Captain Brass! Are you any closer to catching the Headhunter?"

Grissom guessed that Sheriff Burdick and Conrad Ecklie were probably watching the live coverage at this very moment. He doubted that the sheriff was enjoying the show. "No comment," he murmured repeatedly.

"Out of the way," Brass ordered the reporters. "We have nothing to say at this time."

The press protested vigorously but grudgingly let them through. The officer accompanying the two men, whose badge identified him as JOSTEN, led them to a house across the street and two doors down from the Kim residence. "The witness's name is Bryan Deitz," Josten informed them once they were out of earshot of the reporters. "He says he was weeding his garden this afternoon when he saw something suspicious." He knocked on the door, and another uniform admitted them to the house. "We figured you'd want to interview him inside, away from the cameras."

"Good call," Brass said.

They found Bryan Deitz sitting in his kitchen. He was a nondescript Caucasian male with sandy brown hair. Grass and dirt stains on his clothing added credence to his claim that he was gardening earlier. Grissom automatically scanned the man's soiled work clothes and shoes for bloodstains, but didn't see anything incriminating. Deitz looked up anxiously as Brass and Grissom entered the room. "Is it true? Malcolm's been murdered?"

"Probably," Grissom stated. He decided there was no need to agitate the witness by mentioning the missing head. He wondered how well Deitz knew his neighbors. "We're still investigating the circumstances."

"Jeezus." He ran his hand through his hair. He seemed taken aback, but not devastated by the news. "I can't believe this is really happening. This is such a nice, safe neighborhood, you know? And on a sunny Saturday afternoon, no less."

Brass introduced himself and Grissom, then took out his notebook. "You think you saw something?"

"Maybe," Deitz hedged. "I'm not sure if it means anything, but I saw a delivery guy drop by the Kims' house this afternoon. Around three or so."

That's about the right time, Grissom noted. "Making a delivery or picking up?"

"I'm not sure. Both, maybe." Deitz scratched his head. His gaze turned inward as he searched his memory. "Come to think of it, it seemed like he was delivering a box, but I think I remember him leaving with a box, too."

Brass hung on the witness's words, like a bloodhound that had just caught a fresh scent. "Did he go inside the house?"

"Yeah," Deitz said. "He stepped inside and came out a few minutes later, carrying a cardboard box."

Grissom privately wagered that the box had contained Malcolm Kim's severed head. "How long would you say he was in the house?"

"Not long." The witness shrugged. "Five, ten minutes, tops."

Brass nodded. "You get a good look at this guy?"

"Not really," he answered sheepishly. "I wasn't paying that much attention, you know? It was just another delivery on the block. We get them all the time."

"Try to remember what you can," Brass encouraged him. "You might be surprised how much comes back to you."

"Okay." Deitz closed his eyes and tried to visualize the suspect. "To be honest, I only really saw him from behind. He was just a guy, you know? Average build. Brown uniform. Baseball cap. The usual."

"White? Black? Hispanic?" Brass prompted him.

"White, I think. I'm not sure." He opened his eyes and shrugged apologetically. "Sorry, guys. I wish I could remember more, but that's all I got."

Grissom wondered if it was worth setting Deitz up with a police sketch artist. He estimated the distance between the two houses to be at least one hundred yards, which meant that he hadn't really seen the anonymous delivery man up close. *Too bad he doesn't live closer to the Kims.*

A thought occurred to him. "Do you recall if he was wearing gloves?" They hadn't dusted the front doorknob and doorbell at the Kims' house for prints yet, but Grissom privately doubted whether the Headhunter would be foolish enough to make such an obvious mistake. Not after he had meticulously kept his prints off the original shrunken head and its packaging.

"Gloves?" Deitz shook his head. "I don't remember noticing. Sorry."

"You're doing fine," Brass assured him. He took another approach. "Forget what he looked like for the moment. Anything about this guy strike you as out of the ordinary?"

Deitz nodded. He straightened up in his chair, looking pleased to have a question he could actually answer. "Well, the timing was all wrong. Usually, the United Overnight Shipping deliveries around here are as regular as clockwork. Eleven in the morning and four-thirty in the afternoon, that's when the big brown vans come around." His face lit up as he thought of something else. "And, oh yeah, that's another thing. This guy wasn't driving a UOS truck. He was using his own car."

Brass looked up from his notebook. "Come again?"

"I saw him drive away," Deitz said enthusiastically. "No brown truck or van, just an ordinary green hatchback. I remember thinking that was kind of peculiar. Since when do UOS guys make deliveries using their own cars?"

Never that I know of, Grissom thought. The faceless "delivery man" was looking more and more like the probable killer. *And one who makes Saturday deliveries.*

Deitz's face fell. "I guess I should've realized

something was fishy right away." His voice took on a guilty tone. "Maybe if I'd called 911, instead of going back to my weeding, you'd have caught the guy by now. . . ."

"Don't go there," Brass advised him. "Trust me, you're really helping us out here." He let his words sink in for a moment. "Now then, can you describe this car for us?"

"I guess you'd call it a sedan," he said vaguely. "As opposed to a big whomping SUV or something. Nothing too snazzy. It was sort of a pale green, with more blue in it than yellow, if you know what I mean. I mean, it wasn't chartreuse or emerald or neon green, just kind of a muted shade of green. Like jade, maybe. And not too new, like it had been driven around for a few years . . . maybe. Like I said, I wasn't paying attention."

"Make? Model?"

Deitz's short-lived excitement at assisting the investigation evaporated as his memory failed him once more. "I don't know. To tell you the truth, I'm not much of a car buff. I can barely tell a Jeep from a Hummer."

Grissom suspected that was an exaggeration, but let it pass.

"License plate?" Brass persisted.

"All the way from my garden?" Deitz said defensively. "No way."

Grissom feared they were reaching the point of diminishing returns. "How well did you know the Kims?"

"Not too well," he admitted. "I mean, we were friendly and all. Waved at each other if we passed on the sidewalk and all. Knew each other by name. But it's not like we socialized or anything. I've never even stepped inside their house."

Grissom silently lamented the apparently superficial connection between the neighbors; times like this, he wished that Las Vegas was more like a small town where everyone knew each other's business. "Are you aware of any difficulties in the Kims' marriage? Or anyone who might want to harm Mr. Kim?"

"Not that I can think of," Deitz replied. "Like I said, I didn't know them well, but they always seemed happy enough. Who knows what goes on behind closed doors, though?" He smiled ruefully. "Hell, I'm on my third divorce."

Brass's cell phone rang. "Excuse me," he said as he stepped away to take the call, then returned a few moments later. "That was the officer with the paramedics. Seems Ms. Kim is ready to be interviewed." He tucked his notebook into his jacket and nodded at Josten and his partner. "Please finish taking Mr. Deitz's statement and make sure it's sent to my attention." He handed the neighbor a business card. "Thank you for your assistance, Mr. Deitz. Let me know if you think of anything else."

"You bet," Deitz promised. "Say, you don't really think Helen had anything to do with this, do you?"

Grissom assumed that "Helen" was the victim's wife. "We have no reason to suspect that at this time," he said firmly, not wanting to set the tongues of the neighborhood gossips wagging any more than they were already bound to do. "We're just pursuing every avenue of this investigation." The sheriff's scowling face flashed across his memory and Grissom paused on his way out of the kitchen. "And Mr. Deitz? We'd appreciate it if you didn't speak to the press about any of this just yet."

"Really?" Deitz sounded slightly disappointed. No doubt he had been hoping for fifteen seconds of fame on the evening news.

"Think about it," Brass added in his most authoritative tone. "We don't want this suspicious UPS guy to know that we're on to him, do we? It's best that we keep the info between us for the time being."

"Oh, right," Deitz said. "I get it."

Grissom hoped he did.

Leaving the witness behind, he and Brass stepped outside and headed back toward the murder site. It was darker outside now, and cooler, but the media seemed in no hurry to disperse. Would Bryan Deitz be able to hold out against the reporters' relentless demands? Grissom wasn't a gambling man, but he figured the odds were against Deitz's story staying out of the headlines for long. Even if the cooperative citizen managed to fend off the reporters who were probably already trying to track down his phone number, the story of the sinister delivery man was sure to make its way through Deitz's family and friends. And it was only a matter of time before *somebody* talked to the press.

Let's hope we can make the best of this lead, Grissom mused, *while it's still under wraps.*

Braving the gauntlet for a third time, the men waited until they were back behind the police tape and barricades before discussing Deitz's testimony. "Knock on wood," Brass said, "but I think we just caught a break. I'll check with UOS, but I'm willing to bet that they have no records of any calls on the Kim residence this afternoon."

"Probably a safe bet," Grissom agreed. A tentative reconstruction of the crime was already forming in his mind.

Malcolm Kim was lounging at home, doing his crossword puzzle, when the doorbell rang around three o'clock. He got out of his easy chair and strolled to the foyer to answer the door. Unaware that he only had minutes left to live, he casually opened the door to what appeared to be an ordinary delivery man.

But the newcomer was apparently armed—in true Jivaro fashion—with some sort of blow pipe or air gun. A poison dart struck Kim's body but did not take immediate effect. Attempting to flee, the terrified academic staggered into the living room, knocking over the floor lamp in the process. Weakened or immobilized by the poison rushing through his bloodstream, Kim was overcome by the headhunter, who suffocated him with a convenient sofa pillow.

Once the professor stopped breathing, the killer hauled up the body and draped it face-first over the back of the couch, so that the nape of Kim's neck was exposed. A blow from some sharp-edged weapon—possibly a machete or an axe—then severed the body's head from its shoulders. Blood gushed down the back of the couch like a crimson waterfall. The killer collected the head from the floor and hid it in a cardboard box he had brought for just that purpose. The interior of the box was no doubt lined with plastic to keep the blood from soaking through. Within minutes, the Headhunter drove away with his prize, leaving the decapitated corpse of Malcolm Kim propped up against the couch, where his wife found it some three hours later.

And as for the head? Grissom guessed that somewhere in Las Vegas, the killer had already started shrinking it.

I wonder if he's disposed of the skull yet.

Brass was obviously mulling over the details of the murder as well. "Why do you think the killer left the body behind this time? We still haven't found the rest of Dr. Zounek."

"I'm guessing he wanted to get in and out of the house in a hurry," Grissom theorized, "for fear of being caught red-handed with the corpse." According to Deitz, the man in the UOS uniform had only been inside the Kims' home for five minutes or so. "Besides, the body was of no value to him. All he really wanted was Malcolm Kim's head."

15

WHEN IT CAME TO MURDER, the most likely suspect was almost always (a) the first person to find the body or (b) the victim's spouse or significant other.

Helen Kim was both.

Ashen-faced and trembling, however, she hardly looked like a murderer as she sat at the kitchen table of her next-door neighbor's house. She was a thin, somewhat angular woman, whose classical features had a slightly severe look. Her dark brown hair was cut in a stylish shoulder-length bob that had probably looked better a few hours ago. A tan cotton blazer and skirt reminded Grissom that she had been teaching a seminar earlier that day. Tears had smeared the mascara and makeup around her puffy red eyes. Her hands shook as she sipped on a soothing cup of herbal tea. The owner of the house, Paulette Cowan, hovered solicitously in the doorway until a uniformed officer gently shooed her away.

"Thank you for speaking with us, Ms. Kim,"

Brass said. "We understand that this must be hard for you, but it's important that we get a statement from you as soon as possible. While your memory is still fresh."

"I understand," she said tremulously. Her voice was hoarse from crying and probably screaming before. "Although I don't think that I'm ever likely to forget any of it. Every horrible moment is going to be burned into my memory for the rest of my life."

"Just take us through it from the beginning," Brass suggested.

"All right." She took a deep breath to steady her nerves before plunging in. "I got home around six and was expecting to find Malcolm waiting for me. It seemed odd that the lights weren't on inside, but I didn't think much of it; I thought maybe he was taking a nap or something. Then I found the front door unlocked. I went inside, turned on the lights, and called out to him, but he didn't answer. That's when I started to get worried. Then I smelled an awful odor coming from the living room. . . ."

Professor Kim's body would not have decomposed to a significant degree by that point, so Grissom assumed that Helen Kim had smelled the excess blood, as well as the contents of the body's released bowels and bladder. The usual stench of a murder site, in other words.

"I went into the living room and saw . . ." Words failed her as a convulsive shudder rocked her bony frame. She choked back a sob. "I'm sorry. Just the thought of it . . ."

"We understand," Brass said sympathetically. "You're doing fine."

Grissom gave her a few moments to compose herself. "Forgive me, Ms. Kim, but I have to ask. Are you quite certain the body belonged to your husband?"

"I–I think so," she said hesitantly, as though the notion that the decapitated corpse might be someone other than her husband had never occurred to her. "He . . . it . . . was wearing Malcolm's clothes. And he was in our living room." She stared anxiously into Grissom's eyes as a desperately hopeful note crept into her voice. "You think it might be someone else?"

Grissom didn't want to get her hopes up. "No. Chances are, it is your husband. We just need to verify that." He sat down at the table across from her. "How closely did you examine the body?"

"Not very long," she confessed. "To be honest, I ran screaming out of the house as soon as I saw . . . it." She dabbed at her eye with a tissue. "I guess I wasn't very brave."

"You did the right thing," Brass assured her. "For all you knew, the killer was still in the house."

"Oh my God!" She clutched her heart. "Do you think?"

Brass shook his head. "One of your neighbors observed a UOS man visiting the house several hours before you returned. Do you know if either you or your husband was expecting a package?"

"UOS?" Confusion showed on her face. "Not that I know of. Although we do get packages fairly often. Review copies of manuscripts, books from Amazon, et cetera." A thought occurred to her. "Did you see a wedding band on the body's finger? A plain gold ring?"

The open question of the victim's identity was obviously preying on her mind. Grissom almost regretted raising the issue. "I did notice a ring, I'm afraid."

Helen Kim sobbed as her last fleeting hopes faded. "There's an inscription," she murmured weakly. "'To be fond of dancing . . .'"

"'. . . was an almost certain step towards falling in love.'" Grissom recognized the quotation from *Pride and Prejudice*. "We'll check for the inscription."

"But you really think it was Malcolm?"

He nodded solemnly. "I'm very sorry for your loss." He decided to backtrack a bit. "Earlier today, you were conducting a seminar at the university?"

"That's right." She sounded relieved to move on to a less traumatic memory. "A five-hour lecture and discussion comparing the lives and work of Jane Austen and Mary Shelley." She gave them an apologetic shrug. "I teach a course in nineteenth-century women's literature."

"Sounds like a fascinating topic," Grissom said sincerely. "Very different women writing about very different subject matter." As far as he could recall, though, neither Austen nor Shelley had ever written on the subject of shrunken heads.

"How many people attended the lecture?" Brass asked.

"Maybe about seventy," she guessed. "It was fairly well attended."

Not a bad alibi, Grissom thought. Especially if those seventy witnesses could confirm that she was otherwise occupied when her husband was murdered. "And was the seminar well publicized as well?"

"I believe so," she replied. "It was posted on the department website, and I think there was a notice in the campus newspaper."

In other words, anyone could have known that Ms. Kim was going to be away that afternoon. It was the perfect opportunity to steal his head.

"Can you think of any reason someone might want to harm your husband?" Brass asked.

"No!" she said emphatically. "Malcolm didn't have any enemies. He was admired by his peers, adored by his students." She broke down into tears. "It's not fair. Everything was going so well for us. I'm almost done with my book. Malcolm had just been named head of his department. . . ."

Grissom's ears perked up. "And when was that?"

"A few months ago," she said. "Back in January, after Dr. Malke announced his retirement."

"Any hard feelings about that promotion?" Brass asked. "A jealous colleague?"

"Not at all," she insisted. "Malcolm more than deserved that position. Everyone was happy for him."

Maybe not everyone, Grissom thought. "Were either you or your husband familiar with Dr. James Zounek?"

"That's the man whose . . . head was sent to Malcolm, correct? The first victim?" She swallowed hard, trying hard not to lose control. "No. I'd never heard of him before, not until that horrible photo was all over the TV and the newspapers. I didn't even know Malcolm had received a shrunken head until I heard about it on the news."

Grissom arched an eyebrow. "Your husband didn't mention it to you before?"

"No," she divulged. "He said he didn't want to worry me, that it was probably just a prank." She broke down into tears once more. "And now that monster has Malcolm's head! When I think about what he must be doing to it now . . ."

Grissom and Brass exchanged suspicious looks. Why hadn't Professor Kim told his wife about something as outrageous as the *tsanta* before the media firestorm struck? *Sounds to me*, Grissom thought, *as if he was hiding something.*

But what?

16

"So you have no idea where Carlos Vallejo is?"

It was the day after Professor Kim's murder, and the search for the missing janitor had led Detective Sofia Curtis to the offices of Black Jack Cleaning Service, in an ugly industrial park out by the airport. The Grace Tranquillity Mental Health Clinic had contracted its janitorial services through Black Jack, so Sofia was hoping his employers might know where Vallejo was to be found. Ordinarily, she had Sunday afternoons off, but both Brass and the sheriff had made it clear that ordinary working hours were a thing of the past until the Vegas Headhunter was apprehended. Sofia had been trying to reach Vallejo at his home for three days now. She prayed that her failure had not cost Malcolm Kim his life.

"I told you people before," protested the manager of the company. Steve Court was a squat, balding Caucasian with a beer gut and a sallow complexion.

His rumpled business shirt was open at the collar. He sat behind a cluttered metal desk in a cramped office that was more utilitarian than attractive. Metal filing cabinets. A fax machine. A water cooler. The ashtray on his desk technically violated Las Vegas ordinances, and the air-conditioned atmosphere reeked of tobacco, but Sofia got the impression that Court pretty much ran the place by himself. A stack of brightly colored poker chips added a touch of flair while hinting at his favorite recreational pastime. A framed photo of the wife and kids informed the world, and any prospective customers, that he was a family man, a message undercut somewhat by the "Vegas Showgirls" calendar pinned up over the phone. An upright cardboard display on the desk held a supply of brochures advertising the company. "He hasn't shown up for work for three days."

Since Brass and Grissom's first visit to the clinic, Sofia noted. *Wonder if someone there tipped off Vallejo that we're looking for him?* She sat across from Court on an uncomfortable folding metal chair. A copy of the Sunday paper lay unopened on Court's desk. "VEGAS HEADHUNTER STRIKES AGAIN!" shrieked the banner headline.

"Is that typical of him?" she asked.

"Not at all," Court insisted. "Carlos is a good worker and an all-around nice guy. One of my best people, in fact. Been working for me for years." He gestured at the newspaper. "Look, I'm sorry about what happened to that shrink and this other guy, but I'm sure Carlos had nothing to do with any of this. You're barking up the wrong tree."

Court fidgeted uneasily in his seat. Sofia got the impression that he wasn't being entirely forthcoming. It wasn't exactly a scientifically verifiable conclusion, but since switching from being a CSI to a detective, she had learned to rely on her instincts more. And her gut was telling her that Steve Court was holding out on her.

"You wouldn't be protecting him, would you?" she said. "Or maybe the reputation of your firm?"

A poster on the wall bragged that Black Jack used comprehensive employee screening "for your safety." Sofia saw the same claim repeated on the brochures.

"What are you talking about?" he said indignantly. "I run a clean company. Complete drug testing for all my employees. No criminal records."

"Glad to hear it," Sofia said. "I wouldn't want someone to leak to the press that you're not cooperating fully with our investigation. I can't imagine people want suspected headhunters having access to their homes and businesses."

Court stared at her in horror. "You wouldn't!"

"I'm just pointing out that the press is covering this case very closely." She plucked one of the brochures from the display and flipped through it idly. "Who knows what they might hear?"

The manager licked his lips nervously. "What exactly do you want?"

Sofia pressed her advantage. "Do you have *any* idea where I might be able to find Vallejo?"

Court mournfully contemplated the safety poster before giving in. "Okay, he has a girlfriend, Tania Orcharos, up in North Las Vegas. She *might* know where he is."

Now we're getting somewhere, Sofia thought, glad that she hadn't wasted a perfectly good Sunday afternoon for no reason. She took out her notebook. "You got an address or phone number for this girlfriend?"

The man sighed as though he was turning over government secrets to the enemy. Sofia admired his loyalty to his employee. *Guess they go back a long way.*

"That information may be in Carlos's personnel file," he conceded. "As a contact in case of an emergency."

He seemed in no hurry to retrieve the file.

Sofia held up her badge.

"Think of this as an emergency."

"Where's Nick?" Catherine asked.

At Grissom's request, the CSIs had convened in the layout room for a nine P.M. conference on the Headhunter case. Photos from the previous night's crime scene were pinned up on the walls. After a long night processing the Kims' house and yard, Catherine wasn't entirely happy to be back at the lab three hours ahead of her usual shift. Between household errands, and trying to spend some quality time with Lindsey, she had barely managed to squeeze in five hours of sleep that afternoon. She wondered if Nick had accidentally forgotten to reset his alarm clock again.

Wouldn't be the first time.

"Sofia borrowed him to help her track down Carlos Vallejo," Warrick informed her. "She's got a possible lead on his location and wanted a CSI along in case there was any evidence to be processed."

"Like a bloodstained UOS uniform?" Greg said hopefully. "Or Professor Kim's head?"

"Well, those would certainly constitute slam dunks," Catherine said. She mentally apologized to Nick for doubting his punctuality, while wishing he and Sofia luck on their expedition. *The sooner we get this case wrapped up, the better.*

She felt like she had barely seen Lindsey since they'd started collecting shrunken heads.

At five minutes past nine, Grissom strode into the room and took his place at the head of the table. "Sorry to keep you waiting, but I've come straight from the morgue, where you'll be glad to know that we have confirmed that the headless body belonged to Professor Malcolm Kim."

"How'd we do that?" Catherine asked. She wasn't sure she'd recognize Grissom without his head.

"There were multiple identifying factors," he explained. "The cadaver's fingerprints matched numerous sets of prints found on Professor Kim's personal effects, while his medical records revealed that Kim had his left kidney removed five years ago due to a benign tumor. The body we found at his home last night was also missing a kidney. Finally, an inscription inside his wedding ring matched the description given to us by his wife."

"Okay, I'm convinced," Warrick said. "That's one question answered at least."

"True," Grissom said. "Unfortunately, Kim's fingerprints also match the partial Nick found on that dart."

Catherine wasn't expecting that. "He shot himself with a blow pipe?"

"Unlikely," Grissom said. "Doc Robbins found a pinprick wound at the back of his neck, just below where the head was severed. If he was struck in the back of the neck, he was probably fleeing from the killer when the dart hit him."

"Right." Catherine remembered the overturned lamp in the living room. Visualizing the scene, she reached back behind her own head. "He must have yanked the dart out and flung it away from him."

Warrick nodded. "Where it ended up behind the bookcase."

"That's how I see it," Grissom agreed. "He probably didn't realize it, but Kim may have provided us with a vital clue before he died." He flipped through the folder in front of him. "DNA confirms, by the way, that the blood on the dart belonged to the body." He glanced over at Greg. "We got the results of the tox screen yet?"

"Yep. I picked up the results just a few minutes ago." Greg handed the report over to Grissom. "Henry found traces of curare in the victim's blood. And on the dart."

Henry Andrews was the lab's resident toxicologist. A real lab rat, but he knew his poisons. Catherine trusted his results. "Isn't curare the same poison used by the Jivaro in the Amazon?"

"That's the one," Warrick said. They had all been doing too much reading on the subject lately. "Sounds like we're dealing with a real old-school headhunter, all right."

"Authenticity does seem to be a concern of our killer," Grissom agreed. "Curare is a powerful muscle relaxant when introduced into the bloodstream, traditionally by a poisoned dart or arrow. Death results from asphyxia when the lungs and diaphragm stop functioning. The paralytic effect takes effect right away, but may take twenty minutes or longer to kill a human or any other large mammal. Probably not enough to kill Kim right away, but it would have left him paralyzed and at his attacker's mercy."

"What a nightmare," Catherine said, shuddering at the thought. "You think he knew what was coming?"

"Possibly," Grissom said. "If he made the connection with the shrunken head. But there's no way to know for sure. Alas, forensics does not yet allow us to retrieve the final memories from a murder victim's brain."

Maybe that's just as well, Catherine thought. *It might be possible to know too much about just what it's like to die.*

Grissom continued to go over the autopsy results. "Saliva and mucus on the couch pillow, and fibers in Kim's lungs confirm that he was probably suffocated before he was beheaded."

"Any idea how the head was removed?" she asked.

"Multiple blows from an edged weapon," Grissom replied. "Tool marks on the vertebrae suggest a machete."

"That would do it," Warrick said. "So I guess we're looking for a bloodstained machete. I don't suppose you saw a machete at Daniel Skiller's apartment?"

"Forget about Skiller," Grissom said. "He's not our guy. On top of everything else, he was behind bars, thanks to the hostage crisis at the library,

when Malcolm Kim was murdered." He moved on
to the next item in the briefing. "Meanwhile, Brass
has confirmed that the delivery man was an impos-
tor. UOS has no record of a call being made to the
Kims' residence yesterday afternoon."

If only the victim hadn't opened the door, Catherine
thought, even as she wondered whether she or
Lindsey would have fallen for the same trick. *Probably, dammit.* She resisted an urge to call the babysit-
ter and warn her to keep the front door chained, no
matter who came calling. *That's one of the problems
with this job. It can make you paranoid if you let it.*

She deliberately pushed her fears out of her mind.
"So now we know *how* the second murder was committed, but not why." Unlike Grissom, who preferred
to concentrate on the how of things, she was a bigger believer in the idea that deciphering the motive
was an important part of any investigation. "We
need to figure out how the Headhunter is picking his
victims." She looked at Grissom. "Has Brass found
any link between Dr. Zounek and Professor Kim?"

"Aside from the fact that they were both male
authority figures with impressive degrees?" Grissom
shook his head. "No, or at least not yet. As nearly as
we can determine so far, Malcolm Kim was not a
patient of Dr. Zounek, nor was Zounek affiliated
with the university. They also lived in different parts
of the city."

"Male authority figures with big diplomas,"
Catherine echoed. "Gee, who does that sound like?
Better watch yourself, Grissom."

"I'm hardly the only remaining Ph.D. in the city,"
he observed.

Warrick scowled. "But there must be some con-
nection between the victims. What about Professor
Kim's students? Are any of them patients of Dr.
Zounek?"

"I've been going over the student logs from all of
Kim's classes," Greg reported wearily, "starting this
semester and working backward, and comparing
them to a list of Grace Tranquillity's past and present patients, but I haven't found any names in common yet." He spotted Grissom looking at him. "But
I'm still looking," he added hastily. "Professor Kim's
been teaching for a while now, so we're talking
some pretty long lists."

"Keep at it," Grissom instructed. "We don't know
how long our killer might have been nursing a
grudge."

"That's a good point," Warrick said. "I still remember a few college teachers who rode me pretty
hard. Of course, those were the *good* ones."

"Aren't they always?" Catherine agreed. "You
know, maybe we need to start back at the beginning. This all began when Dr. Zounek's head arrived
at the Anthropology Department addressed to Malcolm Kim, which makes the college the only thing
connecting them at the moment. Maybe it's significant that the Headhunter mailed the head to the
college instead of Kim's home? Did anyone ever
search Kim's office at the university?"

"Not that I know of," Grissom said. "It wasn't a
crime scene, and the *tsanta* never even made it into
his hands. It was intercepted by the office manager,
who opened his mail."

That's true, Catherine thought. She wouldn't have

thought to put the professor's office under a micro-scope if she had been on the scene that night. "Maybe we need to backtrack then, and take a closer look at what Professor Kim's been up to at the university lately. Who knows? We might be able to find out why he was targeted in the first place."

"Good idea," Grissom said. He looked over the as-sembled team and made a quick decision. "Warrick, that's your old alma mater. Why don't you join Catherine?" He smiled at them both. "Congratula-tions. You're going back to college."

17

TANIA ORCHAROS'S ADDRESS LED Nick and Sofia to a largely Hispanic neighborhood in North Las Vegas. Sofia parked her unmarked Taurus a block down the street to avoid alerting Carlos Vallejo to their presence, assuming that the missing janitor was indeed hiding out with his reputed girlfriend. They had pointedly not called ahead, in hopes of catching Vallejo by surprise.

"Thanks for coming along," Sofia said as they got out of the car. "Hope I'm not dragging you away from something more important."

"No problem," Nick told her. As a former CSI, Sofia was technically proficient enough to process any evidence she might stumble across, but doing so would be a breach of protocol. Nick was happy to keep her company just to keep everything on the up-and-up. He left his field kit in the car for the time being, carrying only a small supply of CSI gear in his blue vest. "I hope I can be of service."

"Me, too," she said.

It was a clear, moonlit night, and the temperature had mercifully dropped down into the seventies. Nick found himself comfortable wearing just his vest over a T-shirt and light brown chinos. Even though it wasn't even nine-thirty yet, everyone on the block seemed to have settled in for the night. The flickering glow of multiple TV sets emanated from the windows facing the street. Nick and Sofia seemed to have the sidewalks all to themselves. Only the occasional car cruised down the street.

Tania Orcharos lived at the end of the block, in a one-story tract house done up in stucco and Spanish tile. A children's plastic playhouse occupied the front lawn, which looked as if it had been recently mowed. Miscellaneous toys were strewn about the yard. Chicken wire fenced in the backyard. A dusty pickup truck was parked in the driveway. Lighted windows implied that someone was at home.

The scattered toys and the playhouse worried Nick. A past victim of child abuse, he had a soft spot for kids and hated the idea of causing an ugly scene in front of frightened youngsters. On a more pragmatic note, crying kids could complicate any attempt to take Carlos Vallejo into custody, if indeed he was on the premises. Nick found himself half hoping that their suspect was somewhere else. *Maybe Ms. Orcharos can just point us in his direction?*

That struck him as an ideal scenario.

Sofia took the lead as they walked up to the front door of the house. A high-pitched squeak, right beneath his feet, startled him. "What the heck?" He looked down to see that he had accidentally trod on a rubber dog toy in the shape of a bone.

For the first time, he noticed the "BEWARE OF DOG" sign posted in the window.

Terrific, he thought sarcastically. He liked dogs as a rule, but he had to wonder what kind of ferocious canine was waiting for them on the other side of the door. *Why exactly did I volunteer for this field trip again?*

He carefully stepped off the well-gnawed chew toy, trying not to make it squeak again. "Sorry about that," he apologized to Sofia. "So much for the element of surprise."

Sofia shrugged. "I wasn't planning a commando raid."

She rang the doorbell.

Nick heard the chime sound inside. Curtains rustled, and he caught a glimpse of a feminine face peeking out through the drapes. No one answered, not even the dog, and Sofia rang the bell again, just to make it clear that they weren't going anywhere. Whoever was inside seemed to get the message; Nick heard footsteps approaching the door from the other side. A moment later, the door swung open to reveal a fortyish Hispanic woman wearing a tank top, cutoffs, and bathroom slippers. Her curly black hair was still damp from a shower. Her full figure was fighting a losing battle against middle-age spread. Dark eyes inspected them warily. "Yes?"

"Tania Orcharos?" Sofia asked.

The woman nodded. "What's this about?"

Sofia presented her badge and introduced herself and Nick. "We'd like to ask you some questions about Carlos Vallejo."

Orcharos did not invite them in. "This isn't really a good time. . . ."

"We'll try not to take too long," Sofia said. "Do you know where Carlos is?"

Orcharos shook her head. "Out of town some-where. Visiting relatives, I think." Her eyes darted to one side as she momentarily glanced up the road as if maybe she was looking for someone. "I don't know when he'll be back."

She seemed in a hurry to get rid of them. Nick tried to peer past her, but he could spy only a frac-tion of the hallway beyond. To his relief, he didn't see any kids or dogs lurking in the background. Maybe they were already in bed for the night? *That might be for the best,* he thought, although the lack of barking puzzled him. *You'd think the dog would be raising a fuss by now.*

He didn't see Carlos Vallejo, either.

"When was the last time you talked to him?" Sofia asked.

"I don't know," the woman said impatiently. "We're not married, you know."

She tried to close the door, but Sofia stepped for-ward and blocked the door with her shoulder. "He listed you as his emergency contact at work," she pointed out. "Sounds like a serious relationship to me. You have a phone number where we can reach him?"

"Nope."

"Really?" Sofia asked skeptically. "Your boyfriend goes out of town, and he doesn't even leave you a phone number?"

"We're kind of taking a break right now."

"Oh yeah? Why is that?"

Orcharos crossed her arms defensively. "Personal stuff."

Nick wondered if Vallejo was actually inside the house at this very minute, just out of sight. Listening intently to every word. "Mind if we step inside?" He feigned a shiver. "Getting kind of breezy out here."

Actually, he was perfectly comfortable, but, hey, if it got them off the front porch and into the house . . .

"Sorry," Orcharos said tersely. "Just got my kid to sleep." She snuck a peek at her watch, then glanced furtively up the block again. "Look, I can't do this right now. And I really don't have anything to say to you."

Why's she so anxious to send us packing? The nervous way she kept checking her watch and peering up the street made Nick think that maybe she was expecting company. He decided to stall for time, just to see what was up.

"Do you know if Carlos or his family is from Ecuador?" he asked. "Or perhaps Peru?"

She bristled. "What's that got to do with anything?"

"Just asking, ma'am," Nick said affably. "How much do you know about Mr. Vallejo's background?"

By now, the jittery woman looked like she was ready to blow a fuse. "I don't have to answer these questions. I haven't done anything wrong." She tried to close the door again, more forcefully this time, but Sofia refused to budge. Orcharos gave the stubborn detective a dirty look, and Nick half expected her to sic the unseen dog on them. "Come back again some other time. I'm done talking to . . ."

Her voice trailed off as her eyes widened in alarm. Following her gaze, Nick spotted a male figure approaching the house, walking a boxer on a leash. A plastic poop bag dangled from the man's other hand, while the dog appeared determined to sniff every bush and stretch of sidewalk they passed, much to the annoyance of the human, who tugged irritably on the boxer's leash. Between the distance and the darkness, Nick couldn't make out the pedestrian's face, but the presence of the dog—and Orcharos's agitated reaction—caused a surge of excitement to rush through the CSI's strapping frame.

Could it be . . . ?

The nameless dog walker, who was paying more attention to his distractible canine than to what was going on in front of the Orcharos residence, came beneath the lambent glow of a street lamp. The light exposed a short, stocky man in his fifties, wearing a sleeveless wife-beater, jeans, and sandals. A crewcut topped his blocky skull. Sagging jowls and a pug nose added credence to the theory that people often resemble their pets. A thin mustache carpeted his upper lip. Nick immediately recognized the face from Carlos Vallejo's driver's license photo.

Bad timing for him, Nick thought, *but a lucky break for us.*

"Carlos!" Orcharos shouted. "It's the *policía*! Run!"

Vallejo looked up in surprise, belatedly noticing the strangers on his girlfriend's porch. He froze for a moment, like the proverbial deer in the headlights. Responding to his mistress's voice, the boxer tried unsuccessfully to pull Vallejo toward the house.

"Carlos Vallejo!" Sofia's voice rang out over the

quiet neighborhood as she held up her badge. "LVPD! We need to talk to you!"

Vallejo bolted. Dropping both the leash and the poop bag, he turned and ran.

"Hold it!" Sofia hollered after him. Turning her back on Orcharos, she reached for her gun. Nick doubted that she intended to fire her weapon without provocation, but the mere sight of a gun often persuaded suspects to surrender without a fight. "Don't do this, Carlos!"

"Leave him alone, bitch!" Without warning, Orcharos tackled Sofia from behind. She grabbed the cop's arm, trying to wrestle Sofia's hand away from her holster. She wrapped one arm around Sofia's throat while grabbing the cop's gun arm at the same time. "He hasn't done anything!"

"Dammit!" Sofia elbowed Orcharos in the gut, but the other woman refused to let go of her. Sofia grunted in frustration as Orcharos clawed at her face. "Nick, get him!"

He hesitated, torn between going after Vallejo and coming to Sofia's assistance.

"Don't worry about me!" the cop blurted. Dipping her chin, she spun toward her attacker and kneed the woman in the groin. Orcharos staggered backward, and Sofia swiftly moved to place the combative girlfriend in a hold. She twisted Orcharos's arm behind her back while fishing for her handcuffs. "I can handle this. Don't let him get away!"

Nick hated the idea of leaving a partner behind, but decided to take her at her word. *Sofia's no pushover. She can take care of herself.* With one last backward glance, just to assure himself that she had the situation under control, he launched himself after the fleeing janitor. The dog toy squeaked beneath his feet once more as he raced across the front yard and down toward the sidewalk. Adrenaline added fuel to his legs.

To his dismay, he saw the dog charging toward him. *Oh, crap!* Nick thought. The brindle-colored boxer had to be at least seventy pounds and looked like maybe it had a touch of pit bull in him as well. Drool flew from its flapping jowls as it raced down the sidewalk at Nick. The dog's leash trailed uselessly behind it. It barked excitedly.

Nick had no idea if the boxer intended to maul him or just lick his face, but he didn't want to find out. He groped for his gun, then had a better idea. A yellow tennis ball, which looked as if it had already served as a chew toy, lay in the grass ahead of him, and Nick snatched it up on the run. He waved the ball before the dog's eyes, then hurled it away with all his strength. "Good dog! Fetch!"

He held his breath, then let out a sigh of relief as the distracted boxer took off after the ball. Car brakes squealed as the dog ran out in front of traffic, and for a second, Nick feared that he had gotten the dog killed, but then the car drove by and he spotted the boxer alive and well on the other side of the street. *Good,* he thought, glad that the dog had survived. He had a soft spot for animals, too.

He couldn't spend any more time worrying about the boxer, though. Vallejo had a head start on him and was already halfway up the next block. Nick hit the sidewalk running and dashed across the intersection, somehow managing to avoid getting nailed by an oncoming car. His arms pumping at his sides, he sprinted after Vallejo. The soles of his tennis shoes slapped loudly against the pavement.

"C'mon, Carlos!" He almost stepped on the discarded poop bag, but dodged it at the last minute. That wasn't exactly the kind of evidence he wanted to collect right now. "Let's not do this the hard way! We just want to talk to you!"

Vallejo glanced back over his shoulder, but kept on running. Abandoning the well-lit street, he veered sharply to the right and cut across a neighbor's front yard, disappearing between two houses. Nick cursed under his breath as he briefly lost sight of his quarry. Putting on an extra burst of speed, he took the turn as tightly as he could in order to eat up some of the gap between him and Vallejo. As he burst out from between the two houses, he looked frantically from left to right. *Please don't let me have lost him!*

The brilliant moonlight came to his rescue as he spotted Vallejo running north across his neighbors' backyards. Nick stayed in pursuit, not even pausing to take a breath. His sidearm weighed heavily against his hip, but no way was he going to fire wildly in a residential neighborhood after dark. Besides, he reminded himself, Vallejo was just a suspect. There was still no evidence connecting him to the murders. He just happened to have worked for one of the victims—and seemed in no hurry to talk to the police.

"Stop it, Carlos!" he shouted. "You're only making things harder for yourself!"

The overlapping backyards were an obstacle

course of swing sets, barbecue grills, sandboxes, and clotheslines, slowing both men down. Lights went on in upstairs windows as the commotion attracted the attention of the neighbors. Startled voices escaped from open windows. Dogs yapped at the intruders. A back door swung open and an elderly man in a bathrobe stepped outside, clutching a shotgun. "What the hell's going on out here?" he demanded.

"LVPD!" Nick hollered, praying that the man could see his blue FORENSICS vest. A blast of buckshot would definitely ruin his night. "Please stay in your home!"

To his relief, the gun-toting neighbor retreated into his house, slamming the door loudly behind him. Nick could hear more people stirring around the neighborhood and realized that he needed to get Vallejo under wraps before the whole situation got out of control. The way things were going, it was only a matter of time before he ran afoul of another irate dog or homeowner. *I'm pushing my luck here.*

Fortunately, he was in better shape than Vallejo, who was already running out of steam. The man's labored breathing suggested that he couldn't keep the pace up much longer. Nick was grateful for every hour he'd spent at the gym and on the jogging track as he gradually found himself gaining on Vallejo. He was only six yards behind the fugitive and closing fast.

"Give it up, Carlos! You're not getting away from me!"

Vallejo looked back over his shoulder again. His

frightened face was drenched in sweat. Panic filled his eyes. Not paying attention to where he was going, he ran headfirst into a vertical steel post supporting an empty clothesline. Flesh and bone smacked loudly against the post, and Vallejo staggered backward, clutching his skull. Blood seeped through his fingers, glistening brightly in the moonlight.

Ouch. That's gotta hurt.

Vallejo was still reeling when Nick tackled him to the ground, just like an unlucky quarterback back in Nick's football days at Texas A&M. No ref's whistle blew, however, as Nick squatted atop the runaway janitor, pinning him to the grass. Vallejo moaned in pain. Blood spewed from an ugly-looking scalp wound, spilling his DNA all over the lawn. Nick hoped to God the man didn't have HIV or hepatitis or something. The gash on Vallejo's head looked as if it needed stitches, but didn't appear immediately life-threatening. Head wounds just tended to bleed a lot. Treating the injury could wait, Nick decided, until he had his prisoner under control. Yanking the man's arms out from beneath him, he efficiently cuffed Vallejo's wrists together.

"Stay right where you are," Nick ordered, breathing hard. Now that the chase was over, he could feel the adrenaline giving way to fatigue. "Don't give me any more trouble!"

Police sirens disturbed the night. Flashing lights lit up the nearby street as at least three patrol cars converged on the scene. Nick guessed that the neighbors had dialed 911. Or maybe Sofia had managed to call for backup.

Either way, he wasn't going to look a gift horse in the mouth. "Over here!" he shouted, while continuing to hold Vallejo facedown on the ground. Dazed and in pain, the suspect didn't even try to get out from beneath Nick. The collision with the pole seemed to have knocked the fight out of him. "And bring a first-aid kit!"

Vallejo whimpered. "My head hurts," he said in a thick Spanish accent.

"Yeah, I know," Nick said, not without a degree of sympathy. "We're going to get that looked at." He kept one eye on his prisoner and one eye on the street, where he was glad to see a pair of uniformed officers exit their car and come running toward them. Unsure of exactly what the situation was, the cops had guns drawn and at the ready. Nick rushed to identify himself. "Nick Stokes, CSI!"

"One more thing," Vallejo pleaded. *"Por favor?"*

Nick scowled. At this point, he just wanted to turn the suspect over to the unis and check on Sofia. He hoped that Tania Orcharos hadn't roughed her up too much, or vice versa. "What is it?" he asked crossly.

"Just tell me, man," Vallejo said. "Is my dog okay?"

18

THE CUT ON VALLEJO'S head required eight stitches, so it was nearly one in the morning by the time Nick and Sofia finally got a chance to interrogate the suspect, who was now charged with resisting arrest. A large bandage was plastered to his scalp. An orange prison jumpsuit had replaced his bloodstained clothes. Nick had changed, too, into a spare set of blue CSI coveralls. His old clothes, which were liberally splattered with Vallejo's blood, were now bagged as evidence.

At least we didn't need to get a warrant to obtain a DNA sample, Nick thought.

"I didn't have nothing to do with the doctor getting killed," Vallejo insisted. A thick accent betrayed that English was not his native tongue, but there seemed to be no need for a translator. Although he had been read his rights by the arresting officers, he had so far declined legal counsel. A photo of Dr. Zounek's shrunken head rested on the table in front of him. "You want to find out who killed him, you talk to his patients." He nodded at the photo. "Only a crazy person do something like that. That's seriously *loco*, you know?"

"Then why'd you run from us?" Sofia asked. Scratch marks on her face served as reminders of her tussle with Vallejo's outraged girlfriend. Tania Orcharos was currently occupying a holding cell elsewhere in the building, while her dog and her six-year-old daughter had been turned over to a sister who lived a few blocks away from her. The boxer, whose name was Buddy, had turned out to be a real sweetheart, easily rounded up by the officers on the scene. To his credit, Vallejo had acted genuinely relieved that the dog was being taken care of.

Not exactly the kind of behavior you'd expect from a serial headhunter, Nick thought. Then again, Hitler was supposedly a dog lover, too. And so was that freak in *The Silence of the Lambs*.

Vallejo didn't answer Sofia's question. Instead he just stared down at the tabletop with a defeated expression on his face. His uncuffed arms rested limply at his sides.

"Carlos?" Sofia prompted him. When that didn't get a response, she turned up the heat. "Look, you're not doing yourself any favors by clamming up on us. You're in enough trouble already. And so is Tania."

He looked up at the mention of his girlfriend. An anguished expression came over his face. "Please, she don't belong in jail. It's not her fault. She was only trying to protect me."

"Maybe the judge will take that into account,"

Sofia said, "especially if we put in a good word for her. But you have to level with us, Carlos. What was she protecting you from? Why did you run?"

"You know why," he said sullenly. "I'm in this country illegally."

So it seems, Nick thought. Given the hour, they hadn't confirmed things with Immigration yet, but Ronnie Litra in Documents had already pronounced Vallejo's green card a well-made fake. *That would explain why he's been avoiding the police*, Nick conceded, *not to mention why his employer wasn't terribly forthcoming at first.*

Grissom and Greg were searching Tania Orcharos's house at this very minute, but, last Nick had heard, they hadn't turned up evidence linking Vallejo to the murders yet. No leftover beads, no human remains, no UOS uniform, not even a bloody machete. Ground-penetrating radar had failed to uncover any headless bodies in Orcharos's backyard. They were still trying to get a warrant to search Vallejo's own apartment, but Nick was starting to wonder if that was going to be worth the effort. Maybe he was just another illegal alien trying to fly beneath the radar?

Despite the strenuous foot chase Vallejo had put him through, Nick felt sorry for the guy. Even if he turned out to be innocent of the murders, he was probably looking at deportation for sure. "So where you from originally?"

"Peru."

The ancestral home of the headhunters. Nick felt a flicker of excitement. He leaned forward in his chair. "What part of Peru?"

Vallejo picked up on Nick's renewed interest in

his background. "I know what you're thinking." He chuckled bitterly. "You think I'm a headhunter just because I'm Peruvian."

"Kind of a funny coincidence," Nick observed. "You aren't Jivaro, are you? Or do you prefer Shuar?"

The janitor laughed out loud. "What century are you living in, man? I grew up in a slum in Lima. I'm a big-city boy, not some crazy old shaman from the bush."

"You know how to shrink a head?"

"Hell, no. That's old news back where I come from. Maybe somebody's grandfather knew some-body who knew somebody who used to do that kind of thing." He snorted. "I wouldn't know how to shrink a head if you paid me."

Sofia took another tack. "You know how to use a laser printer?

"Huh?" Vallejo looked genuinely baffled by the question. "Like with a computer?"

"That's right," she said. "You ever use the printer at Dr. Zounek's office?"

"Why would I do that? I just mopped up and took out the garbage, that's all." Worried eyes pleaded for Nick and Sofia to believe him. "I got in trouble for watching TV one time, but I never messed with the computers."

Nick nodded, listening. Now that they had Vallejo's fingerprints, they could check them against the prints they had taken from the printer, but most of those prints had already been matched to the var-ious doctors and staffers at the clinic. At this point, the warning note that had accompanied Dr.

Zounek's head had been printed almost two weeks ago. Even if Vallejo did print the note, his prints would have likely been obscured by all the people who had pressed those buttons since. Likewise for the keyboards of the computers at the clinic.

"You ever work for UOS?" Nick asked.

"What?" He looked even more confused than before, which made sense if he was innocent. So far, the UOS angle had not yet made it into the news. "I'm a janitor. You know that."

"Do you know anybody who works for UOS?" Nick suddenly realized that he had no idea what Tania Orcharos did for a living and made a mental note to find that out. "Somebody who might be willing to loan you one of the uniforms?"

"No!" Vallejo exclaimed, sounding like he was running out of patience with the seemingly random barrage of questions. "I don't get it. Where are you going with this?" He leaned forward anxiously. "Tell me the truth, what's going to happen to me now? Am I going to get deported because of this crap?"

"That's up to Immigration," Sofia said. "Not our call."

"*Madre de Dios!*" Carlos pounded the table in frustration. "Why'd that stupid doctor have to get his big head cut off?"

Sofia jumped on his outburst. "Sounds like you didn't like Dr. Zounek much."

"Nobody liked him," Vallejo muttered. "He was a stuck-up bastard who thought he was better than everyone else."

She tapped the photo in front of him. "Well, that's one way to deal with a swelled head."

Nick cracked a grin, but Vallejo didn't find the detective's remark quite as amusing. "You think this is a joke, lady?"

Nick was intrigued to see that their suspect apparently had a temper. "I hear Dr. Zounek tried to get you fired."

"That was no big deal. We worked it out." Perhaps realizing that he was making a bad impression, he made an obvious effort to calm down. "Anyway, I wouldn't kill somebody over something like that."

"Okay then," Sofia said smoothly. "Let's go back to the night Dr. Zounek disappeared. That would be Friday, March 29. You remember that date?"

"Sorta. I remember people talking about the doctor being missing when I came in to work the next week. That Friday?" He shrugged. "It was just another night at work. I came in, did my job, and went home."

"About what time was this?" Sofia asked.

He rubbed his bandaged skull as he threw his mind back in time. "Eight-thirty, nine o'clock maybe. I like it better after everyone has gone home. It's quieter, more peaceful."

Easier to watch TV, too, Nick guessed. *Or play around with the computers?*

"Was Dr. Zounek around when you were cleaning up?" Sofia asked.

He shook his head. "No. There was nobody else around. The office was empty."

"Didn't you notice Zounek's car in the parking lot?" Nick asked.

"The flashy red one?" Vallejo clearly was familiar with the doctor's wheels. "It was gone already."

Wait a second, Nick thought. According to the missing-persons report, Zounek's cherry-red Ferrari had been found parked in front of the clinic on the morning he failed to report to work. "You sure about that?"

Vallejo nodded. "That was one sweet ride. It was hard to miss."

"I'll bet," Nick said. He exchanged a meaningful look with Sofia. Unless Vallejo was mistaken or lying, they had a serious discrepancy here. "What about any other cars? Anybody else parked out front?"

"Maybe. I don't know. I wasn't really paying attention. It was Friday night. I just wanted to finish up and get started on the weekend." He gestured with his hands as he tried to explain. "It's kind of a big parking lot, with lots of other businesses sharing it. There's always a couple cars around, you know?"

Actually, Nick didn't know. He had yet to visit the clinic himself. *I'll have to ask Grissom or Brass about the layout,* he thought. *Find out whether it's possible Vallejo could have missed the Ferrari somehow.*

"Let's move on to the second murder," Sofia suggested. "The killing of Malcolm Kim. I assume you heard about that?"

Vallejo nodded. "On the news, yeah. But I didn't know this Kim guy. I swear to God, I never heard of him before!"

"Professor Kim was murdered yesterday afternoon, around three P.M.," Sofia informed him. "Can you tell us where you were at that time?"

He peered inward, searching his memory. His face reddened suddenly.

"Yesterday, three o'clock?"

"More or less," Sofia said. "You can remember back that far, right?"

"Yeah, yeah. It's just that . . ." Avoiding the female detective's eyes, he looked at Nick instead. Man to man. "If you gotta know, me and Tania, we were . . . you know, enjoying the afternoon. It was a nice day. Consuela was away at a birthday party. The dog was tied up out back. We had a few hours all to ourselves, so . . ."

Beats chopping off an anthropology professor's head. Unfortunately, it wasn't much of an alibi. The only person who could confirm Vallejo's story was Tania herself, whose credibility was suspect to say the least. "I don't suppose anybody else saw you that afternoon?"

"What, you think we sold tickets or something?" Vallejo bristled. "You got a dirty mind, man."

"No offense intended, sir," Nick said. "We need to cover all the bases."

"Why bother?" Vallejo lamented. "My life is screwed anyway." He smiled ruefully, perhaps recalling yesterday's amorous interlude. "Tania and I, we had a good thing going. A nice life. But that's all over now, thanks to this headhunting *cabron.*

His face hardened. His dark eyes fixed on Nick.

"You do me a favor, mister. You get this guy . . . and when you do, tell him Carlos Vallejo says burn in hell forever."

19

A SMALL SHRINE HAD BEEN set up outside Wright Hall at the university. Flowers, cards, handwritten testimonials, and stuffed mascots were piled around a framed color photo of Malcolm Kim. Warrick watched as a weeping coed laid a fresh rose on the makeshift memorial. A black-trimmed helium balloon bore a portrait of a sad-faced angel. "Guess he was a popular instructor," Warrick surmised.

"Not with someone," Catherine said.

It was bright and early in the morning, and the college was obviously still reeling from Professor Kim's murder. A kiosk near the front of the building held a special edition of the campus newspaper, the *Rebel Yell*. A banner headline read: "KILLER CLAIMS 'HEAD' OF ANTHRO DEPT!"

Okay, that's a bit tasteless, Warrick thought. He suspected that the student editor would be hearing from the dean about the morbid pun. Not that the grown-up media had been much more restrained.

You could barely turn on a TV lately without seeing James Zounek's head on the screen. And the on-air pundits had been having a field day speculating about just what the killer was doing with Malcolm Kim's head right now. Warrick had even seen a computer simulation of the shrinking process on the news that morning. *I wonder if they'll wait until we catch the guy before filming the TV movie.*

He and Catherine lugged their field kits into the building. Although Warrick had earned a BS in Chemistry at UNLV years ago, Wright Hall was unfamiliar to him, having been erected after his stint at the college. Nevertheless, the CSIs found their way to the offices of the Anthropology Department, where Vivian McQueen was expecting them. Warrick recalled that the matronly office manager had been the first person to lay eyes on the original shrunken head. That shock was nothing, he guessed, compared with what had happened since.

"I just don't believe it," Ms. McQueen told them, while dabbing at her eyes with a tissue. Her severe black dress was suitable for a funeral. "First that . . . thing arrives in the mail. Now poor Professor Kim. The whole department is in mourning."

She wasn't exaggerating. A flyer posted in the hallway announced a candlelight vigil for Kim to be held in the evening. As Warrick and Catherine conversed with McQueen outside her cubicle, he spotted several students and TAs wearing black armbands.

"We're sorry for your loss, Ms. McQueen," Catherine said.

"Please," the older woman said. "Call me Vivian. Everyone does."

"All right," Warrick said. "Can you think of anyone who might want to hurt Professor Kim? A jealous colleague? An upset student?"

"Not really," she replied. "Granted, there's always a student or two who isn't happy with their grade, and sometimes we hear from an overzealous parent who thinks that an instructor has been too hard on their precious child." She rolled her eyes as her voice took on a long-suffering tone. "But that's par for the course. Nobody's ever angry enough to do . . . something like this."

"You never know," Warrick said. The massacre at Virginia Tech, not long ago, as well as similar incidents across the country, had demonstrated just how much havoc a truly unhinged student was capable of. Hell, this was hardly the first time that Warrick had been forced to revisit the campus for professional reasons. "College kids can be under a lot of stress sometimes. Maybe one of them just snapped."

He wondered how Greg was doing comparing Dr. Zounek's patient logs to the names of Malcolm Kim's past and present students. Discovering that Zounek was treating an emotionally disturbed college kid was just the breakthrough they needed right now. *We're running out of viable suspects.*

"I suppose," Vivian conceded. "But I really can't think of any recent grievances that could inspire anyone to such . . . violence. We generally attract an exemplary class of students here in Anthropology. Stable, studious young men and women with an interest in science." She took a deep breath as she bleakly contemplated the alternative. "I mean, it's not like we're the Arts and Drama Department or something. God forbid."

Warrick let that slide. Sneaking a peek at Catherine, he saw her conceal an amused smirk behind her palm. "Does the name Carlos Vallejo mean anything to you?" he asked.

"No. Is he a student here?"

"I'm afraid not," Catherine said. "Do you know who provides the janitorial and cleaning services around here?"

"Mostly students on work-study. As part of their financial-aid packages." A nostalgic look came over the older woman's face. "I put myself through Bryn Mawr busing tables at the cafeteria for four years."

"I drove taxis," Warrick volunteered, "among other things."

Like working as a bell captain at the Sahara, selling helicopter rides over the Grand Canyon, digging graves . . .

Catherine declined to mention her nights as a stripper. "No connection to Vallejo there," she commented to Warrick.

"Yeah," he agreed. That lead was feeling colder by the moment. *Maybe Nick got a workout for nothing.*

"Who is Carlos Vallejo?" Vivian fretted. "Should I know that name?"

"Probably not," Warrick said. He considered asking her about Daniel Skiller but decided not to bother. Grissom had said to forget about Skiller, who had a perfect alibi for the second murder. "Do you know if anybody has been in Professor Kim's office since his death?"

The woman blanched at the word "death," making him wish that he had been a bit more euphemistic in his phrasing. "A few TAs and such, picking up graded papers and lesson plans. All of Professor Kim's classes are canceled today, out of respect, but, alas, life has to go on. We can hardly deprive our students of their education just because some monster . . ."

Words failed her, and she reached hastily for another tissue.

"What about Ms. Kim?" Catherine asked. "Has she been by yet?"

Vivian shook her head while she struggled to compose herself. "I imagine she'll be along eventually, to pack up his things, but I assure you that nobody at this university is pressuring her to vacate the office just yet. As far as I'm concerned, she can take all the time she needs to get over this terrible ordeal. The poor woman hasn't even had a chance to bury her husband yet."

"We'd like to search Professor Kim's office, if that's all right with you," said Warrick.

"Go ahead," she said, not even asking for a warrant. "You do whatever you have to to catch the savage who took Professor Kim from us." Her voice caught in her throat. "I wish I had never opened that horrible package!"

"Don't blame yourself," Warrick said gently. "You were just in the wrong place at the wrong time." He looked up and down the hall. "So which office was Professor Kim's?"

"Let me show you." She led them to a closed door at the end of the hall. Malcolm Kim's name was engraved on a plaque in a metal frame on the door. "We've been keeping the door closed to dis-

courage gawkers," she explained as she let them in.
"I confess I haven't had the heart even to look in
here since the tragedy."

"Thank you for your assistance," Catherine said.
"We'll try not to be too distracting."

"I'll leave you to your work then." Vivian turned
back toward her cubicle. "If you need me, you
know where to find me."

Closing the door behind them, the CSIs took a
moment to look around the room. Malcolm Kim's
office was about the size of Grissom's, but less ex-
otically furnished. Shelves sagged beneath the
weight of books and manuscripts. Mounted degrees and diplomas testified to the late professor's
academic credentials. A framed photo of an elegant
woman, whom Warrick assumed was Ms. Kim, sat
on the desk near the phone. In- and out-boxes
were piled high with paperwork. A UNLV calendar
was pinned to one wall. From the look of things,
Kim had had a busy schedule ahead of him before
his untimely decapitation. A Navajo peace pipe
rested on a shelf before a row of academic journals.

"Nice view," Catherine observed. A closed window looked out over the campus below. Warrick
spied the Chemistry Building, his former home
away from home, across the grounds. Students
strolled from building to building, some more
briskly than others. Others lounged on the green,
enjoying the sunshine. The dark cloud that had descended over the university was strictly metaphori-
cal, it seemed. Warrick wondered if there were any
potential CSIs among the roaming students. He and

Catherine had both attended the university at different points.

Too bad we never ran into each other back then.

He turned away from the window to concentrate on the office itself. "Any idea what we're looking for?"

"No idea," she admitted. "But this is where this case started, sort of, so it's probably worth a look. Don't forget, Grissom said that he thought that Kim was possibly hiding something from his wife, that he didn't even tell her about the shrunken head until it hit the news. Maybe he knew more about the Headhunter's identity than he let on?"

Warrick swept his gaze over the professor's private sanctum, searching in vain for something out of place. "If so, that was a mistake that cost him."

"Big time," Catherine agreed.

Uncertain where to begin, Warrick started scanning the titles on the bookshelves. To his disappointment, he didn't see anything about headhunting or the Jivaro in general. If anything, Kim's particular field of study appeared to be life on Native American reservations, with an emphasis on the tribes of the American Southwest. Warrick spotted several tomes on the topic, but nothing relating to jungle warfare along the Amazon. After pulling on his latex gloves, he took a stack of manuscripts from a shelf and started sorting through them. They appeared to be drafts and galleys of articles for various academic journals. *Publish or perish,* Warrick thought. It struck him as ironic that despite Professor Kim's scholarly activities, he had ended up perishing anyway—in a singularly gruesome fashion. *Just how cutthroat are the office politics around here?*

While he searched the shelves for something worth killing over, Catherine concentrated on the desk. She rifled through the in-box, then pulled out the long, shallow drawer directly beneath the desktop. A sharp intake of breath alerted Warrick that she had found something even before she spoke. "Oh my God. Warrick, come take a look at this!"

He carefully put the manuscripts back where he had found them and hurried to see what Catherine had discovered. His green eyes widened as he spied what appeared to be a bound thesis lying faceup inside the drawer. The title page of the paper immediately caught his attention: "The Rise and Fall of Headhunting: The Pernicious Effects of Exploitation and Imperialism on a Traditional Rite of Passage," by Amanda E. Knowlston.

"Congratulations," Warrick said. "I think you just broke this case wide open."

"Here's hoping," she said. "But take a look at the date on the front page. May 26, 2001. That's over seven years ago."

Warrick noticed that the report looked a bit faded and dog-eared around the edges. "So how come he's got it right at hand here, like he was just looking at it again?"

"Because that's exactly what he was doing," Catherine theorized. She dusted the clear plastic cover of the paper for prints, coming up with several fresh ones. "Somebody's handled this recently. I'm guessing Kim dragged this out of the archives right after he got the *tsanta* in the mail last week. The question is, was he just researching the topic in general or thinking about this 'Amanda E. Knowlston' in particular?"

Warrick mulled over the possibilities. "You think the Headhunter is a woman? That's not exactly old school." From what he'd read, Jivaro warriors were traditionally male.

"Welcome to the twenty-first century," Catherine said dryly. "Maybe she's a pioneer."

"Yeah," he quipped. "Sally Field can play her in the Lifetime movie." He reviewed the history of the case in his mind. "But didn't that eyewitness see a delivery *man* leaving Kim's home on Saturday?"

"From behind and from two houses away," Catherine pointed out. She lifted the prints onto a strip of transparent tape, which she then transferred to an evidence card. "An unflattering brown uniform, hair tucked under a baseball cap . . . I can see someone mistaking a woman for a man, especially at a distance. Besides, you know what Grissom always says about eyewitness testimony."

"That horoscopes are more reliable?" Warrick had heard their boss expound on the subject on more than one occasion. He also knew from personal experience just how inconsistent and erratic people's memories could be. "Good point."

He picked up the thesis and started skimming through it. Thirty pages long and liberally footnoted, it seemed to be reasonably well written and not overly abstruse. They would have to review it more thoroughly later, but the gist of it seemed to be that Western greed and commercialism had "ruined" the sacred ritual of headhunting, turning it from a profound rite of passage, in which a warrior achieved spiritual power over his enemies, into a way to cadge guns and other luxury items from novelty-hungry white men. As far as this Amanda Knowl-ston was concerned, filthy commerce had corrupted an authentic tribal practice.

"Interesting stuff?" Catherine asked.

"Possibly. Maybe I'm just projecting, but there seems to be a fair bit of anger beneath the acad-emese." He handed the document over to Catherine so she could see for herself. "Maybe even a bitter streak."

"Or maybe it was just written by an idealistic, self-righteous college student with an overly devel-oped social conscience?" She flicked through the pages herself before bagging it for transport back to the lab. Warrick guessed that Grissom was going to want to read it cover to cover. "You remember what it's like at that age," she reminded him. "We were all going to change the world."

"True enough," he admitted. Political activism and college life went hand in hand, at least for some students. "What I really want to know is why Pro-fessor Kim never mentioned this paper, or Amanda Knowlston, to Grissom or Brass." He looked at Catherine. "Do you think he did have something to hide?"

"Doesn't everyone?" she said.

"Thank you for coming," the sheriff said as he stepped up to the podium. "I have a brief statement to make."

The pressroom at police headquarters was packed

with reporters and photographers. Bright lights and flashbulbs hurt Grissom's eyes as he and Brass posed on the dais behind the sheriff. Mounting publicity regarding the "Vegas Headhunter" had compelled Burdick to hold this conference—and demand Grissom's attendance. Privately, the busy CSI suspected that there were better uses for his time than serving as a prop in a glorified photo opportunity, but both the sheriff and Ecklie had made it clear that his participation was mandatory.

"The recent murders of Drs. James Zounek and Malcolm Kim have justifiably outraged the good people of Las Vegas," the sheriff said. His measured tone largely concealed his irritation at having to call the press conference in the first place. "And I want to assure the public that we are using every resource to bring the perpetrator of these heinous crimes to justice." He gestured toward the men standing behind him. "Captain Jim Brass of the LVPD and Dr. Gil Grissom of the Crime Lab are personally overseeing the effort to apprehend the murderer."

Unmentioned, no doubt at his own request, was Conrad Ecklie, who was standing just out of view of the cameras. Grissom was wryly amused by his colleague's reticence; clearly, Ecklie did not wish to be associated with the investigation until there were more positive results to report. *You have to admire Conrad's instincts where public relations are concerned,* Grissom thought. *Catherine always says that he's better at the politics of the job than I am.*

"Nevertheless," Burdick continued, "despite the extreme—and perhaps even excessive—publicity

this case has received, I want to stress that these
were not random killings. We have strong reason to
believe that these were premeditated crimes, targeted at specific individuals, just like any number of
homicides that, sadly, occur every day in communities throughout the world." His stern voice and
steely gaze put the press corps on notice. "Any suggestion that there is a serial killer at work in Las
Vegas would be both inaccurate and, in my opinion,
highly irresponsible."

Grissom wished he could share the sheriff's confidence in that regard. The killings were clearly premeditated, as evidenced by the arrival of Dr.
Zounek's shrunken head at the university nearly a
week before Professor Kim's murder, but until they
knew what criteria the Headhunter was using to se-
lect his victims, there was no way to guarantee that
anyone was safe. For all they knew, the killer was
busy shrinking Kim's head at this very minute. If
they didn't track him down in time, would he mail
Kim's head to his next victim?

Sneaking a peek at his watch, Grissom hoped
that the conference wouldn't last much longer. Besides the ongoing search for the Headhunter, he
needed to review his notes on the O'Malley case before testifying in court the next day.

"Finally, I wish to extend my condolences, and
those of this entire department, to the friends and
loved ones of the two victims. This department will
not rest until the guilty party is behind bars."

Grissom noted that Burdick was taking pains not
to refer to the killer as "the Vegas Headhunter," but
feared that the sheriff's efforts were in vain. Judging

from the headlines, that colorful sobriquet had already caught on with the press and the public. Even the staff at the crime lab was using the term now.

"This concludes my remarks," Burdick said, gathering up his notes. He stepped away from the podium. "As this is an ongoing investigation, I will not be taking any questions at this time."

Vocal protests erupted from the assembled reporters, who jumped to their feet, brandishing their microphones like weapons. Despite the sheriff's pronouncement, questions pelted Burdick as he retreated briskly from the dais, followed by Brass and Grissom:

"Sheriff! Why hasn't the Headhunter been caught yet?"

"Should Professor Kim have been under police protection?"

"What about rumors that these murders are the work of a satanic cult? Are we talking human sacrifice here?"

"What's the connection between the Headhunter and the library hostage crisis yesterday?"

Burdick's face reddened and his composure broke as soon as he was out of view of the cameras. "Yapping hyenas!" he grumbled. "It's like they *want* to scare the tourists away." He whirled on Brass and Grissom. "And where are they getting their information from? It's bad enough we can't catch this lunatic. Do we have to let the whole world know our business?"

Grissom sympathized with Burdick's frustration, but assumed that the question was rhetorical. Unfortunately, when conducting an investigation of this size, it was difficult to keep the press at bay entirely. Counting those at the university, the staff at the mental-health clinic, the innocent bystanders at the library, and Professor Kim's neighbors, dozens of people had been interviewed and given statements about the case, not to mention the various suspects and their attorneys. You couldn't expect all of those people to keep quiet forever.

"I'm confident that none of my people has spoken to the press," Grissom stated.

"Well, somebody has!" Burdick vented. A nervous-looking aide approached the sheriff with the latest editions of the daily papers. Burdick snatched the papers from the underling and waved them at the other men. "Take a look at these."

"VEGAS HEADHUNTER TERRIFIES CITY," read the front page of *USA Today*.

"KILLER STAYS A-HEAD OF POLICE," proclaimed the *Las Vegas Review-Journal*. "Shocking Murders Attract Worldwide Attention."

"WHOSE HEAD IS NEXT?" asked the *Sun*.

Scowling, Burdick thrust the papers at Grissom. "Find this guy, and plug these leaks!"

Is that an order? Grissom wondered.

20

"AMANDA KNOWLSTON?" Vivian McQueen searched her memory. "I think I vaguely remember a grad student by that name, but . . . how many years ago did you say this would have been?"

Warrick double-checked the date on the thesis. "About seven years ago."

"That long?" Vivian shook her head. "I'm sorry, I wish I could help more, but there are so many new students coming through every year. After a while, they start to blur together."

Warrick sympathized. He sometimes felt the same way about murder suspects. "I can imagine."

"Maybe you can ask around?" Catherine suggested. They had already determined that there was no Amanda E. Knowlston listed in the local phone directories. She gave the older woman a business card. "Or if something comes back to you?"

"I'll do that," the office manager promised, tucking the card into her sleeve. "You know, you might

check the registrar's office. They would still have
her student records on file and possibly her current
address. The university makes a real effort to keep
in touch with graduates."

Tell me about it, Warrick thought. He regularly got
solicitations from UNLV's Alumni Association in the
mail. Sometimes, when he was feeling flush, he
even wrote them a check for a few dollars. *Wonder if
Amanda Knowlston does the same,* he mused, *or does she
prefer to donate shrunken heads instead?*

"Good idea," he said. "Thanks."

"Have you been talking to the press, Ms. Rudolph?"

Brass and Grissom had swung by the Grace Tranquillity clinic for a follow-up interview with Liz
Rudolph. Once again, the brittle, auburn-haired receptionist preferred to conduct the discussion behind the closed doors of Dr. Zounek's office. She
stood protectively in front of the late psychiatrist's
desk.

"Why do you ask?" she inquired.

Grissom showed her copy of the *Las Vegas Regis-
ter-Journal,* the same one the sheriff had foisted on
him after the press conference two hours ago. "The
newspaper coverage of the case mentions that Dr.
Zounek's head was identified using DNA taken
from this office. You and Captain Brass were the
only persons present when I collected that sample."

She blushed. "I may have mentioned a few details to a friend or two, but I didn't talk to any reporters." She flipped over the hourglass on the
doctor's desk, as though to signal that she only had

a limited amount of time to spare them. "Not that the phone hasn't been ringing off the hook ever since what happened to Dr. Zounek hit the news. We've even been having to keep the front doors of the clinic locked just to keep people from snooping around."

"We noticed," Brass said. "Thanks for letting us in."

A frosty glance at the two men suggested that she was having second thoughts about that. "Besides, what if someone here did speak to the press?" Rudolph asked. "You didn't tell us not to."

"Fair enough," Brass conceded. "But from now on, we'd appreciate it if no one on your staff volunteered any more information to the media. To be honest, too much publicity doesn't make our jobs any easier—and gets in the way of us actually catching Dr. Zounek's killer."

"But I don't understand," she said. "I read that Daniel Skiller was already under arrest. And Carlos Vallejo, for that matter."

Grissom shrugged. "We're not convinced that either man is actually the person responsible for these crimes." An exhaustive search of Vallejo's apartment had failed to turn up any solid evidence linking him to either murder. At the moment, all they had on him, despite his illegal status and attempt to evade custody, was a minor workplace grudge against the first victim. Not exactly a compelling case for the prosecution. "Which reminds me: Are you quite certain Daniel threatened to decapitate Dr. Zounek?"

"Of course!" she said indignantly. "You don't think I'd make up something like that?"

"Not at all," Grissom replied. "I was just wondering if possibly you misheard him? It strikes me as an unlikely coincidence, should Daniel turn out to be innocent after all."

Not for the first time, he wished that the security tape from the waiting room had included an audio track.

"I don't know anything about coincidences. I just know what I heard," she insisted. Lifting the hourglass from the desk, she toyed with it absently. "Now then, is that all? Between you police and the reporters, I can barely get my work done."

"Not quite," Grissom said. Despite the sheriff's outburst earlier, identifying the source of the news leak was hardly the primary motive for this visit. Grissom had a more urgent matter he wished to discuss with Liz Rudolph. "Does the name Amanda Knowlston mean anything to you?"

Catherine had called him from the university to bring him up to speed on their efforts there. The thesis on headhunting that they had discovered in Professor Kim's desk sounded like just the lead they were hoping for. He couldn't wait to peruse the thesis himself, but in the meantime, he wanted to find out if Amanda Knowlston was the missing link between the two victims.

"Who?" Liz Rudolph said, frowning.

"Amanda Knowlston," Grissom repeated. "Would that be the name of one of Dr. Zounek's patients? Or perhaps a girlfriend?"

She sighed in exasperation. "I believe I've already provided you with a complete list of Dr. Zounek's clientele. Under protest, I might add. And I don't know anything about his personal life. As I told you before, I was not aware of any serious relationships."

"Could Amanda Knowlston be a former patient?" Brass asked. "Or maybe the relative of a former patient?"

Perhaps someone who blamed Dr. Zounek for a negative turn in their treatment?

She shook her head. "Not that I recall."

"What about a former staffer at the clinic?" Grissom pressed her. "Maybe one of those college interns you mentioned before."

"No, no, no," she said, raising her voice. "I've never heard that name before." She kneaded her forehead. "Would you please stop badgering me?"

"My apologies," Grissom said. "I didn't mean to upset you. But we are going to have to reinterview the other doctors and staff members here, in the event that one of them might recognize the name."

"I doubt they will." She let out another impatient sigh. "But if you must, you must." Putting down the hourglass, she stepped away from the desk and opened the door to the hallway outside. "I hope you don't take this the wrong way, gentlemen, but I sincerely hope you find the real killer soon—if only so that you can leave the rest of us alone."

Warrick basked in the familiar sights and sounds of the college campus as he and Catherine headed over to the Registrar's Office, which was only a short walk from Wright Hall. They passed the imposing circular edifice of the Law School and crossed Brussels Street. Glancing north, he spotted one of the campus's most distinct landmarks: a thirty-eight-foot-tall pop-art sculpture in the shape of a giant flashlight. He smiled at the sight of the towering black structure.

"Bring back memories?" Catherine asked him.

"Some," he admitted. His time there had been exhausting, but exhilarating. Growing up socially awkward and bookish in a tough Vegas neighborhood had been rough at times; it wasn't until he enrolled at UNLV that Warrick felt that he had truly come into his own. In a very real sense, this was where his future had begun.

"Wild ones, I bet," she teased.

He smiled at a few particularly risqué memories. College hadn't been all work and no play, and chemistry wasn't the only thing he had gotten an education in. "I enjoyed my college years," he said discreetly. "What about you?"

"Between raising a daughter, working the clubs, and studying, I didn't have a whole lot of time for the college social scene." She sighed wearily. "Just staying awake sometimes was a challenge."

"Like today?"

"Something like that," she said, laughing. They had all been working practically nonstop for nearly a week now. "Except I was younger and had more energy then."

"Could've fooled me," he said. Catherine was one of the strongest and most indomitable people he knew. Frankly, he couldn't imagine handling this job and a rebellious teenager, too. *I couldn't even manage a marriage to a full-grown adult.*

The sight of the Frazier Building mercifully spared him any more ruminations along those lines. The unassuming one-story building was the oldest on the campus. "UNLV" was spelled out in giant red letters on its plain white walls. Palm trees fronted its humble façade. Old memories easily led them to the Registrar's Office, which resembled the lobby of a small bank, with college employees manning a long counter at one end of a large open area. Students were lined up before the counter to deal with tuition payments, transcript requests, changed majors, and other bureaucratic chores. Wooden tables along both sides of the waiting area held wire racks containing all of the various forms required to keep the office running smoothly. More students stood before the tables, filling out forms by hand. Posted notices listed the appropriate deadlines and requirements. A framed oil painting depicted Frazier Hall as it had appeared fifty years ago, when it was the first building constructed on the campus. Warrick marveled at how much the university had grown since then.

And was still growing.

He was taking out his ID, preparing to cut in line, when a voice called out to him from behind the counter. "Warrick Brown? Is that you?"

The voice came from an elderly black woman, whose sparkling brown eyes were magnified by the pop-bottle lenses of her horn-rimmed spectacles. A bun of silver hair crowned her aged head. Laugh lines were etched deep into her face. A bright floral sundress was draped over her petite figure.

"Miss Eugenia?"

The speaker was an old friend of his Aunt Bertha. Warrick remembered her helping him out with his

financial-aid applications when he was just a freshman, in exchange for him placing an occasional bet
for her at the Sahara and elsewhere. He'd had no
idea she still worked for the university.

Catherine shook her head in disbelief. "I swear,
Warrick, you know somebody everywhere we go."

He didn't deny it. As a lifelong resident of Vegas,
as well as an enthusiastic sampler of the city's night
life, he had contacts all over town. "Don't knock it,"
he whispered to Catherine. "Looks like we might already have an 'in' here."

"Work it, baby," she told him.

Despite some dirty looks from the students in
line, the CSIs walked right up to the counter. "Miss
Eugenia!" Warrick greeted the old woman. "I can't
believe you're still here."

"Tell you the truth, they tried to retire my skinny
butt a few years back," she explained. "But they're
going to have to drag me out of here." She grabbed
the edge of the counter to demonstrate her resolve.
"What else am I supposed to do with my days? Sit
around and count out all the pills I'm taking? I like
being around bright young people. Keeps me on my
toes!"

"Well, it sure seems to be doing wonders for
you," Warrick said. Upon closer inspection, Eugenia
Reynolds was smaller and frailer than he remembered, but she still seemed lively and full of pep.
"You look just as pretty as ever!"

She swatted at him playfully. "You keep that
horse manure to yourself, Warrick Brown." Her
magnified eyes sized him up from behind the
counter. "But look at you! I remember you when

you were just a scrawny kid prowling around the old neighborhoods, your nose stuck in a book." She shared a conspiratorial look with Catherine. "Who knew he'd grow up to be such a mouthwatering hunk of manliness?"

Catherine didn't even try to keep a straight face. "Yeah. Who knew?"

Warrick realized there was no way he was coming out of this with his dignity intact. His only consolation was that Grissom and Nick and Greg weren't around to witness his humiliation, although how he was going to keep Catherine from sharing this incident with the entire lab, he had no idea. *Maybe I can bribe her somehow?*

"Anyway, Miss Eugenia . . ."

"Yes, yes," she said indulgently, letting him off the hook. "What brings you back to college, Warrick? I know it wasn't to visit this mummified old spinster."

He tried to adopt a more professional tone. "This is Catherine Willows from the LVPD Crime Lab. We're here on police business."

Eugenia's wizened face sobered up. "This is about poor Professor Kim, isn't it?"

"I'm afraid so," he confirmed. "We're interested in a former student of his, Amanda E. Knowlston. We'd like to take a look at her student records."

The old woman frowned. "You know I can't do that, Warrick. Those files are confidential."

"Maybe you can make an exception in this case." He flashed her his most charming smile, one that had often opened doors for him all across the city. "For old time's sake."

She shook her head decisively. "We take the privacy of our students very seriously."

"This is a murder investigation," Catherine said pointedly. "We take those very seriously, too. Especially when the killer is still on the loose."

But Eugenia remained adamant. "I'd like to help you, young lady. I really would. This whole campus will breathe a little easier when this 'Headhunter' maniac is behind bars, but rules are rules. I've never violated a student's trust before, and I'm not going to start now."

Visibly biting back a sarcastic reply, Catherine shot Warrick a desperate glance, as if maybe he could reason with the woman. Clearly, she didn't know Eugenia Reynolds. "If we have to, we can get a warrant," he finally said.

"Then you do that, Warrick. And then I'll find that file for you. But not before."

Surrendering to the inevitable, the CSIs left the Registrar's Office in defeat. "So," Catherine asked dubiously, "*can* we get a warrant? All we've got is a ten-year-old thesis."

"Found in the top desk drawer in the victim's office, where the other victim's head was mailed to," Warrick pointed out. "It's not a lot, but I'll get on the phone to Grissom. Maybe he can get the sheriff to put some pressure on a friendly judge. We're not the only ones who want to get the Vegas Headhunter into jail and out of the headlines."

"Sounds like a plan," she agreed. "So what do we do in the meantime?"

Warrick considered their options. He was reluctant to head back to the lab with nothing more than an old term paper. "Well, we still need to e-mail those fingerprints to the lab. Confirm that the prints on the report belong to Kim." The scanner and wireless equipment were in the back of their Denali; in theory, Mandy Webster at the lab could match the prints against Kim's within minutes if she wasn't busy with something else. "You want to get something to eat afterward?"

As he recalled, the Barrick Museum had a pretty good cafeteria.

"I have a better idea," Catherine said. "Why don't we track down Professor Kim's wife while we're waiting for the warrant to come through? Maybe she knows who Amanda Knowlston is?"

Warrick recalled that the Kim residence was not far from campus.

"Worth a shot," he agreed.

21

FINDING HELEN KIM took a little longer than they expected. They had to call around a bit before they found out that the widow was currently staying at a Hyatt less than three miles from UNLV. The modest hotel, which mostly catered to families visiting the university, wasn't as glamorous as the big resorts on the Strip, but Catherine figured it had to be better than the bloody crime scene the Kims' home had become. The memory of finding her husband's decapitated body on the couch was surely fresh in the woman's mind. Catherine wondered if Helen Kim would ever feel safe in her living room again.

I'm not sure I would, she thought.

They met with the victim's wife in a fairly standard-issue hotel room on the Hyatt's third floor. Catherine and Warrick sat on the edge of the twin bed, while Helen Kim occupied a chair by the window. Filmy drapes diffused the afternoon sunlight. The remains of a room-service lunch sat on a small circular breakfast table. The meal appeared largely untouched; she didn't seem to have much of an appetite.

And who could blame her?

Catherine spotted a bottle of tranquilizers on the bedstand, next to a well-read copy of *Sense and Sensibility*. She hoped Helen Kim wasn't too doped up to assist them. "Thank you for taking the time to talk to us today." She hesitated, uncertain how to address the other woman. "Do you prefer Ms. Kim? Professor Kim?"

"Just Helen will be fine." Her angular face was devoid of makeup, and her clothes didn't quite match, as though dressing herself had almost been too much for her. Dark brown hair was knotted at the back of her head, more to get it out of the way than anything else. Her voice was hoarse, as though she had been crying recently, but not noticeably slurred. Dark shadows haunted her eyes. "I don't feel much like a professor at the moment."

"We understand this is a very difficult time for you," Warrick said.

She cracked a bitter smile. "That's the understatement of all time. I just don't know what to do, how to cope at all. None of this makes any sense." Red-rimmed eyes moistened, and she reached for a tissue. "To be honest, I'm not sure what I can tell you that I didn't tell Captain Brass before."

"We're just following up some new leads," Warrick explained. "Does the name Amanda Knowlston mean anything to you?"

Her fist tightened on the tissue, crushing it into a little ball. All the color drained from her face and her eyes widened in shock. A gasp escaped her lips.

And we have a winner, Catherine thought. The name had obviously hit a nerve. "Helen?"

"I'm sorry." She took a deep breath to compose herself. Tossing the crumpled tissue aside, she tried to dismiss her reaction with a wave. "Never mind all that. I'm just a bundle of nerves these days." Her face assumed a carefully neutral expression. "What was that name again?"

You heard it the first time, Catherine thought. "Amanda Knowlston."

The woman vacillated unconvincingly. "I'm not sure. Should I know that name?"

Catherine's patience was running low. "Listen to me, Helen," she said sternly, not mincing any words. "The psycho who beheaded your husband, and at least one other innocent man, is still out there. If there's something we need to know, you really need to tell us right now."

She felt a twinge of guilt for exerting pressure on the grieving widow, but she was sick and tired of people obstructing their investigation. Didn't anyone realize that they were possibly dealing with a serial killer here?

"I-I'm just worried about Malcolm's reputation," Helen stammered. "I wouldn't want his memory sullied by any groundless accusations." Her tearful eyes pleaded for understanding. "Can I rely on your discretion?"

"I can't make any promises," Catherine said honestly. If and when this case came to trial, who knew what information would become public record? "But we're not going to air any dirty laundry for no reason."

"What kind of accusations are we talking about here?" Warrick asked.

Helen Kim needed a moment to work up her nerve. Crossing the room, she washed down a tranquilizer with a glass of water before returning to her seat. Her limbs trembled as she spoke.

"Mandy Knowlston was this deranged young woman who became obsessed with my husband. She claimed that Malcolm had seduced her, but of course, that was just some insane fantasy of hers. *She* was the stalker, not Malcolm." She tore at a Kleenex with her fingertips. A note of anger entered her voice. She got visibly worked up just thinking about it. "She even showed up on our doorstep one day, insisting that Malcolm had gotten her pregnant. God only knew who the real father was. Probably some drunken frat boy."

Uh-huh, Catherine thought skeptically. She had never met Malcolm Kim in the flesh, at least when he still had a head on his shoulders, but the shrine in front of Wright Hall had depicted a fairly good-looking man, who had probably been even more attractive seven years ago. She could see how an impressionable young grad student might fall for him. *Wonder just how popular he was with his students, especially the female ones.*

"Forgive my candor," Catherine said, "but I have to ask. Is there any possibility that there was something going on between your husband and Amanda?"

Helen stiffened indignantly. "Absolutely not! How could you even suggest such a thing?"

"Stranger things have happened." Catherine recalled dating her TA during a geology course years ago—and getting an A for her efforts. Maybe Amanda Knowlston's final exam had been a pregnancy test? "Believe me, you wouldn't be the first woman whose husband cheated on her."

"I'm sure you've investigated plenty of sordid dramas in your career," Helen said huffily, "but I assure you that our marriage was rock-solid. Malcolm was a handsome, charismatic man. Female students got crushes on him all the time. So did some male students, no doubt. But he would *never* betray our marriage vows. He wasn't that kind of man." She unconsciously toyed with the wedding band on her finger. "I was the only woman in his life."

Or so you thought. Catherine suspected that Helen was protesting a bit too much. There had to have been some reason for Malcolm not to mention Amanda Knowlston—and her documented interest in shrunken heads—to the police before. If he *had* impregnated a female student years ago, he certainly had a motive for wanting to keep the whole affair hushed up. A scandal like that wouldn't have been good for his career . . . or his marriage.

Still, she didn't see any point in challenging Helen Kim further on this issue, at least not at present. Denial, and the instinct to burnish one's memories of the dearly departed, could be powerful forces. Catherine didn't feel like smacking her head into those brick walls right now. *Maybe later, once we've uncovered more about this alleged affair and/or stalking incident.*

Warrick let the matter drop as well. "Whatever happened to Mandy Knowlston?"

"I wanted to file a restraining order against her,"

Helen said, "but Malcolm convinced me that we should just ignore her." Now that her husband's fidelity was no longer being questioned, her tone became a little less icy. "As I recall, she had a miscarriage and a nervous breakdown, more or less in that order, and eventually dropped out of school. I have no idea what became of her later. Thankfully, we haven't"—she caught herself using the present tense—"hadn't heard from her in years."

Until Professor Kim got that ominous package in the mail?

"When exactly was this?" Warrick asked.

"I'm not sure. Six, maybe seven years ago." The full implications of the CSIs' questions finally sank in. "You think *she* did this?" She sounded appalled by the suggestion, which had evidently never occurred to her before. "But why, after all these years?"

Who knows? Catherine thought. She'd seen a lot of cases of delayed revenge in her career. Sometimes old grievances and painful memories just built up inside people until they couldn't take it anymore. Or perhaps something happened that reopened the wounds and triggered a violent response. Maybe Mandy Knowlston had bumped into Malcolm on the street recently, and everything came flooding back?

But then, why would she kill Dr. Zounek, too?

"Can you describe what she looked like?" Warrick asked.

Helen looked uncertain. "I don't know. I only met her that one time, when she showed up on our doorstep to accuse Malcolm of getting her pregnant."

Her face darkened at the memory, and Catherine suspected that the offended widow could see her rival pretty vividly in her mind's eye. "Pretty enough, not stunning. Trim. Average height. Straight blond hair. Blue eyes." She sniffed testily. "Not Malcolm's type at all."

If you say so, Catherine thought, taking Helen's terse description of Mandy's physical attributes with a grain of salt. For all they knew, the lovestruck coed had been a real knockout way back when. Maybe more than Malcolm could resist? In her experience, blond, blue-eyed college girls were most any man's type.

"Caucasian?" Warrick asked.

"Yes."

Catherine did some quick math in her head. If Mandy was a grad student seven years ago, she'd probably be in her early thirties now. That let out Stacy the blond barista and Karla at Red Noir Studios. It frustrated her that they had no idea what Amanda Knowlston looked like now. "How curvy was she? Do you think she could pass as a man from a distance? If she was wearing a disguise?"

"Maybe," Helen said hesitantly. "She was slim, not voluptuous." She sounded perplexed by the question. "Does that matter?"

"Maybe." Catherine remembered the paper they had found in Malcolm Kim's desk. "Did your husband ever mention Mandy's thesis to you?"

"Her thesis? No, not that I recall." Now the confused widow looked thoroughly lost. "Why? What was it about?"

"Shrunken heads."

Helen Kim clutched her chest. "Oh my God!"

Grissom leaned back in his chair as he perused a photocopy of Amanda Knowlston's thesis on head-hunting. His reading glasses rested on his nose, while the lamp on his desk provided more than enough light to read by. The door to his office was closed in hopes of keeping out any distractions. He had been looking forward to reading this paper, for multiple reasons, ever since Catherine and Warrick had first phoned him about it. Fingerprint evidence had confirmed that Professor Malcolm Kim had read the original mere days before he died. Grissom wondered if it had held any answers for him.

"The Shuar are a fiercely independent people who have successfully resisted the imperialistic depredations of every hostile culture that has tried to conquer them. The mighty Incan Empire failed to steal their land, as did the Spanish *conquistadores,* the governments of Peru and Ecuador, and even the United States. Their bravery and warlike spirit have kept them free for centuries, while instilling fear in the hearts of their foes. History tells of one notable instance when, in 1599, the Shuar staged an epic revolt against the illegitimate colonial government of the Spaniards, killing more than 25,000 avaricious European invaders. After being cheated in the gold trade by a corrupt Spanish viceroy, the Shuar retaliated by pouring molten gold down the criminal's gullet until his bowels burst."

Poetic justice? Grissom mused. The grisly means of execution was not uncommon in ancient history, but was one he had yet to encounter in his own career.

There was a knock at the door.

Grissom scowled, mildly annoyed by the interruption. Still, he could hardly shirk his responsibilities as supervisor. "Come in."

Brass strolled into the office. He glanced at the document in Grissom's hand. "Interesting reading?"

"I'd give it a B-minus," Grissom replied. "There's a laudable enthusiasm for the subject matter, but it lacks objectivity. The author romanticizes the Jivaro warriors to a worrisome degree." He put down the thesis and rubbed his eyes. "I'm reluctant to read too much into this one piece of evidence, but I rather suspect that our killer also identifies with the Jivaro a bit too strongly."

Brass picked up the paper and squinted at the title page. "You liking this Amanda Knowlston for the murders?"

"Maybe," Grissom said. "But it's too soon to put out an APB. Judge Doherty came through with a warrant for Amanda Knowlston's college records, so we should know more after Warrick and Catherine pick them up in the morning." A clock on the wall read one-fifteen A.M. "Plus, I still need to finish reading this paper."

"Well, don't work too late," Brass reminded him. "You're due to testify in the O'Malley case tomorrow."

Grissom had not forgotten that. The timing was unfortunate—he hated taking time out from the Headhunter case—but he also had an obligation to make sure that the late Don Cook received some posthumous justice. Grissom's testimony was key to the prosecution's case against the dead man's father-in-law.

"Don't worry. I'll be there." A freshly dry-cleaned gray suit, suitable for courtroom appearances, was hanging in the corner of the office. His notes on the O'Malley case were already packed away in his attaché case. He'd be heading home early tonight in order to be well rested for his stint on the witness stand tomorrow.

As soon as he finished reading Amanda Knowlston's paper.

"The source of the Shuar's greatness is the *arutam*, a mystical energy created by their ancestors that transcends nature. Only by slaying an enemy in battle can a young Shuar warrior achieve manhood by the taking the *arutam* within him. The Shuar believe that *arutam* renders a warrior invincible and that each new victory increases his power. . . ."

22

"ONE WARRANT, AS REQUESTED."

Warrick handed the legal document over to Eugenia Reynolds. He and Catherine had been first in line when the registrar's office opened that morning, and he was anxious to get his hands on Amanda Knowlston's student file. Despite their best efforts, the CSIs had been unable to track down Amanda or "Mandy" Knowlston via Google, the phone book, and the usual law-enforcement databases. Whatever else the alleged stalker might have been doing for the last seven years, she had successfully managed to fly under the radar, which made the college records their best bet at getting a lead on her current location. *Maybe she's changed her name or moved out of state or something?*

"See, that wasn't so hard," Miss Eugenia chided him.

That's what you think, Warrick thought. Apparently, the sheriff had really needed to lean on Judge

Doherty to get the warrant served in a timely fashion. For the first time, Warrick was grateful for the media circus surrounding the case. "I think you'll find everything's in order."

Eugenia squinted at the warrant through the pop-bottle lenses of her spectacles. Warrick waited tensely, trying hard not to let his impatience show, until the elderly woman reached the end of the court order. "See, this is just what I was looking for," she pronounced finally. "Now I can release these records with a clean conscience."

She reached beneath the counter and drew out a skinny cardboard folder. "I took the liberty of Xeroxing the file for you." Warrick reached for the folder, but Eugenia yanked it back and handed it to Catherine instead. "Now, now, Warrick Brown, didn't your aunt and granny teach you anything about manners?" Her eyes twinkled mischievously. "Ladies first."

"You tell him." Catherine smirked at Warrick as she accepted the folder. "Thanks for keeping him in line."

Warrick felt distinctly outnumbered. Still, at least they had the file. That was the important thing. "If you two are done bonding at my expense," he said lightly, "maybe we can get back to catching a killer?"

"I should hope so!" Eugenia said. She dropped her teasing tone and expression as she looked Warrick squarely in the eyes. "I have faith in you, Warrick. I know you'll get this person in no time." She waved them away from the counter. "Now get going . . . and don't be a stranger!"

A bench in the hall outside the office offered a convenient locale at which to look over Amanda Knowlston's records. Catherine opened the folder on her lap, while Warrick peered at it from beside her. At first glance, the file looked disappointingly skimpy. Just a few application forms, a receipt for dorm housing, and a copy of her college transcript.

A quick scan of the latter confirmed that Mandy Knowlston had never completed her degree. According to the records, her stint at the university had ended abruptly in the spring of 2001, with her taking incompletes in all of her classes that semester, including "Advanced Topics in Anthropology." The transcript didn't list who her instructor was, but Warrick was willing to hazard a guess. He pointed out the listing to Catherine. "If I was still a gambling man, I'd bet good money that Malcolm Kim taught that course."

"Seven years younger," she agreed, "and even more irresistible."

But that was all old news. "Anything more recent?" he asked.

"Not really." Catherine rifled through the file. "No transcript requests, transfers to other colleges, complaints against Professor Kim . . . not even a change-of-address notice. She seems to have completely lost touch with the university after dropping out seven years ago. But we haven't struck out completely." She plucked the transcript from the file. "We *do* have a birthdate, December 14, 1975, and a social security number now."

That's something, he admitted. She read the digits off to Warrick, who scribbled them down in his notebook. "Grissom's in court today, but let me text

that info to Nick and Greg. Hopefully, that's just
what they need to track her down."

He fired off the data, then glanced again at the
file. "Any medical records relating to that miscarriage?"

"Not here." Catherine double-checked the folder.
"Maybe those would be over at the campus medical
center?"

Warrick groaned inwardly at the thought of obtaining yet another warrant, this time for confidential medical records. *Wonder if it's worth the effort?*

"This transcript sure seems to tell the gist of the
story," Catherine said as she looked over the physical record of Mandy Knowlston's truncated academic career. "Looks like her unhappy affair with
the professor, if that's what actually happened, completely derailed her education. Judging from this
file, she never got her master's degree, never transferred to another college, nothing. The affair, or her
obsession with Professor Kim, pretty much wrecked
her college career."

Warrick nodded. "Didn't seem to have hurt Kim's
career any. He ended up head of the Anthropology
Department."

". . . while Mandy Knowlston's bright future
went down the toilet." From the bitter tone in her
voice, Warrick guessed that Catherine was ponder-
ing what might have become of her if she hadn't
managed to put herself through college. Would she
be a washed-up former stripper now? "Sounds like
a motive for murder to me."

"*Tumashi akerkama,*" Warrick muttered. "Blood-
guilt."

* * *

The Headhunter thought of herself as Kakara, a mighty Jivaro warrior with two kills to her credit.

Her former identity no longer mattered.

Slaying her foes, and capturing their souls, had imbued her with *arutam,* the spiritual power she needed to avenge the wrongs done to her in the past. For too long, she had allowed vain, arrogant men to set themselves above her. With every new victim, she felt her strength increase. Once she had been weak and vulnerable, but no more.

Now she was Kakara, the headhunter, and blood-vengeance would be hers.

Unfortunately, her latest target was proving elusive.

Kakara was staked out at a covered bus stop across the street from the Las Vegas crime lab. Several buses had already passed by, but she wasn't going anywhere that morning. The bus stop offered an excellent view of the building's front entrance on Westfall Avenue, so she was right where she wanted to be, watching out for her prey.

Mirrored sunglasses and a wide-brimmed cowboy hat concealed her identity. Despite the heat, she wore a long oilskin duster over a lightweight halter top and jogging shorts. A pair of cheap tennis shoes could be disposed of after the hunt. Deep pockets, which she had personally sewn into the inner lining of the coat, held her machete and bamboo blow pipe. A Ziploc envelope of freshly dipped clay darts rested in her right coat pocket, within easy reach of her gloved fingers. Today's newspaper was on her lap, just in case she needed to hide her face behind it at some point. A leakproof leather satchel waited for her enemy's head.

She was ready. Now all she needed was her prey.

Where are you, Dr. Grissom? You know-it-all sonofabitch.

She had been disappointed, but not too surprised, to discover that the aggravating CSI's home address and phone number were unlisted. *No matter,* she thought. *I know where he works.* The crime lab and its attached parking garage were closed to the public, but that was all right for her; she would never be so foolish as to set foot inside anyplace with such tight security. She hadn't succeeded in her campaign so far by taking unnecessary chances. Better to track Grissom covertly, observe his habits and routine, perhaps trail him to his home. *I can be patient,* she thought, *and wait for just the right opportunity.*

She sucked thirstily on a large bottle of spring water. Despite the shade provided by the roof of the bus stop, the scorching heat was getting to her. The urban setting felt as hot as the Amazon rain forest, if not quite as humid. Surrendering to the rising temperature, she shucked off the heavy coat and draped it carefully over the bench beside her, taking care not to spill the poisoned darts onto the pavement. She prayed to her spirit guides that she wouldn't have to wait all day for a glimpse of Grissom. Surely he'd have to step out for lunch or a smoke or something?

Her teeth bit into a fresh apple as she munched on the snack to keep up her strength. While keeping her eyes fixed on the entrance to the crime lab, she imagined herself deep in the heart of the Amazon, where she belonged. Scaly caimans splashed in the lazy river nearby. Toucans and mockingbirds perched in the lush green canopy above her, filling the day with birdsong. Blooming orchids and magnolias imbued the atmosphere with a heady perfume. Monkeys chattered overhead. She felt deeply at home in this verdant landscape, an unspoiled wilderness whose proud, heroic people had held the soul-destroying oppression of the modern world at bay through their spiritual strength and fortitude. Kakara had never actually set foot in the Amazon, but she had read and dreamed about it so many times that it often felt more real to her than the grubby, depressing reality of Las Vegas. Even now, she could see herself lurking in the dense emerald foliage, waiting patiently for the moment to strike. . . .

A city bus pulled up to the curb, its squealing brakes jolting her from her reverie. A garish banner touting Cirque du Soleil's latest extravaganza was emblazoned on the side of the bus, which blocked her view of the building across the street. A refreshing gust of air-conditioning hit her as the bus driver opened the door and looked at her expectantly. "Well?" his piggish eyes demanded rudely.

She impatiently waved him on.

The bus pulled away, and Kakara experienced a moment of panic as she spotted Grissom ambling away from the crime lab on the other side of the avenue. Her heart missed a beat. *Oh Lord*, she realized. *I almost missed him!*

Adrenaline shot through her system like a gift from the gods. Her pulse racing, she sprang into action. Chucking the half-eaten apple into the street, she leaped to her feet and hastily threw her coat back on. The weight of her concealed weapons swung against her as she strode briskly down the sidewalk after Grissom. She matched her pace to his, keeping both behind and across from him. It was important that she not be too obvious about it. The last thing she wanted was for her prey to realize that he was being followed. She had to be as cunning and coldblooded as the sacred anaconda.

Falling into a comfortable rhythm, she observed Grissom from across the busy avenue. The nosy CSI was dressed more much formally than she had ever seen him before. Instead of his blue FORENSICS windbreaker and baseball cap, he was wearing a neatly pressed suit and tie, as though he was on his way to a job interview. A black leather attaché case swung at the end of his arm. He was easy to keep up with, as he appeared somewhat distracted, dictating notes into a voice recorder as he made his way downtown.

Good, she thought. The more preoccupied he was, the less likely he was to spot her trailing him. She couldn't help wonder, though, what he was talking about. Chances were, he was going over the case of the Vegas Headhunter at that very moment. *What is he saying about me?*

Emboldened by his distracted state and unable to resist the urge to eavesdrop on him, she crossed the street at the first available intersection and fell in behind him. She strained her ears to listen in, but his low, soft voice frustrated her. Was that the word "tsanta" she heard? She couldn't be sure. *Speak up,* she thought irritably. *I can't hear you.* As they turned left onto Las Vegas Boulevard, she found herself torn between the desire to creep even nearer to him and the need to stay safely distant. How close was too close?

She fell back reluctantly, unwilling to risk everything just to satisfy her curiosity. *Who cares what he's saying?* she consoled herself. *He'll been dead soon enough anyway.*

What really mattered was finding the right opportunity to strike, although their current location was hardly ideal. Grissom was heading southwest on the boulevard now, which was too busy, too open, too exposed. Even though they were several blocks north of the big tourist area, with its inescapable crowds and casinos, she still wasn't sure how or when she would be able to claim the CSI's head in this sunlit metropolitan environment. She scanned the sidewalk ahead of them, looking for some secluded locale where she could be alone with Grissom for a few moments. Maybe a convenient bush or alcove?

An alley about a block away called out to her. She ran through the scenario in her head, visualizing every second:

She catches up with him right as he's passing the entrance to the alley. The blow pipe is too cumbersome and conspicuous under these circumstances, so she just jabs him in the side of the neck with a poisoned dart. As the curare takes effect, she drags him into the alley and out of view of the street. She has to move quickly, but a few moments are all it takes. Freeing the machete from its hiding place inside her coat, she chops off Grissom's head with a single powerful blow. Moments later, she's on her way with the captured head in her satchel. No one is the wiser as she confidently strolls down the sidewalk with her prize, leaving the CSI's headless body behind the alley.

"Yes," she whispered to herself. She could do it. The *arutam* she had gained from her previous victories would give her the strength and speed she required to carry out her plan. The power of a true Shuar warrior would shield her from harm. She picked up the pace, her heart pounding in anticipation. Her fingers explored her pocket, closing on a single homemade dart. Her mouth was dry. She licked her lips.

As Grissom approached the mouth of the alley, she glanced from side to side. The spirits of the Amazon were with her. She and Grissom seemed to have the sidewalk to themselves at the moment. Cars and trucks zipped by on the boulevard, not even giving them a second glance. The timing was perfect.

She came up behind him. She drew the dart from her pocket.

Good-bye, Dr. Grissom. For all of your intelligence, you never even saw this coming.

"Grissom! Hang on a moment!"

Kakara nearly jumped out of her skin. She stumbled, missing a step, and thrust the dart back into her pocket. Lowering her head just in time, she saw Grissom pause and turn around. He stared past her at another man, who came rushing up from behind them.

"Hodges?"

The stranger, who seemed to have come out of

nowhere, hurried past her to catch up with Grissom. He was an unimpressive man with lank black hair and a wheedling voice. He seemed slightly out of breath, as though he had been rushing too fast in the heat. Like Grissom, he was dressed in a conservative business suit, although his wide-striped tie was a tad too loud.

"Glad I caught up with you," Hodges said. "You have a surprisingly brisk walk, you know that?"

Grissom looked concerned. "Is there a problem at the lab?"

"What? No, no." Hodges sounded surprised that Grissom would think that. "I'm just testifying myself today—in the Cerota case—so I thought you might like some company on the way to the courthouse." He wiped the perspiration from his forehead. "Not a bad morning for a walk, don't you think? Although not a day you want to forget your sunscreen."

A flash of annoyance crossed Grissom's face, quicky followed by a more neutral expression. He sighed as he tucked his voice recorder into his pocket. Kakara got the distinct impression that he would have rather been alone with his thoughts.

"I suppose not." He glanced at his watch. "Well, if we're going to walk together, let's get going."

He wasn't the only one who resented the newcomer's intrusion. Kakara bit down on her lip to keep from screaming in frustration as Grissom walked past the alley unscathed. She glared murderously at the back of Hodges's head.

A few more moments and Grissom would have been mine!

She soothed herself by visualizing Hodges's throat

beneath her blade. *Who knows? Maybe I'll go after him next.* The man's smug, self-satisfied countenance reminded her somewhat of the late Dr. Zounek. She imagined peeling that face away from its skull. . . .

A few more blocks brought them within sight of the new city courthouse. The Lloyd D. George District Courthouse was an eight-story modernist building whose striking architecture stood out from the more traditional government buildings on the block. A massive steel overhang, supported by a gigantic gleaming pillar, extended high above the wide front steps of the intimidating edifice. At least, Kakara realized, she knew where Grissom was going now.

That explained the business suit, too. *Got to make a good impression on the jury.*

She scowled at the courthouse. She had served on jury duty a few years back and had not forgotten the tight security she'd had to pass through every day: guards, metal detectors, and who knew what else. Hadn't she read somewhere that the new courthouse, which was only six years old, was the first federal building built to post–Oklahoma City blast-resistance specifications?

No way was she going to be able to smuggle her machete in there.

Fuming, she lingered on the sidewalk as the two men climbed the steps to the front entrance. Hodges was continuing to carry on a rather one-sided conversation with Grissom. "Don't forget to turn your cell phone off," he offered helpfully. "You wouldn't want it to go off in the courtroom. I hear Judge Clarke frowns on that."

"Thank you, Hodges," Grissom said with an edge of irritation in his voice. "I have done this before."

Hodges realized that he had overstepped. "Well, I didn't mean to imply that you hadn't. Of course you know that you have to turn off your phone. I just thought you might appreciate a reminder, given that you have so much on your mind right now, what with the Headhunter and all."

His sycophantic burbling faded into inaudibility as they left Kakara behind. Within minutes, they had disappeared through the imposing glass doors at the top of the steps.

Now what?

She ached to follow them into the building, but the metal detectors made that impossible. Instead she looked around for someplace where she could wait for Grissom to emerge. Turning away from the building, she saw that an open plaza faced the old federal building across the street. A pair of towering palm trees, flanking the center of the plaza, offered the promise of shade. Benches waited for weary pedestrians. It seemed as good a place as any to lie in wait for her enemy.

A clock tower informed her that it wasn't even ten A.M. yet, which meant she was in for a long day. *That's all right*, she told herself. *You can be patient. He has to come out eventually.*

A wise hunter knew when to strike—and when to wait for precisely the right moment.

23

NICK WAS IN THE break room, reviewing a transcript of Carlos Vallejo's interview, when he got the text message from Warrick. Grabbing a pencil, he scribbled Amanda Knowlston's birth date and social security number on the back of the transcript and headed for his laptop, which he had left in the conference room. He found Greg there as well, tapping away at the keyboard of his own computer. A voluminous stack of papers was piled at his elbow. Glancing over Greg's shoulder, Nick saw that the younger CSI was entering the details of Malcolm Kim's murder into VICAP.

The Violent Criminals Apprehension Program was a nationwide database containing profiles of crime scenes from all over the country. The CSIs had already searched VICAP for previous shrunken head murders, but had come up empty-handed. Still, the data from the Vegas crime scenes might well help future investigators should the Head-hunter move on to fresher territory.

Let's hope it never comes to that, Nick thought. *I want to nail this guy—or gal—here and now, not somewhere down the road.*

Greg looked away from the screen. "What's up?"

Nick filled him in on what Warrick and Catherine had learned from the registrar's office at the university. "Maybe now we can find out what happened to this Amanda Knowlston person."

"You really think the Headhunter is a woman?" Greg asked. "That doesn't exactly fit the profile. I've been reading up on the Jivaro, and they're not exactly big on nontraditional gender roles. The men hunt and kill, the women stay at home and take care of the baby headhunters."

Nick shrugged. "Remember the Miniature Killer? Serial killing is an equal-opportunity sport these days. Perhaps our headhunter isn't as traditionally minded as we thought." A few other possibilities came to mind. "Or maybe the killer is Amanda Knowlston's new boyfriend. Or an overprotective dad or brother out to avenge her honor."

"Or her sister or her cousin or her college roommate from Ecuador . . ."

"Exactly," Nick said. "At this point, we can't rule anything out. There are still too many alternatives. For all we know, Amanda Knowlston died years ago or is living happily ever after in Belgium right now."

"Let's find out." Greg saved what he was doing on VICAP, then offered his seat to Nick. "You want to do the honors?"

"Don't mind if I do." Nick sat down at the keyboard. An LVPD password granted him access to a wide variety of state and city databases. He decided to start with

the Department of Motor Vehicles. If Amanda Knowlston was driving anything in Nevada—like maybe
a green hatchback—she would be on file with the
DMV. He plugged her birth date and SSN into the
search engine.

Within moments, an image of a driver's license
appeared on the screen. An unflattering color photo
showed a grim-faced Caucasian woman with short
auburn hair who looked to be in her mid-thirties.
"There you go," Nick said triumphantly, until he noticed the name beneath the photo. According to the
screen, that SSN belonged to "A. ELIZABETH
RUDOLPH." "Wait a second. The name's wrong."

"Maybe she changed it," Greg suggested. "When
she got married or something?"

Always possible, Nick thought. "That first initial
must stand for Amanda."

"Elizabeth Rudolph," Greg recited. His youthful
face grimaced in concentration. "Where have I heard
that name before?" He stared intently at the photo;
then his eyes lit up in realization. He grabbed for the
heap of papers at his side and started flipping through
them energetically, like a kid looking for a prize at the
bottom of a cereal box. "C'mon, where are you?"

"What is it?" Nick asked.

"You know how I've been spending hours comparing lists of Dr. Zounek's staff and patients to the
students in Professor Kim's classes? Well, I think all
that mind-numbing tedium is about to pay off." He
let out an excited yelp as he extracted a single sheet
of paper from the files. "Take a look at this list of Dr.
Zounek's employees."

The first name on the list was "RUDOLPH, LIZ."

Nick made the connection. "Isn't she the head receptionist at the mental health clinic?" He had never visited the place, but now he remembered seeing the name in the case files. "The one Grissom and Brass have been talking to?"

"Guess the E in Amanda E. Knowlston is for Elizabeth," Greg surmised. "They're the same person."

Nick's eyes went straight to the address on the driver's license. "Where does she live?"

Warrick and Catherine made good time getting from the university to the Grace Tranquillity clinic. The midday traffic was brutal, but Warrick called on every trick he'd learned back during his taxi-driving days to weave his way across town. The Denali's brakes squealed to a halt as he pulled up in front of the clinic. He was proud to see that he had beaten Sofia Curtis to the scene. The female detective was supposedly en route to join them. Warrick figured she'd be there any minute.

"You really think Liz Rudolph is our perp?" he asked Catherine.

She put away her cell phone. "Sounds promising. Nick and Greg did some more digging. Seems Mandy Knowlston changed her name to Rudolph when she got married a few years back. Started going by her middle name about the same time."

"Guess she wanted to start all over again," Warrick said. "Make a clean break with the past."

"Not clean enough for Professor Kim," Catherine said. "There's more, too. According to Nick, Liz Rudolph does not own a green hatchback, but her late husband did. The car's still in his name, but that doesn't mean she's not driving it."

"Hey, wasn't it Rudolph who told Grissom that Daniel Skiller threatened to cut Dr. Zounek's head off?"

"I think so," Catherine said. "And she was the one who fingered Carlos Vallejo, too."

Warrick snorted. "Nice of her to spread the suspicion around. You think maybe she had an ulterior motive?"

"Hey, if I was a headhunter," Catherine said, "I'd sure want to point the police in wrong directions." She mulled it over as she unbuckled her seatbelt. "But why would she leak the story to the press, like Grissom said she did?"

"To tell the whole world about her revenge? Like I said before, headhunting is all about bragging rights. What's the good of finally achieving victory over your enemies if nobody knows about it?" He got out of the Denali. "Sounds like we definitely need to have a talk with Ms. Rudolph."

"I'll say," Catherine said. "Just watch out for blow pipes."

Sofia pulled into the parking lot just as the two CSIs were approaching the front entrance. They waited for her to exit her Taurus and join them. Warrick was glad to have the cop on hand, just in case Liz Rudolph refused to come down to the station with them. Taking suspects into custody was not actually part of a CSI's job description.

"Sorry to keep you waiting," Sofia said. As usual, she was wearing a dark jacket over a white dress shirt. "Brass and the guys are heading over to Rudolph's home address, but he wants us to take her into custody now."

"Sounds good to me," Warrick said. They didn't have quite enough evidence yet to pin the murders on Mandy Knowlston, a.k.a. Liz Rudolph, but her connection to both victims, as well as her stormy history with Professor Kim, had just vaulted her to the top of their suspect list. He opened the door for Catherine and Sofia. "After you."

Warrick had never visited the clinic before, but thought it looked innocuous enough. He grimaced when he spotted the large-screen television tuned to the local news station; helicopter footage of Professor Kim's house confirmed that the media was still milking the Vegas Headhunter story for all it was worth.

Let's hope we can give them a new headline soon, he thought. *Like "VEGAS HEADHUNTER BEHIND BARS."*

Sofia walked up to the check-in desk. The middle-aged black woman behind the counter bore no resemblance to Liz Rudolph's driver's-license photo, which Nick had helpfully transmitted to them via cell phone. Warrick discreetly scanned the clinic but didn't spot their suspect.

Maybe she was in the back somewhere.

"LVPD," Sofia said, introducing herself at the desk. "We'd like to speak to Liz Rudolph. Is she around?"

"Sorry, officer," the other woman replied. A name badge identified her as JANE ROOP. "Liz called in sick today. We haven't seen her since yesterday, poor thing."

In other words, Warrick realized, *not since the last time Grissom and Brass dropped by to interrogate her.* He hoped that their suspect wasn't already on the run. She could be halfway around the world by now. *Damn.*

Judging from the worried look on his colleagues' faces, the same possibilities were running through Sofia's and Catherine's minds. "Did she look ill the last time you saw her?" Catherine asked.

"Not particularly," the receptionist admitted. "But we've all been under a lot of stress lately, what with Dr. Zounek's murder and the press." She glanced up at the flat-screen TV, where James Zounek's shrunken head was now framed above a blond anchorwoman's shoulder. "Oh God, I should probably change the channel!"

Unable to find the remote, she dashed out from behind the counter and over to the TV. *Sesame Street* replaced *Eyewitness News,* but none of the waiting patients complained. Warrick suspected that everybody present was glad to get the doctor's mutilated remains off the screen. He guessed that it wasn't exactly conducive to mental health and tranquillity.

"There! That's better," Jane Roop said as she resumed her position behind the counter. She smiled at Sofia and the CSIs. "Would you like to leave a message for Liz?"

"No, thank you," Warrick said. No need to spook Rudolph in advance, if she hadn't already made a break for it. Glancing through the clinic's picture window at the sunny street outside, he spied a familiar-looking brown van driving by. A sudden thought occurred to him. "Excuse me," he asked. "I don't suppose you know what Ms. Rudolph's husband did for a living?"

"Charles?" she replied. "He used to drive for UOS—before the cancer got him, that is." She shook her head sadly. "Poor Liz. She took his death pretty hard."

Yeah, poor Liz, he thought. "You hear that?"

"Un-huh," Catherine said. "Want to bet she hung on to her husband's old uniforms?"

Sofia pulled out her cell phone. "I think Brass needs to hear about this."

Liz Rudolph lived in a suburban neighborhood not far from the clinic. A trim, one-story ranch house suggested a solidly middle-class existence. The tidy green lawn was free of weeds and neatly mowed. A high wooden fence, girding the backyard, provided a generous degree of privacy from the neighbors. Overall, the place hardly looked like the lair of a modern-day headhunter, Nick thought, but then again, they were a long way from the Amazon. He and Greg got out of their Denali to join Jim Brass on the sidewalk in front of the house. The detective's Taurus was parked farther down the block.

Nick looked around for Charles Rudolph's green Honda Civic, but the driveway was empty. Maybe the hatchback was in the garage? Liz Rudolph's own red Subaru Forester was also nowhere to be seen. He tugged experimentally on the garage door, only to find it locked. *Later,* he promised himself. *If we find grounds for a search.*

He considered the house itself. The drapes were drawn and the lights appeared to be off inside. A sticker in the front window, as well as a posted metal sign in the yard, warned that the residence was protected by Home Sure Security.

"Think she's home?" Greg asked.

"She should be," Nick replied. "According to Sofia, she's supposed to be home sick today."

That might explain why the lights are off, he thought. *She could be holed up under the blankets getting plenty of rest.*

"Or maybe she's just too busy shrinking the professor's head to show up for work," Brass said gruffly. He strode toward the front door. "Nick, watch the back."

"I'm on it," he agreed readily, although he really hoped that Liz Rudolph wouldn't try to make a break for it via the back door. After his run-in with Carlos Vallejo the other night, he didn't feel like chasing another suspect on foot. Once a week was enough.

Nick circled around the house, looking for a back exit. The fence blocked his view of the backyard, so he called out to Greg, "Hey, bring me that big metal toolbox from the back of the car."

Responding promptly, Greg came running back with the box, a sturdy metal crate holding a wide variety of hammers, wrenches, and pliers. "What's up?" he asked Nick, panting a bit from exertion. "You planning to take this fence apart?"

"Not yet," he answered. "Right now, I just need something to stand on."

He pushed the toolbox up against the base of the fence and gingerly stepped on top of it. The solidly built crate supported his weight and gave him the extra six inches he needed to peer over the top of the fence. He scanned the enclosed backyard.

The first thing he noticed was a largish wooden shed in the southwest corner of the yard. Bigger than a toolshed, it looked like some sort of workshop. Closed blinds covered the shed's windows. A heavy-duty padlock guarded its contents. *Wonder what they're keeping in there? Just some old garden equipment or something more interesting?*

Closer to the house, an outdoor barbecue set occupied a small concrete patio near the back door. In itself, the grill was hardly incriminating—Nick often enjoyed cooking up a big batch of burgers and hot dogs himself—but he also remembered the sooty residue that had been used to darken the *tsanta*'s skin. *Better get a sample of those ashes,* he thought. Perhaps Trace could link them to the ash on the shrunken head? Unless, of course, they came from just your standard charcoal briquets.

Somewhat more unusual was the large stuffed archery target set up against one side of the fence. Straw poked from tears and loose stitches in the circular target. Judging from the accumulation of minute punctures surrounding the bull's-eye, somebody—Liz Rudolph, presumably—had been spending a lot of time developing her aim. *With a bow and arrows,* Nick wondered, *or a blow pipe?* A number of hits in the center of the target suggested that she had gotten pretty good at it.

That's not good, he thought.

Nick's gaze moved onto the yard itself. Unlike the manicured green lawn out front, the grass in the backyard was patchy and brown and in obvious need of watering. *Out of sight, out of mind,* he guessed, *at least as far as the neighbors are concerned.*

By contrast, the garden by the shed showed no such signs of neglect. Woody vines, three or four inches thick at the base, climbed an elaborate wooden trellis. Large heart-shaped leaves sprouted from the vines, as well as clusters of small greenish-white flowers.

Lacking a green thumb, he almost overlooked the foliage, but something about the unusual-looking plants tugged at his memory. "Heart-shaped leaves," he whispered to himself, as his mind conjured up an image from a website he had browsed recently. The mental snapshot clicked with what he saw right before him. "Well, how about that?"

"What is it?" Greg asked. He bounced impatiently on his tiptoes, but could not stretch high enough to look over the fence. "You see something?"

Nick nodded. "I'm no expert, but I think Liz Rudolph is growing curare vines in her backyard."

Curare, of course, was the principal ingredient in the poison traditionally used by the Jivaro head-hunters, as well as the paralytic toxin found in Professor Kim's bloodstream. From what Nick had read online, the Jivaro would crush the roots and stems of the plant, sometimes blending in the venom of various snakes and toads, before boiling the mix down into a dark, syrupy paste that they then dipped their darts and arrows in. One dart could bring down a monkey or a bird in a matter of moments.

"No kidding?" Greg regarded him with a mix of skepticism and admiration. "You actually know what curare plants look like?"

"Not until a few days ago," Nick confessed. He stepped off the toolbox. "But you know this job. It's always an education." He nodded toward the front of the house. "Better go tell Brass."

Greg took off to get the detective, but Nick wasn't alone for long. The other two men quickly joined him by the fence. "No answer at the front door," Brass reported. "If anybody's inside, they're keeping low." His irked expression promised trouble for anyone who might be trying to duck his questions. "You sure about this curare thing, Nick?"

"Reasonably." In a pinch, he could always double-check the website using the laptop in the back of the Denali.

"That's good enough for me." Brass didn't bother climbing onto the toolbox to look for himself. "The hell with warrants. The murder weapon is in sight. To my mind, that gives us probable cause." He looked at Nick. "Okay, football star, how you feel about ramming a door open?"

It had been quite a few years since Nick had served as a fullback, but he liked to think that he was still in good enough shape to tackle a stubborn door. "Let me at it."

Leaving Greg to keep an eye on the back, Nick retrieved the battering ram from Brass's vehicle and bounded up to the front porch. Brass stood to one side of the locked door, his Colt & Wesson already drawn. "Watch yourself, Nick," the cop warned. "We don't know what's waiting inside."

Nick nodded, taking Brass's advice seriously. He'd been at the wrong end of a bad guy's weapon before and was in no hurry to repeat the experience. He took a deep breath to steady his nerves. "All right. Here goes."

An ear-piercing siren went off as Nick smashed the door open. *Right,* he thought, remembering the sign out front. *The security system.* He put down the ram and stepped aside to let Brass take the lead. Holding his gun elevated in the high-ready position, the cop cautiously edged his way into the house. Nick held his breath, waiting to see if Brass encountered violent resistance. The wailing alarm scraped at his nerves. He wished he knew some way to turn it off.

A phone rang inside. *That would be the security company,* he guessed, calling to check on the residents. *We're going to have some explaining to do.*

Sure enough, Brass was still inside, searching the house, when a patrol car pulled up out front. A pair of tense-looking uniforms exited the vehicle and came storming up toward the porch. "You there!" a tall blond officer shouted at Nick. His hand rested on the grip of his sidearm. "Let me see your hands!"

"Ease off," Nick said affably. "We're on the same side here." Holding up empty hands, he stepped off the porch into the sunlight in order to give the newcomers a better look at his blue LVPD vest. His last name was embroidered in white on the upper right corner of the vest, opposite a sewn-on yellow star. "Nick Stokes, CSI."

"For real?" One of the cops warily inspected Nick's ID while his partner covered him from a few yards away. Nick submitted patiently to the inspection, but hoped that it wouldn't take too long. Time was slipping by and he didn't want the trail to get too cold. He breathed a sigh of relief when the first cop relaxed and turned to his partner. "It's cool. He's legit."

The other uniform lowered his weapon. His name badge identified him as JONSSON. His partner was NESKO. "So, what's the story?" he asked.

Nick gave him the *Reader's Digest* version. "We're following up a lead on the Vegas Headhunter case. Captain Brass is inside, conducting a preliminary search of the premises. My colleague, Greg Sanders, is over by the backyard."

"The Headhunter?" Nesko enthused. A freckle-faced redhead, she seemed excited at the prospect of taking part in the pursuit of the notorious killer. "Holy crap. Anything we can do to help?"

"The captain can probably use some assistance clearing the building," Nick suggested. The shrieking siren continued to assail his eardrums. "And maybe you can do something about that alarm?"

"Right," Nesko said with a grin. "That is pretty obnoxious." She turned to her partner. "Why don't you go inside while I call this into the station?" She headed back toward the patrol car. "Let me see if I can get that alarm switched off."

"That would be much appreciated," Nick said.

Jonsson advanced toward the front door, only to bump into Brass, who was already on his way out. "The place is clear," he announced sourly. "No bodies, no heads, no Rudolph." He massaged an aching ear. "I may have lost my hearing, however."

"We're working on that," Nick said. "Ready for Greg and me to get to work?"

"Knock yourself out," Brass said.

Confident that no homicidal headhunters lurked indoors, Nick pulled on a pair of latex gloves and entered the house. Mail was piled up on a dresser in the front foyer. Flipping through it, he found nothing remarkable. Bills and credit-card offers, mostly, as opposed to, say, the new issue of *Headhunters Quarterly* or a catalog from Red Noir Studios.

Guess it couldn't be that easy, he thought.

He did a quick walkthrough to get the feel of the place: living room, kitchen, study, bathroom, guest room, bedroom. The blaring alarm sounded even louder indoors, but it mercifully stopped by the time he got to the master bedroom. *Thank you, Officer Nesko.* Obviously somebody had gotten on the phone to Home Sure Security. The sudden silence made it easier to hear himself think.

Although he had yet to spy a bloodstain or a severed head, the bedroom decor hinted that they might be on the right track at last. The sheets, the curtains, and the carpet all looked as if they had been ordered from same jungle-themed catalog. Leafy green patterns, accented by brilliant-colored tropical birds, proliferated madly over the bedroom, so that Nick felt like he was inside some sort of rain forest exhibit at a museum. Bamboo shutters covered the windows, while a poster-sized photo of the Amazon River occupied one wall. A large clay vase, bearing what looked like some kind of South American Indian motif, rested on a dresser. A portable music player was set up on a table by the bed. The CD case sitting on top of the player promised *Soothing Sounds of the Amazon.* Nick pressed the PLAY button experimentally, and the silence was suddenly broken by the chirping of birds and frogs and other fauna. The drapes and sheets looked relatively new and in good condition; Nick suspected that Liz

Rudolph had redecorated recently. Maybe after her husband had died?

He couldn't help wondering what had become of the missing receptionist. If she wasn't at work and she wasn't at home, where the devil was she? And what was she up to? A quick inspection of the bedroom closet gave him hope that Rudolph might not have fled the city yet. Plenty of clothes and some battered luggage still occupied the closet. Likewise, a carved wooden jewelry box hidden away in a dresser drawer held a tasteful collection of jade and turquoise bangles that Nick assumed Liz Rudolph would be reluctant to leave behind. *If she is on the lam,* he thought, *she's traveling light.*

"Nick?" Greg called from the hall outside.

"In here."

Greg traipsed into the bedroom, lugging his field kit with him. His blue eyes widened as he took in the whole tropical-jungle effect. "Wow. Shades of the Amazon rain forest."

"I was thinking the same thing myself," Nick said. He silenced the CD player. "A Jivaro headhunter would feel right at home, sort of."

Greg looked around. "Where you want to start?"

"You take the living room," Nick suggested. "I'll finish up here." He started to advise Greg on what to look for, but held his tongue. The younger man wasn't an inexperienced lab rat anymore. He knew what to do. "Good hunting."

"Yeah. You, too."

Greg exited the room, leaving Nick alone to continue his search. A second set of closets, opposite the others, awaited his inspection. His and hers? He pulled open the closet door and hit pay dirt. Tucked in amid a full wardrobe of masculine attire was a United Overnight Shipping uniform on a hanger. Nick grinned in triumph as he wondered how the uniform looked on Liz Rudolph herself. Maybe good enough to fool a casual witness?

Probably.

He carefully laid the uniform out on top of the bed. A quick once-over revealed no obvious blood-stains, which dampened his excitement somewhat. After dimming the lights in the room, he put on a pair of tinted orange goggles and inspected the garments under the ultraviolet glow of the ALS. Unfortunately, the bluish light only confirmed his original assessment. There was no blood on the uniform.

That can't be right, he thought. Even if Malcolm Kim was already dead when he was decapitated, how did you chop off someone's head with a machete and not get a little blood on you? *Unless this is just a spare uniform . . .*

The more he thought about it, the more it made sense. Charles Rudolph was bound to have more than a single uniform. Who was to say that his widow didn't use one of the other ones when she made her fatal visit to the professor's house? He decided to bag the uniform as evidence anyway. If nothing else, it was more proof that Liz had access to a convenient disguise.

"Hey, Nick!" Greg shouted enthusiastically. "Come take a look at this. I think I found something!"

Leaving the uniform behind for now, Nick hurried down the foyer to the living room. The jungle motif was less in-your-face than in the bedroom, but Rudolph's exotic tastes were evidenced in a few South American objets d'art scattered around the room. "What you got?" he asked Greg.

The sandy-haired CSI was standing by a partially disassembled sofa. Pleather seat cushions were stacked neatly at the end of it. Using a pair of tweezers, he dropped a tiny round object into a clear plastic envelope. "Found this stuck between the seat cushions." Greg handed the bindle over to Nick. "Look familiar?"

Inside the envelope was a small wooden bead, not unlike the ones decorating James Zounek's shrunken head. Squinting at the minuscule sphere, Nick could have used the high-powered microscopes back at the lab, but he had spent enough time examining the *tsanta*'s beads to recognize another one when he saw it. "Jewelry Essentials Natural Beads." Available at Michaels.

"Bingo," he said. "Good work." He looked at Greg hopefully. "You find any more of these?" He tried to imagine Liz Rudolph sitting on the sofa one night, sewing up Dr. Zounek's eyes and lips while she watched TV. "Maybe some feathers or thread?"

Greg shook his head. He ran a flashlight over the exposed belly of the sofa. "But, you know, there is that workshop out back. . . ."

While Officer Jonsson applied a bolt cutter to the padlock, Greg and Nick took a closer look at the vines growing in Liz Rudolph's garden. The younger CSI mentally kicked himself for not researching curare himself. *Good thing Nick's here,* he thought. *To be honest, I couldn't tell curare from arugula.*

"Well?" he asked. "Is she growing poison or salad?"

"This isn't anything you'd want to eat with blue cheese dressing," Nick answered. He flipped over one of the broad green leaves, revealing a coating of tiny white hairs on the underside of the leaves. "Feel this."

Greg reached forward and tentatively touched the bottom of the leaf. It felt smooth and silky.

"Kind of velvety, right?" Nick asked. "Well, guess what another common name for the curare plant is? 'Velvet leaf.'"

"Okay, I'm convinced." He withdrew his hand. "Ms. Rudolph is brewing her own evil potions, right here in Las Vegas." Using a pocketknife, he clipped off a section of a vine, complete with both leaves and flowers, and deposited it in a brown paper bindle. "Now we just need to find the crazy lady herself."

"And Professor Kim's head," Nick reminded him. "Not to mention the rest of James Zounek." He scanned the unkempt backyard. Weeds sprouted amid the dying lawn. "Remind me to drag out the ground-penetrating radar later on."

Greg knew what Nick was thinking. The fenced-in yard wouldn't be a bad place to bury a body. *Unless she dumped it in the desert somewhere.*

Sometimes he regretted Las Vegas's proximity to Death Valley.

A loud metallic clank announced that the bolt

cutter had done its work. Jonsson stepped back from the shed door as the padlock hit the dirt. Nick had already lifted a set of fingerprints from the lock. "All yours," the cop declared. His partner, Cyndy Nesko, was out front, watching out for Rudolph.

"Thanks," Brass said. He drew his gun as he cautiously pulled over the door. It seemed unlikely that Liz Rudolph had been hiding out in the shed all this time, especially since the door was locked from the outside, but the veteran detective wasn't taking any chances. "Cover me," he instructed Jonsson, "and make sure I'm out of the line of fire if things get dicey."

"Yes, sir!" Jonsson put away the bolt cutter and raised his own weapon. Shooting a superior officer by mistake would definitely be a bad career move for him.

Greg and Nick waited over by the garden. When Brass emerged from the shed a few moments later, the sober expression on his face made it clear that he had found something disturbing. He nodded at the two CSIs. "Take a look, but brace yourselves. It's a freak show."

Visions of bloodthirsty shrunken heads flying through the air to tear out the throats of their enemies raced through Greg's imagination as he and Nick approached the shadowy entrance to the shed. As a CSI, he had been exposed to lots of grisly sights over the last few years, from autopsies to the aftermath of gangland massacres, but a chill still ran down his spine at the prospect of entering the Headhunter's lair. He shook it off, not wanting to show weakness in front of Brass and the others. He was a professional, and this was his job.

Lucky me.

Closed blinds blocked out the sun, so that only a single naked lightbulb, hanging from the ceiling, lit the interior of the workshop, which appeared to have been converted into a homemade shrunken head factory. A variety of knives and razors were spread out on rough wooden counters, alongside a collection of beads, feathers, and seeds. Rocks of various sizes, as well as a quantity of fine desert sand, were stored in labeled Tupperware containers. Ziploc bags held an assortment of dried herbs. A large stainless-steel pot sat on an inactive hot plate that was plugged into a nearby wall socket. An eighteen-pound bag of charcoal sagged against one corner. An unmoving fan failed to dispel the hot, stuffy atmosphere, which smelled of leather and bitter tea. Two bleached human skulls looked down on Greg from a wooden shelf. Their death's-head grins seemed to mock his foolish mortal fears. *This isn't so bad,* he told himself.

Then he looked in the pot.

The partially shrunken head of Professor Malcolm Kim rested inside. Only about half the size of a normal adult head, it looked unsettlingly like the severed head of a child, aside from the distinguished gray hair at its temples and the creases around its eyes and mouth. Frayed hemp cords stitched its eyelids shut. Tiny wooden spikes, about the size of golf tees, pinned its lips shut. The leathery skin was a pale gray shade; apparently it hadn't been polished with ash yet. A bulging jaw gave the face a slightly

Neanderthal look, while the top of the head was already tapering inward on all sides. The bottom of the neck was tied together with a cord. Greg had never seen Kim's face in person, only his headless corpse, but despite the distortions, he recognized the murdered academic right away.

"Yikes." Startled, he accidentally bumped into the handle of the pot, which bounced alarmingly on the hot plate. The shrunken head rattled like a castanet as it toppled over inside the pot. Greg remembered that the shrinking process involved filling the empty skin with hot stones.

"Hey! Careful there!" Nick shouted from a few feet away, where he was examining a set of hanging hammers and saws. "That's evidence."

"S-sorry." Greg stammered. His gloved hands reached out to stabilize the pot, holding on to the handle delicately until he was confident that it wasn't going to move anymore. He couldn't tear his gaze away from the shriveled trophy inside. "You see this?"

"Hard to miss," Nick said grimly. His disgusted expression demonstrated that even after all they had both seen, he still had the capacity to be appalled at the depths to which some human beings could stoop. "I'm guessing Brass has already put out an APB on Liz Rudolph."

"Alias Amanda E. Knowlston." He glanced up at the two skulls, and wondered which one belonged to the head in the pot. *I'll bet Grissom could tell—or that forensic artist chick.* He noticed a newspaper clipping thumbtacked to the shelf under one of the skulls. "Did you see this?" he called to Nick. "It looks like an article from the college newspaper. All about Kim's big promotion to the head of the Anthropology Department." Taking out his camera, he took a picture of the skull and the clipping together. "You think that's what set her off?"

"Could be," Nick said. "Nobody likes seeing their worst enemy doing well. She may have figured he had something else coming to him."

Works for me, Greg thought. He had seen people commit murder for a lot less.

He turned away from the article to check out the rest of the workshop. Nick was still looking over the collection of tools on the wall. "Find anything interesting?" Greg asked.

"It's what I'm not finding that worries me." Nick pulled a Nikon camera from the pocket of his vest and started photographing the scene. The flashbulb illuminated an empty peg. "Where's the machete?"

The hours had flowed sluggishly, like the eternal Amazon itself, but at last, the Headhunter's patience was rewarded. Kakara sat up straight as, after sitting vigil all afternoon, she spotted Grissom exiting the courthouse across the street.

Finally, she thought.

The spirits seemed to be smiling on her, as the CSI was alone this time. The other man, Hodges, was nowhere to be seen. Kakara assumed that he was still tied up in court. She hoped he stayed that way. The memory of Hodges's interference that morning rankled her. She had been so close. . . .

A glance at her watch revealed that it was a quarter after four. The sun, although sinking, remained

bright enough to make it oppressively warm outside. She was tired and hot and her legs were stiff as
she got up from a stone bench beneath a shady
palm tree, but an undeniable sense of exhilaration
swept through her nonetheless. Surrendering to the
heat, Grissom took off his austere gray jacket and
draped it over his shoulder before ambling northeast
on Las Vegas Boulevard. He appeared to be heading
back toward the crime lab.

The hunt was on again.

Throwing on her duster, and making sure to remember her leather satchel, she took off after Grissom. The empty satchel swung at her side, waiting
patiently for the unsuspecting CSI's head. Her concealed machete and blow pipe slapped against her
hips as she crossed the boulevard to fall in behind
her prey. The brim of her cowboy hat shielded her
from both sunlight and scrutiny. From behind the
mirrored lenses of her sunglasses, she glared murderously at the back of Grissom's skull.

She knew his type, all right. Smart, superior, cere-
bral. Another arrogant, condescending male who
thought that his lofty academic degrees meant he was
smarter than her. Kakara's blood pressure rose, and
her fists clenched as she thought about the relentless
way Grissom had been harassing her. To be honest, he
had given her some rough moments, all but accusing
her of fabricating that phony story about Danny
Skiller threatening to cut Zounek's head off and nag-
ging her relentlessly about the comings and goings at
the clinic. Grissom had proven himself a formidable
adversary, endangering her life and liberty, so she felt
more than justified in turning the tables on him. He

thought he was closing in on her? *Hah,* she thought derisively. *All his power will be mine soon enough.*

The police detective, Captain Brass, posed a problem as well, but she felt no particular animosity against him. He was just a cop, doggedly doing his job. He didn't remind her of Malcolm Kim or Dr. Zounek. Although the detective might also have to be dealt with in the future, killing him, stealing his soul, wouldn't be nearly as satisfying. . . .

Processing Liz Rudolph's twisted workshop of horror was a big job. Nick and Greg had been at it for over an hour now, and they hadn't even gotten to the skulls on the upper shelf yet. Nick had already gone through several rolls of film just documenting the scene; not for the first time, he wished that digital photographs weren't frowned upon as evidence, on the grounds that they were too easily manipulated. *Probably save the lab a fortune in film.*

They sure didn't need to play any tricky games with Photoshop here. Assuming that those were indeed Liz Rudolph's fingerprints all over the knives and other tools, they had more than enough evidence to nail her for the murders of James Zounek and Malcolm Kim.

If only they knew where she was.

Sweat dripped from Nick's forehead, contaminating the scene. It had to be more than a hundred degrees inside the sweltering wooden shed, but he didn't dare turn on the fan for fear of blowing away a vital piece of trace evidence. Perspiration glued his shirt to his shoulder blades. He and Greg had been forced to take frequent breaks to rehydrate themselves, with Officers Jonsson and Nesko drafted into making grocery runs to keep them amply provided with bottled water. It wouldn't do anybody any good if one or both of the CSIs collapsed from heat stroke.

Brass stuck his head into the shed. "How's it going?"

"We're probably going to need an extra SUV just to cart all this evidence back to the lab," Nick informed him. "Any sign of our perp?"

Brass shook his head. "Not a peep. We've put out a BOLO on both her and her vehicle, but nobody's spotted her yet." An acronym for "Be on the Look-Out," BOLO was an all-points bulletin that went out to the entire LVPD. "If she's still in Vegas, she's not going to get far."

They had found the notorious green hatchback in the garage, but Rudolph's own Subaru remained missing. Nick hoped that all the commotion surrounding the house hadn't scared her away for good. The conspicuous absence of the machete still worried him.

Where is she now, and what is she up to?

He finished bagging and tagging her extensive collection of knives and razors. Phenolphthalein had detected traces of dried blood on almost all of the blades. Precipitin tests had confirmed that the blood was human. As Nick packed the tools into a cardbox box for easy transport, he spotted a rusty metal handle jutting out just below the edge of the wooden counter. Tugging on the handle revealed a shallow drawer filled with newspaper clippings and printouts from the Internet. Lying on top of the pile was an article about yesterday's press conference at police headquarters. A black-and-white photo showed Sheriff Burdick standing at the podium, looking stern and resolute, while Grissom and Brass posed in the background. Nick recognized the bored, impatient expression on Grissom's face. He'd seen it many times before, usually when Hodges or some other overenthusiastic lab rat was taking too long to get to the point.

But it wasn't his boss's somewhat impolitic demeanor in the photo that made Nick's heart skip a beat. It was the large black circle drawn around Grissom's head and the stitch marks doodled over his eyes and lips. *Oh my God,* he thought, instantly picking up on the significance of the defaced photo.

Liz Rudolph had been trying to figure out what Grissom's shrunken head would look like.

"Greg! Get over here!"

He thrust the article at the other CSI. While Greg stared aghast at the printout, Nick rifled anxiously through the other clippings in the drawer.

They were *all* about Grissom.

"What the hell?" he exclaimed. "Why Grissom?"

Greg gasped out loud. "It's just like Catherine joked in that meeting the other night. Grissom fits the profile of the victims!"

"Come again?" Nick blurted. "What meeting? What are you talking about?"

"That's right, you weren't there," Greg recalled. "You were off chasing that janitor with Sofia." He steadied himself and started over again. "Anyway . . . we had a conference on the Headhunter case and Gris-

som commented that both victims were male authority figures with impressive academic credentials. Catherine teased Grissom by pointing out that the same
description fit him to a tee."

Damn, Nick thought. "Looks like Liz Rudolph made
the same connection. And I don't think she's joking."

He snatched his cell phone from a pocket on his
vest and dialed Grissom. To his frustration, Grissom's
voice mail picked up instead. "Grissom! This is Nick.
You're in serious danger—call me back right away!"

A beep cut off the call and Nick swore under his
breath.

"Isn't he testifying in court today?" Greg asked.

"Right!" Nick realized that Grissom had almost
surely turned his phone off. "Oh God, of all times!"

He rushed out of the shed. "Brass!"

Kakara stalked Grissom along Las Vegas Boulevard.

Lost in thought, his jacket slung over his shoulder,
the head CSI appeared totally unaware of her presence as she followed him down the sidewalk. She
took pains to stay about half a block behind Grissom
at all times. This far north of the Strip, pedestrian
traffic was light, but there were still enough people
about to help Kakara blend into the crowd. On the
flip side, those same passersby denied her the privacy
she needed to claim Grissom's head. There were far
too many witnesses around.

That hadn't been the case during her previous
victories. Those killings had gone off like clockwork.
For perhaps the hundredth time, she relived the
murders in her head, savoring every detail, just as
she had every day since the first time.

Dr. Zounek was practice, at least to a degree. For years, she had put up with his demeaning treatment and superior attitude, how he had ordered her about like a flunky, just because of the fancy MD after his name. How he had denied her raises and overtime while spending a fortune on his snazzy sports car and cosmetic surgery. But it wasn't until she came up with the idea of sending Malcolm Kim a shrunken head before killing him that she realized who the perfect "donor" for that head would be. Using Zounek's head to warn Malcolm of his impending doom was like killing two birds with one poison dart. Plus, she'd have a head to practice on before she shrank Malcolm's treacherously handsome face. After all, it was one thing to read about how to make a tsanta in academic journals and field guides; it was another thing to do so with your own hands. . . .

At first, the entire scenario had just been a wild fantasy, something to obsess about late at night while she brooded over how her life had gone off-track, thanks to Malcolm wrecking her college career by getting her pregnant and then abandoning her. But after a while, the fantasy became all she could think about, eating away at her, until she knew it was the only way to make things right.

She would always be a victim until the blood-guilt was avenged.

Once she made up her mind, the rest was easy.

Pleading car failure, she tricked Zounek into driving her home that night. Luring him inside with the promise of a drink and perhaps more, she caught him unaware with a syringe full of curare. By the time he realized what had happened to him, he was already too paralyzed to fight back. The baffled, terrified expression on his face before he lost consciousness was a thing of beauty, something she would treasure for the rest of her days. She waited *until it was nearly three in the morning, and all the lights in her neighbors' houses had gone dark, before dragging his lifeless body onto the patio behind her house, where her sharpened machete waited. Darkness and a high fence guaranteed her safety from prying eyes. Anticipation only made the pleasure all the greater as she raised the blade above Zounek's exposed throat. For the first time in her life, she truly felt like a warrior. Her right arm, conditioned by years of upper-body exercises at the gym, gave her all the strength she needed.*

A familiar thrill raced through Kakara at the memory. She couldn't wait to feel that intoxicating sense of triumph again. Without even realizing it, she quickened her pace, closing the gap between her and Grissom. Her right hand crept into the outer pocket of the duster, fingering the grip of the machete through the lining of the jacket. She sized up Grissom from only a few yards away. His head was bigger than the others'. It was going to take longer to shrink.

Too bad there wasn't time to send Malcolm's head as a warning.

Killing Zounek was just the warm-up to her greatest victory, when she finally revenged herself on Malcolm Kim for ruining her life all those years ago. She waited patiently, monitoring his activities, until she knew he would be alone all afternoon. Disguising herself in one of Charles's old uniforms, she drove to his home and rang the doorbell. She hid her homemade blow pipe behind her back as she waited for him to come to the door. A cardboard box, lined with plastic, rested at her feet. Her plan was to drug him with the dart, just like a true Shuar warrior, then shove her way inside before he even realized who she really was.

Unfortunately, he saw through her disguise the moment he opened the door. Apparently the "gift" she had sent him earlier that week had indeed stirred his memories of their affair way back when, of how he had denied her and their unborn child, who might well have lived had not the heartbreak of his betrayal led to her miscarriage. He tried to slam the door shut, but she kicked the box into the doorframe in time, wedging it between the door and the jamb. "What are you doing here?" he protested in a low voice, no doubt afraid of causing a scene in front of the neighbors. "It's been seven years for God's sake. Leave me alone!"

"I just want to talk," she lied. "Do you want to do this inside or out here in the open?"

Even then, only minutes away from death, he let his concern for his reputation and his marriage override his better judgment. He hesitated in the doorway long enough for her to pull the blow pipe out from behind her back and press it to her lips. His eyes widened at the sight of the weapon and he turned and fled back into the house, forcing her to waste a dart or two before one struck him at the back of the neck. Crying out in pain and fear, he yanked the dart from his neck and flung it away from him, but it was too late. The dart had pierced his skin. The curare had entered his bloodstream. He made it as far as the living room before collapsing onto the carpet.

She was amazed at her own calm and resolve as she quietly closed the front door behind her and extracted her machete from the box. With no time to lose, she had taken only a few moments to relish the sight of her seducer lying helpless before her. Malcolm was older than she remembered, but she still recognized the distinguished features that had led her astray so many years ago. If he hadn't taken advantage of her, she might have fulfilled her life's dream of becoming a brilliant anthropologist instead of dropping out of school and ending up in a dead-end job only a few miles from the university. Who knew? If not for Malcolm, she might be conducting research along the Amazon right now or maybe be the head of her own department somewhere. It wasn't fair that his academic career had prospered while hers had never happened. And that their child had died because of his callous treatment of them. Malcolm Kim had destroyed two lives, both her own and her baby's. The blood-guilt was his.

But now at last, she would even the scales.

His bloodshot eyes pleaded for mercy, but Kakara the Headhunter had none. With no time to wait for the curare to kill him, she sped the process along by suffocating him with a convenient sofa cushion. Holding the pillow down over his face, she counted the seconds before his chest fell still and silent. His paralyzed body barely twitched as he expired.

Five minutes later, she left the house with his head in a box.

The *tsanta* was shrinking nicely back at her workshop. She intended to mail Kim's head to his wife when it was finished, as payback for turning her eyes from the truth years before, but first she had Grissom to deal with. Another pedantic know-it-all who thought he could bully her with impunity.

She couldn't wait to skin the flesh from his skull. . . .

"Hell!" Catherine swore as Grissom's voice mail picked up once more. She angrily killed the call. "Turn on your cell phone, dammit!"

Warrick glanced at her as they rushed out of

the police station, where they had been updating Sofia on everything they'd learned at the university. The female detective had just been called away on another case when they'd got word from Nick that Grissom was in danger. "Still not getting through?"

"No!" Catherine blurted as she took the steps down to the sidewalk two at a time. According to the DA, Grissom had left the courthouse on his own several minutes ago and was presumably on his way back to CSI headquarters, only a block away. For all they knew, Amanda Knowlston, the Vegas Head-hunter, was lying in wait for him at this very moment or was already coming at him with her machete and poison darts. Catherine frantically scanned the sidewalk east of them, but didn't spot either Grissom or Rudolph. For the first time, she cursed the attractive greenery surrounding the crime lab. All at once, the wooded campus seemed the perfect site for an ambush. "Hurry up!"

"He'll be okay," Warrick promised. "We'll get to him before she does."

Catherine prayed those weren't just empty words. The image of Grissom's shrunken head, his eyes and lips sewn shut for all time, flashed before her mind's eye.

What if we're not in time?

Grissom remained oblivious to his danger as he turned left on Westfall Avenue, but Kakara was boiling with impatience. They were almost back where they'd started that morning, and she still hadn't managed to catch him alone. Her hopes of waylaying

him in the downtown alley that had tempted her before had been frustrated by a pair of rollerbladers
zipping down the sidewalk at just the wrong moment. She had missed her chance again.

Her anxiety mounted as they neared the wooded
campus surrounding the crime-lab building. The
spirits of her fallen enemies were strong within her,
bolstering her confidence, but what if Grissom disappeared back into the secure facility before she
could strike? In a pinch, she could get her car and
wait outside the lab's parking garage in hopes of
spotting his car when he finally left for the day, but
what if she missed him? She didn't even know what
kind of car he drove.

No, she thought. *It has to be now.* Every hour Grissom remained alive gave him more time to investigate her. She couldn't afford to let him live any
longer. *It's him or me.*

Palm trees and shrubs led to a stone pathway
leading toward the building. Perhaps the foliage
was all the shelter she needed to carry out her at-
tack? If she moved quickly and ducked beneath the
bushes, she might be able to claim Grissom's head
and get away in a matter of minutes. *I won't even
wait for the curare to kill him.* She had never decapitated someone while he was still alive, but now
that she thought of it, she found the idea appealed
to her. She looked forward to seeing the fear in his
eyes as the blade descended—and maybe even afterward. She'd heard stories about guillotine victims, back during France's Reign of Terror, whose
heads were supposed to have remained alive for
seconds after their executions. Would Grissom's

head be aware of its fate before she tossed it into her satchel?

She certainly hoped so.

Grissom entered the campus. Kakara looked around to see if anyone was watching, but the gods of the jungle appeared to be with her. The sidewalk was momentarily deserted. The bus stop across the street was unoccupied. Cars and trucks zoomed past on the avenue, but she assumed that their drivers were intent on the traffic, not her. It was risky, she decided, but she might never have a better opportunity.

She followed Grissom onto the pathway. The shade of the palm trees lent her a comforting sense of detachment from the busy street only a few feet away. It was easy to imagine that she was back in the heart of the Amazon rain forest. She reached into the inner pocket of her duster and drew out the hollow bamboo blow pipe. Her other hand fished a poisoned dart from her pocket. She loaded the dart into the pipe.

Grissom paused in his tracks, as though suddenly remembering something. For a second, she feared that he had heard her arming herself, and she ducked behind the trunk of the nearest palm tree. But instead of looking back at her, he retrieved a cell phone from his own pocket and turned it on. Almost immediately, its shrill ring violated the peaceful atmosphere of the campus. Grissom pressed the phone to his ear. "Hello?"

His body tensed as he received some sort of urgent message. "What? Are you sure?" He turned around, his eyes anxiously scanning his surroundings, and spotted Kakara.

Dammit. He sees me.

"Nick!" Grissom shouted into the phone. "She's here! Right outside the lab!"

He reached instinctively for his gun, only to remember that he wasn't wearing a holster. Kakara realized that his court date, as much as it had tried her patience, had ultimately worked in her favor. Unable to carry a gun into the courthouse, he was now conveniently unarmed.

She stepped out from behind the tree and raised the blow pipe to her lips.

"Ms. Rudolph!" He swung his attaché case in front of him like a shield. "Please don't do this! You need psychological help!"

"All I need is your head!" she snarled. Her cheeks bulged as she blew hard on the blow pipe, sending a lethal dart straight at Grissom's face. His celebrated gray matter wouldn't do him any good once she chopped it up and flushed it down the toilet. *You'll never persecute me again!*

To her dismay, however, his reflexes were faster than she expected and he blocked the first dart with the leather case. She swore under her breath as she hastily loaded another dart into the pipe. But her second dart went wild, making her wish that she had spent more time practicing in her backyard. *Why isn't this working?* she thought furiously. *The spirits are with me. He's supposed to die!*

"Liz! Listen to me!" Grissom's eyes pleaded with her over the edge of the attaché. "I've read your thesis. I know what you're thinking now. But this isn't the Amazon. You're not a Shuar warrior from a hundred years ago. Shrinking people's heads is not going to make you stronger or more respected. You're only getting yourself into more trouble!"

Liar! she thought. What did he know of the sacred rites, of the power of the *arutam*? Refusing to waste any more breath trading words with Grissom, she placed another dart in the pipe and called upon the captured souls of Zounek and Malcolm. Grissom was frozen before her, unable to turn and flee without presenting an even better target to his destined slayer. Taking care not to let her eyes betray her intentions, she took aim at his belly, just below the upraised attaché case. *Third time's the charm,* she thought confidently.

This time, she would not miss.

"Liz Rudolph! Mandy Knowlston!"

An unfamiliar female voice called out from behind, addressing her by a name she had put behind her years ago. Spinning around, Kakara spied a blond-haired woman charging toward her, followed by a handsome African-American man. The blonde gripped a gun in both hands. "You're under arrest for the murders of James Zounek and Malcolm Kim!" she shouted. "Put down your weapon!"

Startled, Kakara fired at the newcomer instead. The dart flew from her pipe, striking the blonde squarely in the chest.

"Catherine!" Grissom yelled in alarm.

The woman yelped, but kept on coming. Kakara found herself paralyzed instead, uncertain what to do next. Who were these people, and where had they come from? How did they know what she was up to?

All at once, it seemed the spirits had abandoned her.

"Keep back!" Kakara shouted, frantically reaching for another poison dart. But before she could ready her pipe once more, Grissom's attaché case slammed into the back of her head, knocking her to her knees. The pipe went flying from her fingers, and she collapsed onto the hard stone walkway. Grissom's knee dug into her back, holding her down. Over the ringing in her skull, she heard the other two CSIs running toward them. Although dazed by the blow, she thrashed beneath Grissom, trying to throw him off, until she heard the click of a gun only inches away.

Lifting her head, she found herself looking straight up the muzzle of the blonde's Smith & Wesson. "That's enough!" Catherine said. "Don't give me an excuse to put a hole in your head. We wouldn't want all the loose marbles to fall out."

The name on her blue windbreaker was WILLOWS. The dart was still embedded in her chest, right above her heart. *I don't understand,* Kakara thought. *Why are you still standing?*

Grissom sounded equally puzzled. "Catherine?" he asked, his voice full of concern. "Do you require medical attention?"

"Not really," she chortled. She waited until her black companion had Kakara's wrists cuffed behind her before peeling off the windbreaker to reveal a Kevlar vest underneath. "I figured Little Miss Headhunter here would never aim for my face."

"A wise precaution," Grissom agreed.

24

"So, JUST TO BE CLEAR," Sofia asked, "Daniel Skiller and Carlos Vallejo had nothing to do with the killings?"

Sofia and Catherine faced Liz Rudolph in the interrogation suite. The suspect's short auburn hair conflicted with Helen Kim's description of Amanda Knowlston as a blonde, but that was hardly enough to exonerate her, especially after they found blue eyes behind her chestnut-colored contact lenses. *Guess she changed her look as well as her name,* Catherine thought. *Too bad she couldn't put the rest of her past behind her.*

No lawyer accompanied Liz Rudolph. Apparently, fierce Jivaro headhunters did not hide behind attorneys. Besides the murders of James Zounek and Malcolm Kim, the captured headhunter was now also charged with the attempted murders of both Grissom and Catherine. The woman's blow pipe, machete, and poison darts had joined the overwhelming amount of physical evidence Greg and Nick had collected from the workshop out behind her house. Catherine figured they already had enough evidence to convict her, but a confession would put a cherry on top of the case, and maybe spare the state a costly trial.

So far, though, Rudolph wasn't talking. The stone-faced woman had merely glowered at Brass for an hour, before Sofia had suggested that given Rudolph's history and profile, the suspect might be more willing to open up to another woman. Fed up with Rudolph's mute stubbornness, Brass had gladly turned the interrogation over to Sofia, although Catherine knew that both Brass and Grissom were watching intently from the other side of the one-way mirror.

Let's see if we can give them something worth watching.

"So, Liz, Mandy, Amanda," Catherine addressed her, "what would you like us to call you?"

The woman broke her silence at last. "Kakara."

"Ohh-kay," Catherine responded, dragging out the first syllable. Assuming the name was some sort of crazed affectation, she resisted the urge to roll her eyes. If Liz Rudolph was going for an insanity plea, it was going to take more than a spooky pseudonym. "Look, *Kakara* . . . you might as well come clean. You know we found your little arts-and-crafts shop in your shed. We've got Malcolm Kim's head, your tools, your beads, your weapons, the curare garden, et cetera. We know you had access to the printer in Dr. Zounek's office. We even found Dr. Zounek's headless body buried in your backyard, plus traces of his blood and DNA on your back patio. And then, of course, there was that little business with the blow gun earlier today." Catherine tapped the spot on her chest where the Kevlar vest had saved her from the poison dart. "We've already got more than enough to send you straight to Death Row, so you might as well fess up. If you're going to pay the price, why not let the whole world know what you did? That's what this was all about, right? Avenging your honor? Coming out on top in the end?"

"You know it was!" Rudolph hissed.

Sofia picked up on Catherine's lead. "And they deserved it, right?"

"*Tumashi akerkama*," Rudolph whispered, nodding. "Blood-guilt." Her eyes lit up with glee as she basked in the memory of her victories. "I didn't just kill them, you know. I captured their souls for all eternity."

Catherine was appalled at the woman's lack of remorse. Okay, so Malcolm Kim screwed her over when she was in college, and Dr. Zounek was, by all accounts, a jerk and a bad boss, but that hardly justified going on a killing spree—and trying to kill Grissom as well. Catherine shuddered when she thought about just how close she had come to losing her friend. "You do realize you're facing the death penalty?"

Liz Rudolph snorted derisively. "Lethal injection? The Shuar would sneer at such a feeble means of execution. You can only kill my body, not my spirit." She glared venomously at Catherine. "Unless you behead me, my vengeful ghost—my *musiak*— will haunt you forever."

Catherine thought of all the murderers, rapists, and other felons she had already helped put away.

"Take a number."

Afterward, as Sheriff Burdick was in the process of calling another press conference, Catherine found Grissom in the morgue, taking one last look at the original shrunken head.

"Saying good-bye?" she asked.

"More or less," he admitted. "After Doc Robbins completes his autopsy of Dr. Zounek's body, and we get the tox screen and DNA results back, the head, skull, and body are all being released to Zounek's next of kin. I understand that they intend to cremate the remains." He contemplated the *tsanta* mournfully. "A shame, really. It's a beautiful specimen."

"Too bad you can't keep it as a souvenir," she sympathized. The shriveled trophy wasn't exactly to her tastes, but it would have fit right into the eclectic collection in Grissom's office.

"Exactly," he agreed. "I was toying with the idea of making one of my own someday, perhaps using the head of a dead pig or a goat." He put the head back on its slab and slid it into its refrigerated niche. "It could be a fascinating experiment."

"Or," Catherine suggested, "you might try finding another hobby instead."

Acknowledgments

The writing of this book was complicated by a temporary medical crisis, now happily resolved. I want to thank my doctors, Hugh Bonner, Joel Fuhrman, Deborah Kulp, and Edouard Trabulsi, plus the terrific staff at Thomas Jefferson University Hospital in Philadelphia, for helping me through what needed to be done. I also need to thank my editor, Ed Schlesinger, for his patience, as well as for thinking of me for this project in the first place. Thanks also to my agents, Russ Galen and Ann Behar, and all my friends, colleagues, and relatives for their good wishes and support. Believe me, they were deeply appreciated.

Writing a CSI novel takes plenty of research. Below are just a handful of the books I relied on while working on *Headhunter*:

Ultimate CSI: Crime Scene Investigation, by Corinne Marrinan and Steve Parker, DK Publishing, 2006.

CSI: Crime Scene Investigation Companion, by Mike Flaherty, with case files by Corinne Marrinan, Pocket Books, 2004.

Forensics for Dummies, by D. P. Lyle, MD, Wiley Publishing, 2004.

Crime Scene: The Ultimate Guide to Forensic Science, by Richard Platt, DK Publishing, 2003.

Forensic Art and Illustration, by Karen T. Taylor, CRC Press, 2001.

Hidden Evidence: 40 True Crimes and How Forensic Science Helped Solve Them, by David Owen, Firefly Books, 2000.

Scene of the Crime: A Writer's Guide to Crime Scene Investigations, by Anne Wingate, Ph.D., Writer's Digest Books, 1992.

In addition, I eagerly devoured many of the earlier novels in this series.

Also helpful were Aurore Giguet at the Marjorie Barrick Museum in Las Vegas, Pat Bleech at Salongome Exotic Exports, and, on the Web, "Doc Bwana's House of Shrunken Heads" and
. Karen T. Taylor, in particular, generously took time out of her busy schedule to spend an enjoyable afternoon discussing facial reconstructions with me. (Any errors or fudging on that topic are strictly my own doing, however.)

Finally, I couldn't have done without the genuinely heroic efforts of my girlfriend, Karen Palinko, who nursed both me (and our dog!) through our respective surgeries and convalescences. She truly deserves a medal—not to mention a vacation!

P.S. The dog is fine.

About the Author

Greg Cox is the *New York Times* bestselling author of numerous books and short stories. He has written the official novelizations of such films as *Daredevil, Death Defying Acts, Ghost Rider, Underworld,* and *Underworld: Evolution.* He has also written books and stories based on such popular TV series as *Alias, Buffy the Vampire Slayer, Farscape, The 4400, Roswell, Star Trek, Xena,* and *Zorro.*

He lives in Oxford, Pennsylvania. His website is www.gregcox-author.com.

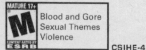

Not sure
what to
read next?

Visit Pocket Books online at
www.simonsays.com

Reading suggestions for
you and your reading group
New release news
Author appearances
Online chats with your favorite writers
Special offers
Order books online
And much, much more!